ZOLA BLUE

Courage of One

CONVICTION TO STAND

Book Three of the Mejuarian Series

Copyright

Dedications

As always I want to thank the wonderful Holy Spirit, my husband. Too, my special, always BFF, Jackie.

Chapter One

The Night Nomad

Thick growths of mangroves cluttering the marshy everglades, the old man trudged through the swamplands, trying to reach one of the lakes feeding the swampy marshlands. Sawgrass entangled his legs, securing his woolen pant legs like thin slimy tentacles attempting to hold him captive. Effortlessly he untangled himself, gently pulling his legs out of their twine, so as not to harm the biological creatures giving life to the everglades. He carried only an oil lamp, and although he appeared old and feeble, his eyesight was as keen as a bird hunting for prey.

Through the damp brush and treed terrain, eagerly he maneuvered across the twenty acres, enjoying the solitude of the night's journey. The protective roar of a crocodile making him look down; two yellow cores, like big firelights, peered up at him. The old man moved around the large reptile, warming himself upon the dry bank in the hot tropical temperatures. "Sorry, my friend," he said, offering his heartfelt apologies to the swamp's resident his booted feet almost trampled across.

Occasionally he stepped on one of the swamp's creatures; however, he tried not to. It insulted the reptile trampled upon, and not to mention, it was dangerous if he did not know the humiliated brute. Nevertheless, the creatures in the everglades were his friends, and when he mistakenly trod across one of them, most kindly accepted this mistake. Large grouchy bullfrogs, buried beneath weeds were the worse. When he lifted his feet angrily, they leaped away and croaked loudly to warn others of his presence. This created quite a disturbance in the peaceful swamp. Most amazingly, too, if the old man entangled his face in the body of a python, swinging from a pond cypress. The long burly snake simply lifted its body out of his way or fell upon his shoulders and joined him for the rest of his journey. After he happened to walk across one of the massive reptiles resting upon the bottom of the cold swamp, it only glared back at him and waited for his apology.

Sounds of the glade's darkness frightened him most. Nevertheless, the deep croak of a bullfrog, growl of a gator, crunch of the grass when a snake slithered across the moist ground soothed the old man's nervous temperament like musical lyrics. Sometimes, the occasional bark of a hound who wandered into the glades added to the harmony of sounds. The midnight hours' soft sounds were his favorite, though, because they were the sounds of nature itself in the everglades. At night, afraid to enter the everglades, town folk did not hunt, and there was safety for all in his homeland.

At last, the old man reached his destination, so he examined the water's edge. The prying eyes of a glossy yellow and black python, draped across a thick branch of a cypress, watched him closely from a tall tree that sat at the lake's edge. Near enough to grab him in its deadly hug, its dark shiny eyes stared at him, so the old man said, "Hello my friend. Let's see what I can do to these waters," stepping into the warm border of the lake.

A factory upstream dumped its noxious waste into the river that fed the large lake and swampy everglades. Even with all of his elixirs, these industrious chemicals slowly destroyed his home. A cloudy film covered the top of the water. Trapped within the grass's seams, the oily goo looked like a rainbow that rested across the dark water. Within the thick sawgrass, a school of tiny minnows swam across the top of the water, popping their small heads out of the murky, rainbow coat on top of their home. Evidently, flushing of the factory's machines had recently occurred. A pungent odor of ammonia drifted up from the lake and made him almost ill.

No Fishing, No Swimming

A sign posted at the dock warned the unsuspecting visitor of the deadly waters. Swimmers and fishers protected by warning signs, the town removed the threat of human consumption of the contaminants found in the water; however, those that lived in the lake and animals survived off its bounties could not read. Still, nothing was safe to eat in the lake, the city council refused to close the factory. For this reason, the old man had to take matters into his own hands. He needed to ensure that the water's purity was constant enough so that all the creatures continued their symbiotic relationship. In a certain way, this made the old man one with all the animals.

The everglades on the outskirts of a place now called Parryville was his home since he could remember a world existing. Each day of his long life, his residence grew sicker. Although he tried to heal the lakes, his efforts were temporary, and he only prolonged the eventual destruction of his beloved way of life.

Wading out into the deeper parts of the lake, he trudged out farther until the water grew colder. Weeds bound him tight, jerking at his clothing, the old man knew he was not alone, since there was life in everything. "Another treatment." The old man exhaled, gazing at a test-tube of pre-measured white powder. He poured the mixture into the murky water.

The powder fizzed savagely, spreading across the lake in a foam of white bubbles, renewing the tainted water, replacing it with fresh liquid. Its bubbling growing angrily, the powder absorbed the oily residue before turning a myriad of colors. A pleasant aroma of sage growing in the air, eyes from creatures hiding in the heavy brush peeked out curiously, enticed by the sweet smell coming from the lake. Moments later, turning into dark smoke, the cleansing mixture drifted away.

Once again, the lake was clear under the moonlight. A school of minnows floated around Luken's legs in the water's shallow areas, darting about, striking at anything smaller than themselves. Such a sight gave the old man pleasure. The shadow of the moon upon the dark lake was beautiful, creating the illusion that he might walk upon the beams of light coming from it into space. Once he left, though, he might leave Earth behind for good.

The old man knew he might take the trek back to the lake in a couple of weeks, but for now, closing the rusted metal lunchbox, he left to return to his cabin. When he reached the woods around his house, she was waiting for him. The old man smiled happily and rushed towards his wife.

Skin that glimmered a golden lime under the weak lighting, silver strands of hair twisted into a long braid that fell down along the side of her face, she was as beautiful as the day he first met her. The old man loved her so. "Talulah," he cried out cheerfully, and she ran to him. A leather fighter's tunic tight upon her chest, and leather pants clinging to her bottom and legs; the fierce warrior, after so many years, still held her loveliness and strength.

"Luken, my love. Too long have I desired to see you again."

"I, as well, my beloved Talulah." The old man took her in his arms and held her tightly. Dropping the bow she had in her hand to the ground, his beloved caught his face in her hands and kissed him. The taste of her berry breath gave him comfort, and he missed her; he kissed her deeply and never wanted to let her go.

"I shall never forget the thrill of my heart when you hold me, my darling Luken." The old man smiled happily, taking her cold hand in his; he looked over at her and blushed. Talulah smiled at him and did not care about her cold flesh. The old man was glad when he came home and she was there to greet him.

"So, how was your day, dear Luken?"

"I fear that I soon will not be able to keep the lake's water pure."

"Do not say such things. As the Earth changes, so do you. Your mixtures will grow in strength because you will make them better." Lovely, shaped orange glossy, plump lips smiled at him. "This is our home, and we will not allow others to take it from us, dear Luken."

"They held their annual hunting contest some days ago. I have spent most of my days of late cleaning up death."

"Such a fretful one tonight. I come to see my husband, and I am greeted by a stranger. I want to see Luken."

A strong warrior, she fought by his side once. Talulah was his strength and, on many times, saved him. Luken did not want her to see him in such a condition, but the everglades' deterioration disturbed him. "Of course, you are right. You are always correct, my lovely Talulah."

"Such a beautiful night."

She was right. The moon was at its ideal angle and looked like a perfectly spherical orb floating above the earth. Its shimmering blue light gave off just enough light so that he saw the lovely outline of her face in the shadowy places along the way. "I made you something."

"Did you? Well, really, Luken you are full of surprises. Tell me now, what is it?" Talulah beamed beautifully.

"You will find out when we return to the cabin."

"Oh, you are such a dragon. Luken, tell me please, my darling."

He laughed. Genuine happiness, escaping him for so long, returned tonight. Finally, the two of them reached his tiny, weather-beaten cabin. Strings of bright light hanging from poles stuck into the camp's ground, the brightly tiny home came into view. Looking no larger than a garden shed, broken boards with nails protruding out of them hung around the dilapidated building from its outside. A single small window upon its front face, its glass was so dirty it looked as if it were stained in a caked-on gooey surface. "Your present is just behind those doors."

"Luken, you can always just tell me what it is." She winked at him, and Talulah pulled him closer to her and kissed him once again.

"That not going to work." He laughed.

"Luken," she giggled. "Here, carry my bow," she grinned and ran off as a child towards the front door.

The old man took the bow from Talulah, watching her run away. Luken loved the weapon. It was the only thing he kept from the times of his old life, in his new one. Although it hung safely in a treasured case against the wall inside of his home, she took it out and carried the precious weapon every time he saw her. Luken thought of times long ago.

Chapter Two

Another Story Many, Many Centuries Ago

Talulah was the most beautiful female in his clan, Luken felt. Along with two other hunters, she stood at the well, polishing her thin blade. Long hair matted in places, blades of grass and twigs sticking out of her silvery locks, even though she was back from a hunt and dirty, she was still very pretty. Luken stared at her; his heartbeat quickened, creating a nervous tension within. A hammer he was using fell from his hands, and the hefty instrument clattered against the steel anvil loudly, making an awful sound. Talulah and her friends looked over at Luken, and she smiled at him. However, the other two in her hunting party laughed and then went back to cleaning their steel. Fine weapons he or his father crafted.

Her smile might have made Luken hopeful that she was noticing him; this was not the case, though. When he was trying to pick up his hammer, he stumbled and knocked over a small pan of coals, burning his hand. This was her way of attempting to make him feel a little bit better in his embarrassment and pain.

A member of the Glade Dragonor clan, they were hunters, and Luken knew she had been on a chase. Dragonor females dressed just like the males and wore garments of polished animal leather dyed black. Tight tunics across their chests and tight pants, the two groups looked identical, except for a few lumps upon their chests and curves along their backside. Besides those few features and a difference in hair color, it was hard to distinguish in their muscular agile bodies. Like the coloring of scaly reptiles, their skins varied in all the neutral tones. Too depending upon their mood or the temperature of their bodies, their skins' hues would change.

Black leather pants clung to her body as she moved, and her figure-hugging tunic, a vest-like garment, although stained with mud and animal blood, she was most admirable and yet beautiful. Slender arms, lime in color, too soiled in dirt, it was hard to see their scaley pattern. Even so, Luken wanted her for his mate and desired nothing more than to love her. Talulah was the daughter of Lord Ephenio, the leader of the clan of Glade Dragonors. Only the son of Tinzadri, a blacksmith nobody for the clan, his father held no position of authority, and marriage between himself and Talulah was very unlikely. Luken did not own a dragon, and his secret love owned one of the quickest and largest in the clan. Luken knew the only way for him to gain a position of notice was to win the Challenge of the Cypress.

The Challenge of the Cypress was the most challenging game the Dragonors held. Every five years, both the Northern and Western Prairie Dragonors and the Glade Dragonors participated in this event. With physical endurance and mental problem-solving skills, the clans' leaders tested the young Dragonors in all-around skills. A grueling challenge on the back of a dragon, the participants had to compete in a battle with their dragons to test their dragon-riding abilities. Although he did not have one, Luken was going to need to ride a dragon. By then, he hoped to have gained enough allies out of his friends that they might allow him to ride their precious companions.

"Hi, Luken. I hear you have entered the Challenge of the Cypress." Raphazk said, grinning at him. A long back braid rolled atop his head in a bun, matted in twigs as well, his clothing also was mud and bloodstained. It was evident the two of them were together. Luken felt a twinge of jealousy when Talulah walked up to him and placed her hand on the young Dragonor's shoulder.

"Wonderful news Luken. Is it not fabulous that you joined? All the luck of the glades with you." She smiled at him again.

Two grins in one day; he truly felt honored. "Have you entered, Talulah?"

"Ha. I bet Luken doesn't make it past the first event. I've only seen him make a sword but never yield one."

Laughter from Raphazk upset him. Luken felt anger growing within, but he said nothing, only continued peering at Talulah.

"Luken can handle a sword. I have seen him do so."

Flattered that she would take up for him, he blushed lightly. Cheeks growing hot, he was sure his emerald-green skin turned darker upon his face. Respect for her compliment, he bowed his head and said, "Thank you, Talulah."

A stern glare given to her companion hunter, he answered, "Yes, I can handle a blade, and quite well, as you will find out." Luken felt nervousness around Talulah. There was no fear or lack of confidence in himself for her comrade. Luken could not wait to go against him in the games.

"Will you compete in the games, Talulah?"

"No, my father won't let me. He knows I will make all of you all look like weaklings," she laughed, slapping Raphazk against the back, then grabbed him around the chest and held him in a gentle bear hug. Talulah peeked over his shoulder at Luken.

Eyes the color of the sky, their bluish color mesmerized him, even though she played with her hunting partner so carefreely. Luken stuttered, "I have no doubt of that," looking away from their antics.

"Luken, come to the gathering tonight. Everyone is going to be there."

"He has no time. I am sure he has a lot of gear to make for others in the competition. My father, of course, has Dalardus craft our weapons," he commented, winking smugly at Luken.

"You are a real idiot sometimes," she said, shoving him away from her. She approached Luken. "Do not worry about his words. Come to the lake."

Kindness from her as well. Talulah had never spoken to him, in such a way, all of their over ninety years of life. "It is possible I will come, Talulah."

"Great. I hope you do." A smile once again came across her lips, and she beamed at him for the first time. Three smiles in one day. Luken was happy, and when he finished at the forge tonight, he might clean up and go to the lake.

Luken left after making seven arrows with engraved platinum tips for Lemet, went home, changed out of his grungy work tunic, and left for the swamps. Arriving much later than the rest, the younger Dragonors had already taken the choice spots. They lazed around the marshy lake upon couch-lily pads, resting while cooling themselves and enjoying the lethargic sensation the cold water provided.

Talulah was not in the lake. Accompanied by her hunting companion, she sat talking with Raphazk on a leather blanket on the moist ground several feet from the pool. "Luken, come join us." Tonight she traded in her tunic for a comfortable white dress draping loosely over her body. Moonlight shining upon the sheer white garment, Luken dared not look down and gazed at her lovely face, illuminating it from the gleam of the fabric.

Luken walked over and sat next to Talulah.

"Well, I might as well say welcome Luken," Raphazk commented disrespectfully.

Luken nodded.

"So, you ready for the big challenge tomorrow, Luken? Maybe you should be sleeping. You don't know how exhausting long days are like the rest of us," he smirked, lying back on the blanket, resting his head upon his arms. Raphazk gazed at the sky, not bothering to look at Luken.

"Of course, he is ready. You are a perfect cow, aren't you, Raphazk?"

She had taken up for him again. "I am ready. Do not concern yourself with my ability to beat you, Raphazk," Luken replied.

"Like I told you, I have not seen you handle a blade or bow," he laughed. "So, this should be interesting."

Under the moonlike, his blue skin looked black. Combined with his dark hair, he was indeed an intimidating Dragonor, and others in the clan thought him to be the next leader of the village. Larger in build than Luken, he looked mighty and fierce, like the Dragornors of legends. Luken understood why Talulah might like him. He, however, wanted to hit him in the face to stop the dark yellow haughty gaze in Raphazk's hateful stare.

"Ra..."

Before she could finish her response, Luken touched her hand gently. "As for me, I shall be prepared, Raphazk. I hope that skin of wine has not dullened your abilities. Since I was, in fact, looking for a challenge." Talulah giggled.

"Perhaps he is right. Do you believe that your confidence might betray you tomorrow?" Talulah giggled, gazing at Luken. For once, the loud young Dragonor had nothing to say and only lay brooding.

"The night is nice," Talulah spoke up.

"Yes, it is."

Raphazk apparently stewed for a bit, thinking of what to say. "My confidence shall never betray me. It is this blacksmith that should worry. He does not have a dragon. How is he to complete the final event?" Raging agitation in his voice, he and Talulah looked over at him, disturbed by his sudden outburst.

Although haughty in his ways and attitude, he told the truth, so Luken held his tongue. Others could not know of his plans right now, which might hinder some kind Dragonor from lending him their trusted comrade.

"I will let Luken ride mine. You are rude, too."

With a smugness in his manner and tone, he smirked, "Are you mad? You can't let anyone ride Magnus. Your father will not allow it."

"He is my dragon. He chose me so no one, including my father, will tell me what I will do with him."

"Thank you for your offer, Talulah, but that is not necessary," Luken told her.

"It is what I would like, Luken. Do not listen to Raphazk. Don't you think he has had too much wine?"

"I have not had nearly enough if my ears heard you said. Allowing Luken to ride Magnus!" While still lying on his back, Raphazk put the wineskin to his mouth and drank out of the opening; the contents spilled down the corners of his mouth.

"He is right. Magnus is a great dragon, and I…"

"What, now you are too arrogant to accept my gift!" She stood up, and glaring at the both of them she said, "I am off to bed."

"I will walk you."

"No, both of you stay away from me," she retorted and stormed off.

Luken sat in silence for a moment. "What just happened there?"

"Talulah is convinced that because she is female, her opinion does not matter. Some type of female trauma thing, I think." A chuckle came from his lips. "She knows Lord Ephenio will not let you ride Magnus too."

Luken liked the sudden outburst of spirited behavior in Talulah. Although her display was confusing to him, she had so much life flowing from her, intoxicating him by her passionate aura. "I like," he began to say, yet it was not wise to let his foe know of his attraction.

"What did you say?"

"Nothing really," he responded and walked away.

Luken awoke that morning smiling, and he knew why he was so happy. An unexpected closeness from Talulah revitalized him and gave him even more confidence in its own way. Lastly, offering Magnus for his use made his heart flutter.

Barely peeked through the tall cypress trees, the sun was just starting to come up when Luken prepared to leave. The challenge scheduled to begin at daybreak, so to get there bright and early would be to his advantage. Many secrets and shortcuts were told as stories

14

by those competing in prior events, boasting tales of glory and success.

Luken rolled his long black hair behind his head and tied it with a leather band; putting on his black tunic and greaves, he left the house, ensuring that his tall black boots were clean. Clean boots were a compulsion with him, and also unsoiled leathers. His small knife stuck into the top of his boot, and his travel sack carrying twine, wire, and lead stones, he was ready.

Dragonor Past

Prairie Dragonors and Glade Dragonors had little or no contact with each other unless they met on neutral ground, and even then, they were hostile to each other. They fought each other and killed out of anger or hate, but for the most part, they were like any other civilization, some were good, and others were not so good.

Bizarre oddities, infused with dragon blood, and created by magic, each of the three clans were ruthless killers. A progeny of three magic driven warlords, Tovar, Wiona, and Tylerious, the Dragonors fought aggressively for thrills. Too, they gave them power over herds of dragons to use in their horrible skirmishes. The warlords kept the clans separated until they fought deadly battles against the humans and other warlords. Infused with hate, they desired only to win for their warlord. As time passed, the wars stopped going on, and the Dragonors and dragons wandered throughout the dungeons deep below the castles. There, they waited for their warlords to return and release them; however, they never did.

A stranger visited all three clans one day. This peculiar being told them that they had the power to destroy them because they should have never been created. All life is sacred, he added. Instead of death, the mysterious man who spoke as a woman at times, gave them and the dragons they rode a new life. Beautiful lands separated by tall mountainous peaks; the stranger placed each clan within its own corner of the vast territories. On one side in the lush, warm area was the Glade Dragonors, and many miles away in the dryer plains, the stranger gave homes to the other two clans.

Each of the clans was transported to lands where there were no humans or isolated small groups. The stranger cast spells that allowed them to live above the ground. Their hair colors changed, their skin complexions turned brighter, and their eyes adjusted to the bright light. At last, instructed they must not live among the humans, each of the clans received an orb of passage. Instructions were, they would know when the time was right. Over time, most of the Dragonors forgot about the sphere, and it stayed in the hands of the High Priestess, passed down through the generations.

Relationships between the Glade and Prairie Dragonor clans developed into those of more than hate. Ultimately, the warrior groups started developing emotional relationships and friendships that made some clans uncomfortable. This blending of the racial traits made them less aggressive for some reason, and although the stranger promised them to refrain from war, these younger Dragonors refused all of the old ways. Many Dragonors also believed that clans should not unite, and this mixture of races was wrong, and once again, the three mighty groups of warriors broke away from each other. Glade Dragonors, the most docile of the three groups, younger Dragonor with new ideas tagged along with these and became part of their community. Over time, the ways and attitudes of the Glade Dragonors changed, and they became almost alien to the other two groups of Prairies. They held on to the past's hurts that would not heal and closed off their villages except to deliver goods, and only to those holding tickets to play in the games.

This will tell his worth

When he arrived at the meeting site, many of the older Dragonors stood around chatting, which was their usual custom. On this one day, Glade, Eastern and Western Prairie Dragonors talked in peace and shared stories of victory in the challenge. Conditions were much warmer in their dry, sunny region. These Dragonors were similar to Glades; however, they had bright sandy blonde hair colors, both eastern and western, and their skin colors were more brilliant. Their complexions appeared washed in white light as well. Because of the warm colors in the desert, too, they wore brighter and less clothing. Thin garments, ranging from dark brown to tan in their colors, their wardrobes and hairs singled them out among the Glade Dragonors.

Luken stepped up to his father, who was speaking with Lord Belegornor, of the Prairie Dragonors.

"This is my son, Luken."

The big Dragonor glared at him and grinned. "Looks like you spit this one out. You ready for the challenge, young Dragonor?"

"I am," he replied, looking around for Talulah.

"My son makes steel as well."

"Good lad. Make your father proud." Luken was not aware his father was close friends with a prairie; nevertheless, chatting like chums, he listened in on the stories.

"Contestants, to me." The loud voice of Lord Ephenio resonated through the crowd.

"Excuse me, Lord Manorer," Luken told him, bowing; he ran over to join the other contestants.

First One Down

He left home with nothing more than the clothing on his back and a few tools, a competition requirement. The first challenge: to roam the forest around the everglades, and in three hours, fashion the perfect weapon, take down, and return with a wild catch. This might have been easy for Luken since he was a blacksmith himself. However, he did not have the steel or heat to create any steel weapon more considerable than the knife he carried.

While he darted through the forest, looking for something to make a weapon out of that might kill a panther or big boar, Luken did not pay attention to where he was running. A few moments later, snagging his foot against something on the ground, he stumbled but did not fall. Luken mumbled angrily at himself for not being careful. Gazing down, he noticed a perfectly thin branch lying across the pathway. Luken picked up the thin curved branch, running his hand along the length of the sturdy stick, examining its strength and curve. An ideal piece of tree formed for a bow, with twine and knife in his sack, he might create the perfect weapon.

Later, stepping into a clearing, he looked up at the sun and realized he had been out for at least half of the three hours. Positions of the sun and moon used like a clock, he knew exactly what time of the day it was. Luken had to find something now and return soon. A small bunny hopped out in front of Luken, he laughed. "Absolutely impressive, Luken, return to your love with a rabbit." With his foot, he shooed the bunny away and kept hunting.

Finally, picking up a large animal's tracks, a panther, most likely, Luken cautiously stalked the beast. Its footprints made it appear to be a massive creature, and big cats in the everglades were deadly. A member of the clan, he was a natural hunter of small animals, rabbits, snakes, deer, small boar, and some crocs. Still, as the son of a blacksmith, studying metals and smithery, he never really hunted anything too deadly. Luken had no choice this time, he had to win the competition. Weaving through the dense woods, he trailed the tracks. A few moments later, Luken saw the big cat. All the time hunting with his father, he never came so close to something so dangerous. Directly in front of him stood a big orange panther, camouflaged by the thick trees and brush.

The panther stopped its slow lumbering movements, sniffing at the air, its massive head at least the size of a berry basket, looked back. Dark black eyes glaring at Luken, the panther bared its sharp white teeth. The beast had seen him. A part of Luken wanted to freeze because of the cat's menacing glare; nevertheless, he knew if he ran or did nothing, the panther would tear him apart. An arrow in one hand and the bow in the other, aiming the weapon, he hoped he had enough time to use it. The panther turned quickly, sprinting towards him. Luken let the arrow go, striking the big cat in the chest, which only agitated it more. The cat growled viciously, but it kept coming towards him. Luken had no time to reload the bow with an arrow and aim, so stepping backward, he grabbed one of the arrows out of his belt and prepared for its attack.

Long fangs bared, bouncing at Luken, the panther growled loudly. Luken held the arrow with both hands and leaping towards the big cat, while it lunged at him, he collided with the massive creature in mid-air, thrusting the arrow upward. Knocked back to the ground, the cat's weighty lifeless body forced him down. Luken struggled, attempting to free himself before the panther attacked again. The cat did not move; it was dead, although its immense weight was still holding him pent to the ground. Laughter grew within Luken, and he laughed happily. At last, freed from beneath the heavy panther's weight, he saw the second arrow buried deep into its neck.

Drenched in its blood, the sticky substance dripped down his body; however, he did not have time to clean himself. Twine and sticks banded together to make a stretcher, Luken laid out the panther and ran back to the village.

All the other hunters already back, they were standing around admiring their catches. When he saw Luken, his father ran up to him, stared down at the stretcher to see the giant animal, and then back up at him with an expression of pride pasted across his face.

"Blood. Boy, are you hurt?"

"No, Father, I am not." His father gave him a big grin.

"Look at this beast!" he yelled out to the others, boasting of his son's accomplishment.

His father's prideful brags on his side, Luken's kill was broadcast throughout the village. Everyone came running to see the large panther. "Come, my son, show them your skill as a great hunter."

"That boy killed that. Good lad." A giant prairie dark Dragonor told him, slapping him upon the back, shoving Luken forward.

Lord Ephenio walked up to him. "Well done." He looked to his father and asked, " Tinzadri, is this your son?" His father was smiling broadly, and that beam was enough to carry him through the rest of the competition. "As fine in the hunt as his father is in making a blade."

"Most certainly, my lord."

With all of the judges and leaders of the other clans inspecting his kill, he felt satisfied. For the first time, did he experience the self-satisfaction that most Dragonors carried deep within them. Luken radiated himself, and the cloud of shame for being a mere blacksmith seemed to lift, like the smoke from his forge. Luken, at last, felt special.

"Luken, how did you do it?" Talulah asked, "You were alone and took down this monster."

Although the bow was not the weapon actually used to kill the panther, Luken held it up proudly.

Talulah took the bow and held it. "It is beautiful."

Luken felt the bow useful and, of course, well made, but beautiful would not be how he described the weapon. Luken shyly smiled. "Would you care to keep it?"

"You made the lovely bow for the games," she replied, holding the weapon next to her closely. "Do you think I can keep it?"

"I want you to have it."

"Should I take it, then you must ride Magnus. You do not get to say no to me either."

Luken wanted to say no since borrowing her dragon made him somewhat indebted to his love. There was no choice in this matter. "Then, I will not say no. And I am indebted to you forever. I will smooth out the roughness on the bow for you if you like."

"I would like that very much."

"Competition number two is about to begin," someone yelled out to him.

Luken turned to walk away, but before she was out of his sight, he waved goodbye. A corny sentiment, of course. Then again, it was better than turning around and holding her in his arms and kissing her.

They were put through arduous climbing and hanging challenges that relied strictly on their body's strength. Their ability to fight and protect the clan was also tested by several challenges: weapon handling, archery, spear throwing, and sword-wielding. Luken was a master in all of these skills, and he knew how to wield every weapon he made skillfully, although he was not a hunter.

Each of them had to read the runestones and correctly give a message to the clan confirmed by Lord Ephenio. Luken had no problems in reading the runes either; he had help. His father, who learned the runes from his father, who read them for Lord Granor. The clan leader refused to read them because he felt them cursed; therefore, everyone in his family was taught rune reading as young Dragonors.

Anyone wanting to compete in the challenge had to train for many years and start as a child developing him or herself mentally and physically for the challenges. At age ten, he knew he loved Talulah. Such low self-esteem, he thought himself beneath her love. The only way to earn her endearment was to do something spectacular in the village, making him stand out. From his youth to win her love, he readied, trained, and pushed himself in secret for many years. A few months from village adulthood, it was time for him to prove himself. Possibly the most challenging, the last test was the one that concerned him—dragon battling. Luken tutored with dragon instructors, like all the other young Dragonors; the large beasts were not his fancy as he favored being on the ground.

Talulah stood around, talking to him and Magnus while Raphazk glared angrily at him. A massive dragon, dark red in color, dull black scales covered its ferocious body; it was one of the most enormous dragons in the village. Long jagged wings spread out behind it, towering over Luken while Magnus glared down at him.

"Magnus is my best friend, did you know? You will fare well with him. Trust him, Luken."

"I will have no problems. I am sure of that. He is just a dragon," Luken remarked, pretending this challenge did not worry him since, in his heart, he was not very confident at that moment in battling upon a dragon's back. Nervous tensions grew within him. Exhaling deeply, he looked up to see other Dragonors and their dragons flying about gracefully. Magnus' snubbed snout nudged him roughly, causing him to move forward slightly. Luken turned to see the gigantic dragon's mouth opening in a giant yawn, exposing rows of big sharp teeth. Magnus laid his head down at his feet.

"See, don't you think he likes you?"

"I hope so."

"You will love him," Talulah said to him cheerfully. "I have an idea. Do you think it might be lovely to ride with me sometime?"

Talulah was a mystery to Luken. Why did she not just say it would be lovely that the two of them should ride together? An adoration for her beautiful speech pattern, as well, Luken could not find anything about her he did not like. Nevertheless, this question was the most challenging test of the competition so far. Stunned that she was asking him out, fear of looking silly held him speechless for a moment. Talulah stared at him.

"We don't have to ride if you do not like to."

"Oh no, I think I would like that very much."

"A date then." Talulah softly touched his hand. "I will bring the dragon."

"And I will bring the…um… the meat basket."

"Sounds like a plan then. Oh, I forgot to give you this." Talulah reached into a tiny pouch she carried with her and pulled out a lock of hair.

A lock of her beautiful hair tied in a lovely black ribbon. Luken ran his fingers across the silky strands of hair. Such an intense desire to be close to her, without thought, he put the hair up to his nose, sniffing the violet smelling locks. Talulah giggled. Flooded with embarrassment, snatching the hair from his nose, he gazed down as if guilty of committing a crime.

"It is for Magnus; my hair calms him. If he gets unruly, just rub it across his neck."

"Yes, yes, of course," he stuttered. The precious thoughts of Talulah giving him her hair was a pleasant emotion, if he only experienced the joyous feeling for only for a moment. "I will return it when I get back."

"Oh no, you keep it. I can't paste it back on," Talulah told him, turning to leave. "Time for you to go." A big smile grew upon her face, and she walked away.

Luken glared at the large dragon; its large eyes were open, but soft snoring sounds came from its mouth. Magnus was asleep. Lifting himself upon the back of the enormous beast, he climbed up the thick tendrils along the spine of its neck. The dragon moved only slightly, and soft sounds continued coming from him.

"Dragon Battle, begin," Lord Ephenio cried out.

"Time to go, Magnus," Luken cried out, holding on to the dragon's tendrils tightly. However, Magnus did not move but continued to lay there. Like Talulah instructed, he rubbed the piece of hair on the dragon's neck, but it did not move still. "Let's fly. "

Laughter broke out among the onlookers. "Magnus won't budge for the boy."

Everyone in the village knew that dragons were not livestock trained to follow their owners. Dragons did whatever they intended, went wherever they planned, and listened to whoever they fancied. This one evidently did not like him and did not heed his commands. Humiliation from the laughter of others, Luken wanted to fade into the dragon and disappear. "I have completely embarrassed myself. Everyone is laughing at me. I certainly hope this is as hilarious for you as it is for them." Magnus lifted his massive head, glassy orange eyes glared intimidatingly at him, and he winked at Luken as if to have him understand who the boss was.

Without warning, the massive beast stood up and dashed upward, startling him. Luken almost fell off his back. He held on to the thick tendrils tightly, swinging from the dragon's spine as he soared upward. Laughter below still mocking him, he refused to fall and held on until Magnus leveled out and he could crawl back upon its back.

"Not funny, Magnus." The dragon let out a small stream of fire.

The dragon was enormous as it flew through the skies, and Luken felt as if he rested upon lumpy, hard bedding. Slowly he relaxed while studying the others flying about, battling with their dragons. Magnus flew around the combat, too, watching all that was going on and never attacked, even when assaulted.

"We have got to fight at some time, Magnus." Just as the words left his mouth, Luken felt a stream of heat against his back, and he peered behind him to see a stream of fire coming from a dragon ridden by Mongol of the Prairie Dragonors. Quickly, he laid forward and buried himself between the thick tendrils on the dragon's back, attempting to avoid the flames. "Mongol is behind us." Magnus never swerved or speed up. Seconds later, Mongol was next to him, jabbing a spear at him. Buried within the tendrils, Luken grabbed his own spear and fought back against Mongol as his foe's dragon moved closer, snapping Magnus's neck.

Luken stabbed at Mongol, who was now standing on his dragon and cautiously staggering to get closer to him. Magnus remained oblivious to what was happening with him, uncooperative in the battle and protecting his stray tendrils from the snapping of the other dragon's vicious mouth. Unlearned in the dragon-fighting art, he was not familiar enough with his companion, so Luken dared not stand upon its back to battle. With the tip of Mongol's spear much closer than Luken felt secure, he had to do something because he could not fall or even partially fall off, or the game would be over for him.

Spear attacks against Mongol held him away and protected him for a while; nevertheless, he knew he had to do something else. Luken had an idea, so he swung his spear sideways, slicing the eye of Mongol's dragon. The colossal beast screamed loudly in pain, almost stopped in mid-flight, and jerked backward. Mongol almost fell off his companion, but the Dragonor warrior hung on until his dragon stopped wailing.

"One down," Luken bragged.

"What treachery," Mongol shouted at him.

All was fair in Dragonor games, even death at times occurred. Warlords of old did not care how they defeated their foes, only that they won the war, and such as it was in their games.

"Thanks for the help, my friend," he said mockingly to Magnus. "I'm quite well. I did not require your help." While he bragged of his own accomplishment, Magnus dropped downward quickly, circled over a Glade Dragonor female, and in seconds, the massive beast snatched her up in his deadly talons.

"Foul," she cried, struggling to free herself.

"That was him," Luken yelled down at her while Magnus was placing her on the ground. Gentle placement of an adversary on a surface was courtesy of the great beast since already there were two rider deaths from falls. Magnus turned his big head and peered at Luken. At last, he understood the great beast. From that point on, through the remainder of the battle, the two of them fought brilliantly together. Too, Luken felt that he won a friendship, which might not hurt since the dragon was Talulah's devotee.

"Only you and I left Luken," Raphazk mocked. "So, you got this far. I must admit, for the son of a blacksmith, you did pretty well. Zatra and I are going to crush you both now. Unless you want to just give up." Brazenly he mocked Luken, then winked wickedly at him.

The words *son of a blacksmith* seeped out of his mouth with hateful scorn. Luken knew this was his last chance. Magnus on his side, he knew this was his destiny, and he would defeat Raphazk. Monstrous smoky flames jetted from the frightening black dragon's nose. Almost the same size as Magnus, Zatra's sleek body curved like a large snake, and his thick tail whipped viciously. Two horns in the center of his bulbous head, his wings, like those of a bat, fanned out around his massive body.

Magnus flew quickly towards Zatra. Luken held on while the two dragons clawed and bit at each other viciously. Pinned against the back until the uproar settled, he stayed out of the way of the flames thrown by Raphazk's massive beast. Sharp talons clicked together, and deadly roars came from their mouths. Zatra's sharp claw swiped at Magnus' neck, scrapping the metallic-like scales upon his skin again, triggering him to cry loudly. Vigorously, the fierce dragon backed away from the battle, and Luken searched his neck for an injury. However, he saw no bleeding.

Magnus flew away from Zatra's hot searing flames as he hunted his dragon down. Raphazk laughed loudly. "Give up, Blacksmith." At this point, all Luken could do was protect himself. Raphazk and his dragon kept pursuing the two of them; he chuckled loudly while his vicious dragon chased Magnus.

Magnus flew straight downward. Luken held on tight, knowing the clever dragon was going to do something probably extremely dangerous to him. As was his nature, without any warning, he stopped and turned around directly in front of Zatra, caught the broad neck of the dragon in his claws, and held him. Wild flames came from Zatra while Magnus swung him around like a toy.

Luken hid from the heat, shielding himself with the great dragon's body until Magnus let go of Zatra. With Raphazk still clinging to him, the massive black beast hurtled into the distance like a stuffed toy. Magnus followed the shocked dragon, then rammed his enormous body into the chest of Zatra. Again, defending himself against Magnus's grueling attack, his vast body flipped backward, and both rider and dragon lost their bearing.

With this opportunity at hand, although the contest was officially over, Luken's confidence was soaring as high as he flew on the back of the dragon. While Zatra regained his composure, Raphazk climbed back up to his seat. Skipping along the spine of Magnus and out onto the front of his wing, Luken bounded upon the neck of the black dragon. The dragon and his companion's attention focused upon Magnus' continuous attacks; Luken quickly maneuvered his agile body in between the spines and surprised Raphazk.

"What do we have here," Raphazk said haughtily to Luken.

"You have already lost, but I want you to know, Raphazk, that I am taking Talulah from you."

"You are still just the son of a blacksmith," Raphazk snarled, stood up on the back of Zatra, and jabbed its deadly tip at him. "And not if I kill you."

Luken jumped to his feet, quickly grabbing the tip of the spear, he held on to it. The sharp metal cut through the animal skin glove on his hands, but he held on. Anger overtook him, and with all of his might, Luken moved his bleeding hands up the spear, ramming it and Raphazk back. Farther and farther from the center of the dragon, he shoved him until his foot slipped off the dragon; however, cleverly, he grabbed one of the dragon's tendrils and hung on tightly. "Help me, Luken." Some part of him wanted to spear his enemy's hands, causing him to fall to the ground below, prevailing over any compassion within him to help Raphazk. Luken reached down, pulling him back onto the dragon. Swiftly, he punched the arrogant Dragonor in the face, and he fell forward and laid motionless on the back of his own dragon. Magnus realized the fight was over; relenting his attacks, he forced Zatra to the ground with Luken upon his back.

When he landed, Talulah ran up to Luken and hugged him. "You are most wonderful, Luken."

Luken enjoyed the hug and closeness; in respect for his new friend, he had to be fair. "It is Magnus who is the true champion here." He winked at the dragon.

"Oh yes, he is," she returned and rubbed the snout of the dragon.

Luken glanced over and saw Raphazk brooding; he chuckled. "What is happening between Zatra and Magnus? There is hate there."

"Oh, yes, it is a long story."

Later that evening, as customary, called for revelry throughout the entire village. For this one night, the three clans put aside their differences, even the tragic deaths that occurred during the competition, and celebrated as one.

Luken and Talulah sat together, talking under Magnus' great body's shadow while he slept near the lake.

"Did I tell you, you were just wonderful today, Luken?"

Luken grinned shyly, "Yes. And did I thank you today for the use of Magnus?" A nervous tension upon him, he stuttered, "A... And for being you."

She laughed, "Luken, that is so you. Why shall you thank me for being me?"

"Many ways. You offered me Magnus. You gave me your hair, and because you smiled at me."

"Luken, I smile at everyone." Talulah beamed when she smiled, and her lovely complexion was enchanting tonight. Luken reached down and held her hand, hoping she did not snatch it from him. Closer, she nudged over to him, and the two of them sat together under the moonlight.

"An excellent show today, Luken," Lord Ephenio commented, walking out of the shadows.

Quickly he let go of Talulah's hand, stood, and replied, "Thank you, Lord Ephenio."

"Sit back down and enjoy your evening," he told them, strolling off.

"My father is always the lurker." Talulah said, taking his hand in hers when he sat back down.

"I don't think he likes me."

"Don't be silly. Does the great Lord Ephenio like anyone, including me? You know that I like you, though?"

Today could not get any better for Luken. Champion of the Cypress, and now Talulah just said that she liked him. "I know I am only a blacksmith right now. I want to know if maybe we could…"

"Do you want to be together, Luken?" She asked, staring intently at him.

"Well, yes. I've won the championship. My weapons give me a lot of prosperity."

"Luken, quiet," she told him, placing her finger against his lip. "I never cared if you were a blacksmith's son. That was Raphazk. I liked you before but you never spoke to me."

Satiated in love for her, Luken took her fingers between his and kissed them gently. "Shall we join the others before your father sneaks over here again?"

"No, should we stay for a bit?" she asked him, drawing even closer to him. Luken's skin began to tingle, putting his arm around her, he held her close to him.

"Why did Magnus attack Zatra so ferocious today?"

"Did you not know that they were brothers?"

"No, I did not know that."

"Well, they are, and Magnus was born a couple of minutes later than Zatra…"

***

Over the years, after winning the contest, Luken and Talulah grew closer than friends, and he and his family earned greater respect as members of the village clan. Lord Ephenio invited his father to join the village council, which delighted him very much. Luken's weapon crafting popularity grew and soon Dragonors from all the clans wanted to purchase his weapons. Luken still didn't own a dragon, however, Magnus was always available to him.

More than fifty years later, his marriage day was upon him. Talula stood before him, so beautiful, and her long silver strands hung flawlessly to her waist and braided with small yellow flowers that matched her skin. His heart beat faster when she stood next to him. Her blue eyes glistened and sparkled under the sun, and her golden lips puckered, like she was eating a small fruit as she said her vows. Delightful sounds from the waterfall behind them joined in, forming lovely choruses harmonizing with the wooden flute and the harp's soft sounds. Crystal waters slowly streaming down emerald-colored rock walls behind her radiated a bright green glow around her. Talulah shone beautifully. Lord Ephenio, the great clan leader, presented the grandest wedding for his daughter, and for once, Luken even believed he was happy.

"I do." Talulah said, grinning happily.

Words of the promise of love exchanged, High Priestess Zorlaida placed magic stones around both of them, and a rainbow of lights filled the air around them.

Many years later, Tinzadri, his father and a council member, wanted Luken to join Lord Ephenio's advisers. So did Lord Ephenio. Luken wanted a life as an adventurer, and through his union with Talulah, he also found that she too had a spirit of inquisitiveness. On the back of Magnus, the two searched the lands between the Prairie Dragonors and their home.

On the back of Magnus, Luken, and Talulah traveled back to their village after spending several days with the Prairie Dragonors. Since it was her great dragon, Luken sat behind her, enjoying the pleasant evening and the company of his beloved.

"Luken, my darling, I do think that soon, I will not have the fortitude to join you on your journeys."

"Why not? I see no reason why you must stop. You are my muse, and I need you."

"Well, that might not be our decision to make soon." Talulah placed his hand across her belly. "We might have someone else to consider?"

"A baby." Luken held her tight. "Talulah, my darling, how happy you have made me this day."

"Are you happy?"

"Of course I am, my darling. We shall live together in love and happiness forever."

"I am so happy also. I cannot wait to tell my father and mother."

Luken grinned. "I have loved you since I first saw you. How can such a dream come true for me?"

"For me as well, my dear Luken."

"We should be home soon, and we will have a great feast and announce it to our family."

"Oh, how wonderful. Let's do that."

Chapter Three

Given and Taken Away

Luken had no prejudices; a deal was a deal, a word was a word, and he trusted the Prairie Dragonors, as well as those within his own clan. All three of the clans, created by the same maniacal magic users, so he and Talulah took very long journeys across the mountains to sell his valuable weapons. Since they were different, the two of them were a sort of amusement for the others in the stern, ill-tempered villages, and some even accepted them secretly into their homes to rest the night away.

As wonderful as his life began with Talulah, it ended just as tragically. Humans came from across the great seas, where the Dragonors once resided, and fought bitterly for the warlords. Many centuries passed, and the men's villages expanded into their realms until soon run-ins with them were familiar. And these meetings of the two groups more likely turned disagreeable, than pleasant.

It was told to Luken that as soon as the stranger sent them to the new lands, isolated contact with small groups of humans occurred from time to time when they traveled across the ground on foot. Sometimes, when Talulah was unable to go with him on the long journey, Luken took the two-week-long trip through the mountains and came across natives of the land who lived in tents and migrated across the region. These humans, he and Talulah found of the acceptable sorts, and sometimes they traded bows and arrows for furs and meat. Luken treasured these natives and learned a lot about their mannerisms and ways, which reminded him of his own village.

Nevertheless, the new population was different. Barbaric, angry, and hateful; Luken supposed they were like the Dragonors once. The men with guns and other powerful weapons began to flourish so close that they even hunted and set bounties on the dragons spotted flying across the lands. They pursued the Dragonors, who they called demons that needed to be destroyed. Life was in ruins for the clans. They suffered a shortage of food and other supplies because they hid away from humans to stop their altercations. For the glades, the wildlife diminished, it seemed overnight. Dragonors knew the great waters no longer shielded their world, and they would have to fight to keep their homes. Most of them had never known real battle before. They had only heard their great ancestors' stories of battle hunger; however, they existed in times of peace and were hunters of the land and no longer vicious warriors. That was part of the deal with the stranger.

Life for Luken and the others changed almost overnight, it seemed. As wonderful as his life began with Talulah, it ended just as tragically.

***

Lord Ephenio strolled through the forest, studying the damage that the human was doing to the lands. These terrible monsters frequently visited the everglades now. Carcasses of snakes, crocodiles, and alligators lay rotting, their skin's gone, hastily removed for its value alone. A shudder came over him as he placed the decaying meat on the litter he pulled behind him. Villagers burned the rot later that night, hoping to ward away the disease of human savages.

Lord Ephenio heard laughter; it was the precious sounds of his granddaughter, Shanara; he listened as she played happily. The two of them should have never entered the forests alone. Hate grew within him that his granddaughter had to search for berries with her mother around such death. Shanara was not stupid, though, as she knew about the human invasion.

When he stepped into the open, he saw Talulah forging for berries across the stream while his granddaughter played blissfully in the water. Around the stream, small berries with nuts inside them were a treat for his daughter, and although warning Talulah about the dangers of being out alone, he knew she was strong and could take care of herself. Such a proud grandfather; his granddaughter would follow in his footsteps and perhaps become the clan leader. Luken, a hardworking young Dragonor by her side, he was pretty sure the two would rule greatly. Lord Ephenio watched his daughter and granddaughter with adoration. Turning, he walked away.

"Mother… don't. Stop hurting her."

Lord Ephenio froze and ran back to the edge of the stream when he heard his granddaughter's screams. Unsure at what he was seeing was not an illusion, panicky gasps came from him when he saw the horror of two humans attacking Talulah. A big brute, wearing a raccoon skin cap and dirty vest, held her around her chest, trapping her in his tight grasp. As swiftly as possible, Lord Ephenio swam through the rapid flows to save his daughter and granddaughter. To him, time seemed to stand still while he watched what was occurring on the other side of the bank.

The scoundrel was laughing as Shanara struggled to free herself. "I am not going to free you, girl," he chuckled.

"Free my mother now!"

Shanara fought hard, pulling the other attacker's leg that wore a scraggly beard and curly matted hair. As the large goon approached his daughter with a sharp blade. "Piss off," the man with the sword told his granddaughter. Grabbing her by her hair, he slung her small body into the stream like she was nothing more than a doll. She cried loudly, and Lord Ephenio blood ran as icy cold as his heart for the humans.

"Don't touch my daughter," Talulah screamed, lifted her legs up, fell forward, and rolled her and the curly top attacker forward. Releasing his grip for a moment, she got to her feet and stomped hard on his stomach. Curly top groaned loudly.

"I'm gonna cut you bloody neck."

"Don't touch my daughter," Talulah screamed. Turning to save her daughter, she did not realize the other assailant was directly behind her. Before she could stop him, the man in the dirty vest took the butt of his rifle and struck her across the head.

"You cheeky cow," the man in the vest told her, kicking her while she lay on the ground.

"Leave her alone," Lord Ephenio yelled, running toward them. Tired but driven, wading out of the stream, his great blade out of its sheath, he put his granddaughter down on the bank along the creek and dashed to help his daughter. It was too late.

The curly top assailant bolted to his feet, anger pasted upon his face; darting over, the man plunged the sword deep into his daughter's chest while she lay upon the ground. "Stop," Lord Ephenio screamed. Shanara stopped writhing, and without thought, Lord Ephenio grabbed him by the messy curls of hair, shoving his head back. The long blade in his hand, pushing it through the man's neck, up to its hilt, then he yanked it out just as fearsome as his attack. The man's body fell atop of Talulah, but he had no time to worry over this offense of his daughter's body.

"Don't hurt me," the man with the dirty vest cried out. "Please, I did not kill her. It was him, and he's dead now. I won't come back, I promise." The man in the dirt vest pleaded for his life but his words evaporated at Lord Ephenio's unhearing ears. Swiftly, the man darted away through the forest. Within moments the great lord caught him by his shirt's neck and threw him to the ground.

"Please, mister, don't kill me." Lord Ephenio's features grew dark, and a fit of anger beyond all rational thoughts overcame him. The great lord raised his sword above his head, plunging it deep into the heart of the pleading man, he watched him wiggle in agony. Moments later, yanking his steel back out of the man's body, he left to collect his granddaughter and his daughter's body.

Lord Ephenio rushed Talulah back to the healers, sent out riders to locate Luken, and prayed for his daughter's health. For days she held onto life. The blade pierced her heart, and they were unable to save her with their medicines or dragon remedies.

     ***

The messenger did not tell him anything; he flew on Magnus' back for a day and a night without a break because he feared something dreadful happened. Luken sensed that the dragon felt the same since the great beast was with him for the short journey to trade a special-order shield to Lord Belegornor of the Prairies. When he returned to the village, Luken's worst nightmare faced him. What he feared all the way home was upon him. Talulah lay in Lord Ephenio's arms, lifeless. Overwhelmed in sorrow, Priestess Zorlaida stood by his side and Shanara ran to him, tears streaming from her precious eyes.

"She tried to wait for you. She only left just an hour ago." Priestess Zorlaida told him.

"What shall we do, Daddy?"

No words came from his mouth. Luken could only hold his child close and glare at his mate's lifeless body. Priestess Zorlaida took Shanara from his arms, and he painfully took Talulah from the ailing lord. Luken saw dead bodies before, but never had one been so close. He looked down upon her frozen, sunken face. Lord Ephenio and Priestess Zorlaida took Shanara and left him to be alone with his beloved. A single tear fell and Luken vowed never to cry again. When they returned to take her away, he could not let her go; they had to pry her from his hands.

After Talulah's death, he stayed within the village, making more valuable weapons, honing his skills to become a better blacksmith than his father. Rarely he left to deliver the weapons himself now and stayed near the village to make sure that Shanara was cared for. As she aged into a young Dragonor, found her own buddies and realized interests of her own, Luken's heart once again longed to explore. This time, it was because of pain and not excitement, and he only wanted to be alone. Luken took journeys to heal the pain eating away at his heart, and they were not nearly as wonderful as the times he and Talulah had on their explorations. Talulah went away, Shanara had a life; Luken had no reason to stay in the village.

Luken left on foot, leaving Magnus behind because, like him, the poor dragon did not have the spirit anymore to travel across the skies without Talulah. Shanara did not bond with the great beast like her mother, and his daughter had actually grown attached to another great creature called Buderous. On a trip through the lands to sell an ax and sword to the prairies, Luken decided to change his route and took an unfamiliar path through the caves in the mountains. For safety, inside the recesses of the dark hollow, he would rest for the night to stay out of the way of the humans. Although it was still early and the sun still shined, he could travel many more miles but Luken did not want to. The days and nights were his now, and right now, he was not expected anywhere.

To his surprise, deep in the recesses within the cavern, the mountains opened to expose an alcove of heavenly gardens with fountains of water springing up, creating a small pond within its luscious, colorful center. Oddly sized mushrooms sat around the pond, and in the trees, little houses fashioned out of branches and leaves decorated the miniature buildings. And, flittering around the little village were small creatures that resembled tiny humans, but with wings.

"Who are you?" A faint voice asked. Luken peered around to see a little creature floating upward. Long blue hair and blue scaly skin of blue as well, his tiny blue wings flapped quickly, emitting flashes of blue light around him. The little guy levitated before him with his arms crossed in what he supposed was his intimidating stance.

"I am Luken, and may I be permitted to ask who you are, my friend."

"You may. I am Grantium. This is the Kingdom of the merfey."

It seemed the stories he heard as a child were right. They were not the only unwanted creations of the warlords. Luken had heard about the merfey, and like many other glades, having never seen one himself, thought them only a myth, told by the prairies.

"It is my honor to meet you." Luken nodded his head respectfully.

"Why are you here? We get no visits from the Glade Dragonors. Only the Prairies come to visit us."

"I am on a journey to visit the prairies now."

"Why no dragon? This is indeed odd. You must come to see our Queen."

The sun showed brightly from a hole within the rock around the gardens, causing their wings to sparkle brightly while the merfey flittered around. As curious children, scrutinizing the newest kid at school, they flocked around him. The sound of their combined wings flapping triggered a ringing in his ears, which annoyed him. Nevertheless, he was in their lands, and it seemed, for now, he was safe. Eagerly they followed him and all their tiny giggles and their suspicious big bubbly eyes upon him. Luken grew a bit unsettled.

"He is different."

"Yes. Is he one of the ones the Queen told us about?"

Chatter throughout the group, Luken grinned, trying to reduce the anxiety within him. "Hi, everyone. I am Luken. I am a Glade Dragonor."

"Hi, Luken." They all responded at once, like a chorus, then more giggles broke out.

"I am new in these lands."

"New in these lands," they giggled.

At last, he followed Grantium through a doorway into a tunnel in the mountainside, which Luken had to bend over to move through. Through another maze, the little merfey led him down a rock hallway. His back was beginning to tighten from the uncomfortable bent position he put himself in. Tiny fire-lit torches, along the wall giving off its light, allowed Luken to see down the dark tunnels. At its end, a large room waited. Finally, almost crawling through a taller doorway, he noticed a tiny throne with a female merfey sitting upon it. Luken straightened his back and stood proudly while approaching the little queen.

Rock walls covered in green vines with broad leaves, red, orange, and yellow flowers grew upon wet surfaces. Vines attached themselves snugly to the walls, like a motif fantastically painted, appearing almost too realistic. If it were not for the water dripping down the walls, forming a stream along the bottom of the wall, he might have thought the walls had been painted upon the rock mountain exterior. On a clean dirt floor, blue and yellow mushrooms sprung from the ground shaped like tables. The pretty vegetation sat around the room and resting on their tops were platters filled with berries, flowers, and tree bark.

The queen sat on a throne made of platinum, which Luken was sure the Prairie Dragonors formed for her because the little merfey did not look like they had the skills or fortitude to forge metal. Rods of platinum designed as delicate vines, similar to those in the cave, created lovely legs and curved arms. The seat and back of the prized little throne, padded in pink pillows, revealed her white form brilliantly, and the merfey queen looked quite delightful upon her tiny chair. When Luken stepped into the doorway of her throne room chambers, the other merfey turned around.

"My Queen. I do apologize, but I found this stranger." Grantium said, bowing before her.

The little white merfey glared at him. In fact, he felt a bit put out by the stare in the Queen's stern gaze. "My Queen, I am Luken." In an attempt to follow Grantium's example, Luken bowed politely.

"Jazhazra. My name is Queen Jazhazra to you," she said, scowling, and her pretty little face actually had a frown in its expression.

"I am delighted to meet you, Queen Jazhazra."

"This is my village, and these are my merfey." The little queen proudly told him. "So, tell me Luken, why are you here?"

"I am on my way to deliver a weapon to the Prairie Dragonors, and before you ask, I will tell you. I don't have a dragon, so I must go on foot."

"Why no dragon? I thought the dragons were your people's pride," she commented and laughed. Grantium joined in on the laughter.

"For some of us, that is true." Luken wanted to tell her about Magnus. That would lead to the entire conversation about his wife, so he held onto his secret.

"Dragons, smagon's, they are the same to me. Useless vile creatures."

"Yes, that is true as well. My Queen, you are very preceptive," he said, aiming to flatter her arrogant ego. The queen stood up, floating atop of her chair, sparkles like diamonds on her wings; they shimmered when the little creature fluttered about. White from head to toe, even the crown upon her was platinum, which made her quite peculiar.

"I had another visitor with your kind today, Gathon, of the Prairie Dragonors. Evidently, they are forming some type of departure council to leave our homes."

"So soon? I thought that might be held later." Lord Ephenio spoke to him before he left about the glade elves departing and asked him to join the council. None of that mattered to Luken right now; he just needed time to be alone, so Luken told him he would think about it and let him know when he returned.

"Yes. I am called to my lands and go to yours in a day or so. Evidently, there has been an attack against the Prairie Dragonors. Oh yes, and I did hear that the humans killed one of yours. What a shame," she said and sat down on a swing hanging from a limb on a tree behind her little throne. Luken held back his words of fury at her for speaking in such an uncaring attitude. It was his mate that the humans killed. Sleep was better inside of the caves than outside in the open, with the humans roaming about, though.

"You are to be on that council. Your father as well, I am told, along with Lord Ephenio."

"I will not go back now. Let Lord Ephenio find another." Luken realized his temper flared, and he did not want to offend the little dictator before him. "I apologize for my tone, Queen Jazhazra. I am afraid I never confirmed any such decision that I would sit on the council with Lord Ephenio."

"Nonsense, you will go back Luken, you are a member of the clan. Is that not your main concern? Its safety."

Queen Jazhazra went on lecturing Luken; however, she had no idea of the pain that awaited him when he returned home. "Yes, you are right. My decision is made, though. I will continue on my journey to the Prairie Dragonor."

"Who is on their way to your village. That is lunacy, Luken," she laughed. This laugh was not pleasant and sunny, but evil. Luken stepped back. "If I must make this senseless journey, then so shall you. It is settled, you will travel with me."

"I am sorry and I don't mean to offend you, Queen Jazhazra, but Lord Ephenio must find another."

As if she heard nothing he told her, the brash little merfey said, "I will send word to Lord Ephenio that you will accompany me. We will leave in three days."

"I thought you must be there earlier."

"No one tells me what to do," she scowled. "Now, leave me."

Luken sat around with the little merfey most of the night, chatting with them and answering their intrusive questions, putting up with their rude comments. Since the merfey were friends with the prairies, there was comfort in the tiny village for him; nevertheless, the odd little merfey actually disturbed him. Three little merfey flying towards him held a plate too large for one of them to carry alone, topped with berries, flower petals, and grilled minnows. Hunger pains attacking his stomach, he took the food and actually enjoyed its pleasant taste. Later that night, with some of the little merfey completely smashed from wine, Luken sat around with them listening. The drunken merfey told him tales about the Queen while he sat chewing on maple tree bark, enjoying the sweet substance dried on it.

Although he was much larger than the whole of them put together, he believed the little creature quite formidable under the Queen's direction. Luken did not trust Jazhazra, and he did not want to end up captive to the lunatic petite pixie. Crazed, he believed her, and he saw it when she spoke to him. Drunken merfey told him her magic was much more significant than others in the village, which was another concern since he watched the little creatures forming fireballs and lightning strikes for his amusement. Their tongues, much too loose, said one day she and Fruitpip, her assistant, taunted the past queen, and in the end, the two of them took control over the Kingdom, and Jazhazra's electrical strikes fried the little Queen alive.

Before the sun rose that morning, not having any intention of returning with the Queen, Luken left the cave to continue on with his journey.

Such an uncaring nature in Jazhazra caused him grief, and his pain was beginning to overwhelm him. Along his path, he came across a rabbit trapped in a stick cage, lured there by some morsel now long eaten. The poor creature appeared to be trapped for several days and seemed to be thirsty and famished. *How ironic, to end up even hungrier than you were before you were deceived by the trap. Nothing is without consequence, my little friend.* Luken freed the frightened little animal; timidly, the poor creature arose to its feet and hopped weakly away.

"Don't be that silly again."

Like the rabbit in the trap, he realized that he was as the creature. Trapped in a cage of his own making by not letting go of his own web of pain and anger. Everyone said it was time for him to let it go, even Shanara, and he was struggling to hold onto it. When Luken freed the rabbit, it felt like he released himself from his own cage in some strange way. Talulah would not want him to keep mourning her and he knew she would tell him what he just said to that rabbit. Luken turned around to go back home.

That night, in a cave far from the little merfey, Luken slept peacefully and dreamed for the first time since his mate's death. A dream of the happiness they had together, and he awoke smiling. When he opened his eyes, she was sitting next to him. Talulah gently rubbed her fingers through his hair. Luken knew he was awake; he stayed deadly still, not wanting to disturb the beautiful vision.

"If this is a dream, I do not want to wake up," he said softly. Talulah's heartening touch continued; he reveled in her closeness.

"I am home, Luken. I left you too early, and I can't go to be with my fathers. I won't." Talulah leaned over and kissed him. "I couldn't come to you earlier because you were so sad. When you get back home, I will be there waiting."

Luken closed his eyes. The sensation of her touch was missing. Immediately, he got up to continue his journey back home, happier than he had been in a long time.

When he returned back to the village, he was greeted by several of his friends who were concerned about his welfare. A polite speech and a thank you were the most that Luken gave them. Respectfully, he took his leave to see Lord Ephenio. The Glade Dragonors could leave; however, Luken couldn't leave the everglades now. Talulah was waiting for him at their home; he just knew it.

"I am surprised at you, Luken, surely I thought you would understand and above all of us desire to leave," Lord Ephenio said to him with surprise and anger in his voice. "My daughter, your wife, is no longer here because of humans. Your daughter does not have a mother, and I will not stand by and allow another one of my people to be killed by them. We will leave if the others decide we must."

"Then I will stay," Luken told him boldly. Never had he ever wanted to disrespect Lord Ephenio, but he could not leave now. "I have not forgotten Talulah: every second, she is in my thoughts, and she always will be."

"Then what of Shanara? She is your child."

"I know that. That is why I am against the Dragonor's leaving."

"This day had to come, Luken. The stranger gave the orbs to the merfey, the Prairie Dragonors, and one to our village. I believe our time is done here. We will move on. You will find another to love."

"I will never love another, my Lord Ephinio," he said gruffly.

"Why, Luken, I do not understand your argument."

Although he might believe him insane, Luken replied, "Talulah is here. I am not sure how. I saw her and have spent time with her." Lord Ephenio stared at him as if he had gone insane. "I have a life again, and a life with her. I cannot explain it to you, and I hope you do not ask me to try. All I know is I have to stay here to be with her."

"You cannot be serious. Even if this were true, Luken, she is nothing more than a spirit. You cannot love or touch her. For the rest of your years, you will want more. I know you still suffer."

"I do not suffer, Lord Ephinio." Luken raised his voice, took a deep breath, and exhaled. Softly, he continued, "She has touched me. I felt her touch last night, and this day I will see her, Lord Ephinio. Talulah is here."

"How can you stay alone with humans? Talulah, how is she here? Have you gone mad, Luken?"

"No, I have not. You will see your daughter. I am sure she will come to you." Luken knew he would never believe him and hoped she would show herself to her father.

"Luken, even if she is here, I have the Dragonors to think about. We cannot stay here as we will all die or end up going to war. I do not want this blood on my hands."

"Then she will be alone. Do you not see why I can't leave?" Lord Ephenio's expression remaining stern and grave, he glared at Luken. "I have lived all my years in the everglades. I have wonderful memories of my life here with Talulah, and now that I know she is with me again, I will not leave her behind. You must understand, my Lord Ephenio, I do not want to beg you to stay, but I will."

"This is not my decision to make, Luken. We can bring it up to the others in the delegation."

"Thank you, Lord Ephenio." He really did not want to pressure the great lord anymore. His decision was made, and now all he could do is wait. "Has that caddy little merfey arrived?"

"Not as of yet but be assured most cannot wait to lay their eyes upon her. Have you seen her?"

"Yes, I have. Do not be swayed by the little imp's size either, she is as big or bigger than any in mouth."

When Luken returned home, as she promised, Talulah was waiting for him.

"How long has it been since our home is so quiet, Luken darling?" Shanara, now living with Lord Ephenio and Priestess Zorlaida, the home was once again empty. Luken rushed to her and took her in his arms and held her tight.

"Oh, how I have missed you."

"And I you," she told him.

"You must go to the others also, Talulah. Shanara and your mother and father's grief are hard as well."

She stopped smiling and said, "I cannot. I am only for you, my dearest Luken. I will expect you to tell me all about them. What is my dear daughter like?"

"No, there must be a way for them to see you. No one believes me." Talulah peered at him with an expression of disbelief.

"I cannot. Please never ask me that again. No one ever believed in our love as we did, Luken."

Time disappeared that night for Luken, and the two of them talked most of it away. When he awoke to ready for the meeting, she was gone. There was no fear in his heart, though, for Luken knew she would return, and he was never going to leave her.

Chapter Four

Council of Departure Meets

At her command, the little merfey carried baskets of fruits, berries, and cut up portions of cooked meat, performing the function of perfect hosting and serving the other lords and High Priestess politely. An array of food, placed on the back table in the grand meeting hall, the room smelled like a cooking hall. Dragonor meetings were never this charming or whimsy.

When Luken, Lord Ephinio, and Tinzadri arrived at the meeting, the other departure council members were already there. They sat around the table, including the Queen of the merfey, who sat on the table, while her busy little merfey attended to their needs. The grand spectacle was almost comical. This did not surprise him, though, since the little queen coveted control. Her small throne, placed at the end of the table near Lord Ephenio's seat, proudly she sat there, directing the merfey.

"What do you think she is up to?" he asked.

Lord Ephenio stared at her and remarked, "Quite tiny, isn't she?"

Luken chuckled; he knew that by her taking the position at the table's head, the little merfey was making a point.

The council consisted of three delegates from the two groups: The Prairie Dragonors, Glade Dragonors, and only the Queen for the merfey.

"Hello, Lord Ephenio. I have heard many things about you," scowling angrily, the little queen gave him her small hand. "Much of it, I see to be true, and I am pleased."

Lord Ephenio looked curiously at the small merfey. "Touch it," Luken leaned over and whispered to him. "She never gave me her hand." Lord Ephenio touched the Queen's hand politely.

"Very well, I guess we should start the meeting now," she said, motioning for the others to take their seat. "Merfey, leave the room."

Caught off guard by her arrogance, Lord Ephenio sat down as she commanded with a look of astonishment upon his face.

"I see you did make it back home anyway, Luken."

Luken said nothing. A gaze in her eyes seemed to pierce deep within him, and her transparent sparkled wings were almost eerie. A silver tiara upon her small head, white hair and skin, and white gown covering her body, in the bright light of the meeting chambers, Luken thought her appearance scary. In secret, the others told him that she was old as eternity and never died. Other merfey died, nevertheless, she did not. Of course, Luken believed it was rubbish. The Dragonors live very long lives; they were ancients, though not immortal. This disagreeable little creature was no god. A brilliance brighter than the other merfey, which they told him made her magic stronger; this he was unable to deny.

"Thank you, Queen Jazhazra," Lord Ephenio replied, evidently finally able to find his tongue again. "I believe we shall start now."

In attendance were Lord Faerverer, the leader of the eastern Prairie Dragonors, and his two captains, Oldhinor and Perchaladon. The Western Prairie Dragonors captain, Lord Belegornor, was there also, and accompanying him was Gwessil, and High Priestess Faur. Each of them turned their attention to Lord Ephenio. Luken saw already there would be disagreements. Dragonors were incapable of getting along together.

"Yes," Lord Faerverer agreed. Skin the complexion of a peach, having a darker triangular pattern upon it, combined with golden thread weaved through his auburn hair and shining silver plated armor, he was quite impressive. "It is time for the Dragonors to leave Earth, and we have made plans to use our passage orb."

"Thank you, Lord Faerverer. May I hear from the others," Lord Ephenio gave respect where it was due, but his own strength allowing him to speak forcefully when it was time. Luken did not worry over any disrespectful attitudes in the room. The old Lord was at least a century older than his father-in-law, Luken knew. Both great Lords impressive to Luken; he sat quietly watching the stately Lords prepare for combat.

"We are only here to invite anyone who wishes to come along with us. My people are ready to leave, and we have no desire to remain here. The warlords are not returning, but they gave us a way out to live in peace," Lord Belegornor belched out loudly.

Queen Jazhazra stood from her throne, floating gracefully, she started to speak. "Several of my friends and my subjects whom I sent out to forage, have not returned. I sent out a party to continue looking for them. Some we found did not have a happy ending."

"Too bad," Lord Belegornor grouched. With an appearance of genuinely being sorrowful, the other Lords and High Priestess listened intently to her. Luken was not buying her sobs.

"I know, of course, you have all heard the reports of how the humans lock us in containers. Do they not understand that we cannot survive," she asked with sadness, gazing down? Moments later, another merfey flew up and stood on the table next to Lord Ephenio

"This is my assistant Fruitpip. I sent her out and others to look for the missing."

Fruitpip's wings began fluttering fearfully. "Hello," she stuttered nervously, "My Lords and High Priestess Faur, I am afraid that what our Queen Jazhazra says is true. I found my own sister Lenishu in one of these containers that the humans used to hold her. My poor heart, they sealed her in a clear container with grass at its bottom. We are still not sure what the grass was for."

"The humans are harsh," said High Priestess Faur. A sheer white gown draped over her slender dark grayish, almost black body. Luken saw the outline of her slim body and breasts. Long golden hair, cut in the shape of a V, fell behind her and lay neatly upon the ground around her chair; he never realized how beautiful she was. Faur was very dark to be a prairie, so the story goes she was once a Glade Dragonor caught in the middle of the split of clans. Because of marriage, just like Lord Ephenio, who was only a young man at the time of the separation, they both had to choose sides. Softly she spoke; her words of confidence and authority betrayed her naïve presence. "I fear it will only get worse for us with the humans, and we too are prepared to leave."

Perchaladon spoke up and snarled, "At one time, we were hopeful that we could live with the humans and even set up trade with some of them, but soon we began to notice the greed that was in them and their barbaric ways. It should give some comfort for you to know that this behavior is not just against us; they treat their own the same way." A relatively short Dragonor, less than six feet tall, his height did not appear to affect his severe demeanor as he argued with the others.

"Since trade with them did not work, as warriors, we should fight and protect ourselves. They want to destroy us," Oldhinor spoke up.

"But we are not warriors any longer," Priestess Faur responded.

"The Glade Dragonors do not wish to fight," Lord Ephenio replied roughly.

"We have to fight now, or we die." Lord Faerverer told them.

"That is true Faerverer, fighting is our only defense now, but still, they come into our forest and attack our weak and helpless when there are no warriors about."

Luken immediately thought of Talulah when Lord Ephenio spoke and knew the grieving Lord was referring to his daughter. Her death no longer pained him, because she was back in his arms.

"Certainly, you do not think the merfey are going to put together some type of army and march to war against the humans, do you?" Jazhazra smirked.

Perchaladon sprang from his chair angrily. "I will fight, if it is necessary, but the dastardly humans want dominion over everything." Angrily he paced about the room. Heels on the bottom of his boots making a thud as he moved across the wooden floor.

"Sit down, Perchaladon." Lord Faerverer growled. A bold burly Dragonor. If the races were still true warriors, he was the perfect example of how one would look. His build more considerable than the average, slender Dragonor figure, he was a giant among them, and his shoulders extended beyond the back of the chair he sat in.

"This talk of fighting is useless. We leave, and that is the final word from my clan," scolded Lord Belegornor.

"Enough of this bantering back and forth. Let us vote," Lord Ephenio told them.

"We should all agree," said Lord Belegornor. The huge lord hated Lord Ephenio for a reason unknown to Luken, but it was evident how he scowled at him during the meeting. "The Dragonors and dragons must leave as one. The merfey are welcome to come along.".

"We have no home with you," Lord Ephenio snarled. One of the clan members who believed in the separation between the Dragonor clans, he was none too happy with Luken and Talulah when they journeyed to the prairies' region. "We have developed a life separate and distinct from both the Prairie Dragonor clans and that will not change. We separated ourselves again after the warlords separated us, and we will leave it that way. We received an orb as well."

"You are a Dragonor, like the rest of us. A cast-off surely, but now we all belong together," barked Lord Belegornor. "The warlords should have put us together from the start."

Luken saw by Lord Ephenio's change in demeanor that there was a real offense to the prairie's lord's words. "We are cast offs. You sent us away, and now you want us to join you?" His words growing heated, the two of them glared at each other.

"Please, Lord Ephenio, Lord Belegornor, this is not the time. We fought and destroyed each other and the humans across the water many long years ago, and for centuries, we lived in peace. However, our instincts are only for hate. How sad," High Priestess Faur solemnly remarked.

"It is true. That is the way of things," Luken spoke up in defense of Lord Ephenio.

"Our clans belong together. I, too, believe the separation was a mistake," Faur agreed.

"Whether the separation was a mistake or not, it was made for the good of our clans. Today, that is the thing I consider; the issue is the safety and comfort of my clan."

"Where will you go if you do not come with us?" Faur asked.

"We are studying the star map now. We As he spoke, some of the other Dragonors yelled angry protests against his decision. Without regard to their complaints, the Lord kept his confidence, speaking loudly over their objections. "Currently, the High Priestess Zorlaida is solving this riddle for us. She has already found two places, and there are more. Wherever you decide to go, we will go in another direction."

"That is impossible," bellowed Lord Belegornor. "You are Dragonors, and you should go with us."

The High Priestess Faur, his wife, reached over and gently touched Lord Belegornor's hand. "It is possible to teleport to another place. We know the stones can only be used once, though, and you do realize if you do not go with us, we will be lost from you forever."

"They are already lost," chuckled Lord Faerverer. "What does it matter? Let them go where they want to go. They hate us, we hate them… leave them to their own fate."

"We realize that," Lord Ephenio said politely, settling his temper back down. Luken was quite impressed that his clan leader was holding the meeting together. Without warning, Lord Belegornor stood up and barked.

"I will not have it. You will go with the rest of us."

Lord Ephenio stood up. "We cannot be civil in this meeting room. How do you expect us to live together?"

"He has a point," Olinder told them.

For hours they argued over whether the Glade Dragonors would leave with the others. Lord Ephenio, Luken, and Tinzadri refused to budge on their opinions and began to loudly object.

Finally, the High Priestess Faur said, "This has to end, we are all brothers, and this is not the behavior of the Dragonors. The contamination of humans has started to change us. This is why we have all agreed we must leave. I have changed my mind, and I think the Glade Dragonors should go where they want to. If they do not believe that they belong with us, so shall it be. Let them start a new life for themselves." She closed her eyes, as if searching for peace in the disorderly room.

"Thank you, High Priestess Faur. We can argue this point forever, but the facts are the Glade Dragonors are not going with you."

"Yes, I agree, this subject is growing tiring." Lord Belegornor said.

"Merfey will gladly go with the prairies." Queen Jazhazra peered over at Lord Ephenio. "I will let my subjects know they are free to join you as well, but I am almost certain we will leave with the prairie Prairie Dragornors."

"The merfey are welcome to come with us, and any homeless dragons in our region we are taking them with us as well."

"Dragons that do not want to leave, for them, it is certain death. They do not fear death, however. I hate to say it, and they can be troublemakers," Tinzadri said.

"As we know, dragons, yes," agreed Perchaloden.

"I would once again caution you, Lord Ephenio. You will forsake the life of the Dragonors forever if you take this path."

"I thank you, High Priestess Faur, for your advice. As a clan, we have decided that it would be best for us to leave and find our own home." They all sat quietly for a few seconds, as if digesting what just happened. Lord Ephenio broke the silence of the group. "There is something else that I would like to ask the council to consider."

A silence came over the room, which made the situation quite tense for Luken because he knew this conversation would be about him.

"What is it?" said Lord Belegornor asked harshly, "You Glades have decided to re-write all of the rules. So, tell us what you desire now." The angry Dragonor waved his hand at Lord Ephenio dismissively at him.

Lord Ephenio evidently decided to ignore the remark of Lord Belegornor. "Luken would like to remain here. He feels the Earth needs him and has called out for him to stay. Before any of you say anything, let me say this. Luken was married to my daughter. Her death was at the hands of hunters in the forest. So you can see that I, too, was surprised by his desire to stay. At first, I objected, believing him mad. I listened to his words, though, and I will allow him to remain on Earth."

Luken waited for him to finish to hear the verdict of the council's decision. He prepared himself for the fight with the others to defend his request.

"Why is this?" said Lord Belegornor. "The Earth belongs to the humans now. He has no right to stay."

"I have lived all my life in the glades…" Luken replied, a bit agitated at the gruff lord.

"We understand that. Such is true for all of us." Oldhinor replied, a look of confusion and unbelief covering his face. "What we do not understand, Luken, is why do you want to stay on Earth alone?"

"I was married in the glades, as Lord Ephenio said. My mate died in the glades, and now I truly believe my life is still in the glades. With her. If I leave, then I leave her, and I cannot bear that. Surely I will waste away if I am required to leave." Luken's voice broke in sorrow.

"How is Talulah still here, Luken?" Lord Faerverer asked. "Surely, you do not expect us to believe that her spirit still lives in the everglades. Is this why you say you cannot leave Earth?"

"Yes, that is what he wants us to believe, Lord Faerverer," Lord Belegornor said condescendingly. "What else will these Glade Dragonors ask for?"

"I cannot expect that you would understand, Lord Belegornor and Lord Faerverer. But I mean no disrespect to either of you when I say you cannot possibly appreciate the situation that I find myself in." Luken paused for a brief second, fighting his sentiment of offense by the two of them. "Lord Belegornor, this is not a Glade Dragonor request. As far as I am aware, I am the only one that has asked to remain."

"Luken's heart is in the everglades and is it not possible that he feels my daughter's essence here? The only place they both have ever known?"

Luken knew that it was more than Talulah's essence. Only he saw her, though, and he could not convince the others that she was truly here with him. Listening to them argue, he remained quiet, hoping that Lord Ephenio could persuade them to let him stay.

"If I still have a vote, I say no," Lord Belegornor huffed.

"Well, I agree he should stay," High Priestess Faur said and touched the hand of her husband, Lord Belegornor, to try and calm him down.

"If my opinion counts, I think he should be allowed to stay. There will be dragons left on Earth, so I believe he should stay. I do think that we do not have the right to make everyone leave if someone has a desire to stay," Gwessil spoke up.

"This is my only son and my strength. I will miss him, but if he has made the decision to stay, allow him," his father spoke up and patted him on the back.

"I will leave no merfey behind, and I will require them all to leave. If only for my kingdom's safety," Jazhazra said authoritatively. "My merfey are not equipped, such as Luken, to take care of themselves. Nonetheless, if Luken wants to stay, I think he should, but only because of his closeness with death. No other should be allowed to stay."

"How can you all agree to this," Lord Belegornor bellowed. "He must not remain here."

"I see no harm in it, as long as Luken recognizes that he should never acknowledge or reveal himself to the humans," commented Lord Faerverer. "I have lost loved ones here that passed too soon, so I can understand how he feels. Allow him to stay."

Lord Belegornor threw his hands in the air, stood up, and marched out of the room.

Luken heard what the council said. "I will keep my distance from the humans. I do not wish to stay for them. I am here for the everglades, the forest around it, and for the one I love. I thank you all."

"Then, the agreement is done. Luken can remain on Earth as he promises to keep his distance from humans." Lord Ephenio turned to him. "Luken, acknowledge before us that you understand that you will never return to us and will live all your long life on Earth alone."

Luken nodded, then replied. "Yes." To his surprise, except for Lord Belegornor, all council members agreed to him remaining behind.

"If this is your wish, then Luken, I will give you my ring of identity. It has passed down through my family for all our generations. Said to be made by the warlords themselves, it will hide your identity from humans, revealing what you wish them to see of you."

"You will need that boy," Lord Faerverer remarked.

"I thank you very much, Priestess Faur," Luken told her. "I have made and sold to most everyone at this table my blades and weapons. This is indeed a sorrowful time for me, and I will miss each of you."

"As we will miss you, Luken," Faur replied.

***

Lord Ephenio and his council studied the skies' maps passed down with the orb in the days that followed. These charts diagramed the heavens and revealed dark outlines of locations they believed they could travel. Glade Dragonors chose a small place many light years from the Earth and at the opposite end of the heavens from the Prairie Dragonors. For a week, Dragonors packed their valuables, food, materials, clothing, and weapons upon wagons. They gathered their livestock together, as well, to remove everything from their existing life to their new lands through the portal. With the dragons' help, they broke apart structures and gardens, leaving no trace of their existence behind, except Luken and his few possessions.

At sunrise, the warlords' magical creations agreed to leave the Earth and teleport to the place of the clan's choice, destroying the orb forever. The merfey decided they would travel with the Prairie Dragonors, and homeless dragons that roamed the region agreed to go with the Glade Dragonors to their new world.

Luken said goodbye to all his friends, mother, and father and watched them move to the front to enter the portal first. Before he left, the great lord summoned for Luken, and the two met near the waterfall where he and Talulah were married.

"Are you sure you want to stay here, Luken? You are family to me now, and I wish that you would come with us? And you know that Shanara does as well."

"Thank you, my Lord Ephenio," Luken said. "However, I have thought long and hard on this, and I must stay."

Lord Ephenio handed him a small pink stone charm that glowed bright pink. "This belonged to Talulah. When she married you, I kept it. Now it belongs to you. It is her heart."

Luken looked at the stone. It was beautiful and honestly reminded him of Talulah. Its bright sparkles seemed to pulsate with life, and joy filled his heart. "I thank you, my Lord Ephenio," Luken said, bent down on one knee and lowered his head in respect for his father-in-law. Lord Ephenio patted Luken on the shoulder. Standing to his feet, the two walked together to the departure area.

Dragonors and dragons stood around, waiting for the time to leave. All of them had their arms full, overloaded wagons, livestock, and dragons with big bundles loaded upon their backs. All waited patiently for Lord Ephenio to lead them into the new world.

When the two arrived at the site, Lord Ephenio said goodbye and walked over to the mystics that waited for him. Shanara ran to him and hugged him tightly. "Father, I am going to miss you so much."

"Shanara, you are my and your mother's dream. Our lives continue on with you, and our memories keep you safe."

"Remember me always and tell Mother how much I love her."

Lord Ephenio placed the map on the ground. Chanting the words of relocation over the map, he positioned the orb on the scroll at the place of their new home. A planet on the heavenly map named Ercutis. The stones began to glow, and the Dragonors began chanting, "Ercutis, ercutis." The louder their voices grew, the brighter the orb glowed, creating a fog that soon disappeared to reveal a doorway leading to a place that looked similar to the home they were leaving. Dragonors cheered happily.

"Go now, my darling daughter."

"Yes, I shall." Shanara weaved through the mass of Dragonors and stood next to Lord Ephenio, High Priest Zorlaida, and his parents. Luken waved at the three of them one last time, then watched as they walked through the portal. All that day, he stood next to the exit, waving goodbyes to his friends and comrades one by one before they left to go to their new land, taking the only world Luken knew with them. At last, Magnus, who waited to the end -Luken never knew why but he thought maybe the giant dragon did not want to leave Talulah as well- winked at him, as if to say goodbye, and walked through the portal.

Luken stood and gazed at Magnus until he disappeared, and for a while longer, he continued to stand there and stare at the opening. *This is your last chance, Luken, go or stay.* For a brief second, he thought he would go through the portal, but then he heard Talulah calling his name. "Luken, Luken." Its opening began to blaze bright orange, and small sparks of fire shot from it, and before he could move back from the intense ball of red flame, it blew up, knocking him backward. The fire burned out. Luken was on Earth forever. Lifting himself up from the ground, he walked back towards the only thing left in the village, his home. When he got there, she was waiting for him, and Luken grinned happily.

***

Jazhazra glared at the bottle of black fluid she got so many centuries ago when Thire-los cast her away, her gooey friend, who never took on a form around her. Before she left, the witch breathed a little bit of herself into the small bottle. Jazhazra was immortal, strong, angry, and she did not want to leave Earth.

Movement of her litter pausing, she knew they were at the portal to leave and go to the new lands. Where, she did not know or care to know.

"Are you in there, Jazhazra?"

"Yes, High Priestess Faur, she replied and poked her head out of drapes on the litter carrying her. "It is such a sorrowful time for me. I must just stay in my place to keep my merfey from pain."

"I do understand, my little queen. We are all quite sentimental this day as well."

"Yes," she said, pretending to wipe tears from her eyes.

"All of the lords are entering first. We do invite you to join us, to be the first to enter the new lands."

"Terribly perfect, how thoughtful of you. I must decline, though, until I am well. We will celebrate our new lands with you on the other side."

"Do take care, my dear," High Priestess Faur told her and left.

Jazhazra lay back down, feeling the motion of her litter while the merfey approached the portal doorway. "Fruitpip," she called.

"Yes, my queen." The little merfey looked into the drapes at her.

"I am unwell. I will enter last through the portal."

"Yes, my queen."

"Do not disturb me either. I will leave my quarters when I am ready," she scowled nastily. Nearly time for the litter to cross through the portal, Jazhazra covered her bright body, shielding her radiant glow from the other merfey. The little ones happily cheered, flittering through the opening of the portal. Her litter porters, too, not watching her, she crept from her carriage and slipped behind a large rock. Finally, her litter passed through the opening. It closed momentarily behind them. Jazhazra inhaled deeply, "Freedom," she said, took out of the black potion, and took a swallow of it. "I believe I will go and live among the humans." Jazhazra transformed into a pretty maiden carrying a milk jug, and she strutted off to the nearest human town. "This is going to be so much fun."

Chapter Five

Gone but Not Forgotten

At long last, the celebration of the new mewlings' birth was upon them. Alejandro beamed with pride over his success in getting the Dragonor village prepared for the Dodekatheon in the short time the king gave him. Under the instruction of King Teloby, he agreed and faithfully accomplished, with a few other Mejuarian, to set up for the festivities. Alejandro directed the Dragonors through ceremony requirements, although, when he first started his arrangements, the prancing Mejuarian felt the location they had for the celebration hopeless.

Wet, swampy, continuous grounds that moved, fearful creatures in the waters, and very little colorful flora, within the Dragonor village was not very impressive. Alejandro found the region quite unappealing; he wondered how the others might find it since the lack of natural resources were meager compared to the Mejuarian Kingdom's abundance. With such deficiency in resources available to him, in the end, he believed his extraordinary talents gave the drab place a bit of fancy. Frankly, Alejandro did not care who disagreed.

Dragonors never seemed to celebrate like the Mejuarian and this concerned him in the beginning. Rigid and stiff, the Dragonors always were a bit too inflexible and proud, in his opinion. They were the exact opposite of himself: over-enthusiastic, loud in speech, and outgoing, amiable personality. From the start, he took control over all the decorations, preparations, and layout. This did cause some minor squabbles between the opinionated Mejuarian and obstinate Dragonors. However, Alejandro would not allow anyone to interfere with the ceremony's liveliness and excitement. It would be as successful as he had planned, even under the circumstances. Alejandro increased his charm and good-natured personality, infused with calmness auras—a gift from Thire-los—kept peace between the two groups. Bland fighters and hunters, freed of their inhibitions, the Dragonors clowned around with him, and on these days, Alejandro would swear—on his beloved black boots—that they smiled. In the end, he turned the nightmare gardens into a grand festive environment. Today, the ships were arriving from the

Kingdom, and all the Mejuarian would be delighted in the lovely atmosphere he created to birth the new mewlings. Although the mewlings might not birth in their parents' kingdom, Alejandro would make sure they entered their new lives in beautiful, inviting surroundings.

Many of the elders did not like Alejandro's ways and delightful decoration. The prancing Mejuarian knew why too. His relationship with Atrurso, an animal naturalist, was an unnatural pair in the eyes of the elder Mejuarian and spawned mistrust and belittlement of him and his work. Not only were they of different Mejuarian talents, families, and birthed with distinctive gifts from Thire-los, but they were also both males. Taboo within the minds of the old Mejuarian that held on to old beliefs, regardless of what exquisiteness he created, he knew his efforts might not please them. Alejandro, nor Atrurso, cared about their mockeries or comments when they were together because the two of them were in love.

Yes, he did wear entirely too much red, comments he frequently heard. Alejandro dressed in a red leotard from head to toe that covered his long arms and legs, which hid his thin ankles. From the ankles up, though, he wanted to show off his muscular, strapping form. Only his dark cherry, slightly furred, face, hands, and thin slinky tail, were not covered with fancy garments. The hair upon his head and tail, a secondary color of black, he wore a satiny black cloak and tall black boots and was quite the striking subject. Alejandro was one of the smallest Mejuarian in the kingdom, only five feet in height; nevertheless, the little Mejuarian carried the nature and pride of the others in the village.

In appearance and attitude, he owned more of the traits of the goddess Lotus' offspring feline features, and possibly a bit of Os, because of the black hairs in his hair and tail. Two prick ears stood upright, and a mass of silky red and black hair, he sported a long ponytail that dangled down along the side of his face. Black thin short furs upon the deep ruby   red over   his   short,   rounded muzzle, Alejandro wore a designer stub on his face. Fashioned as part of his artistic personification, the prancing Mejuarian was one of the few Mejuarian that used the furs on their faces in a decorative fashion. Bubbly bright red eyes gleamed as spry as his personality and within the center of his right eye was his Mejuarian marking. The image of a black flame with its pupil flared red when he was excited.

On his way to make sure the final preparations were being completed for tonight, Alejandro ran into Tinzadri one of the Dragonors that helped him ready the gardens for the celebration.

"Thank you very much, my friend. This is sure to be a most grand event ever. I, Alejandro, have amazed myself again."

"I am glad that you were able to get done what you needed to, Alejandro." The tall Dragonor towered over him. A dark blue complexion, with squiggles and patterns in his skin, monotone speech, he was the epidemy of boring. And in Alejandro's mind, his black leather clothing certainly did not spruce up his dreary presence.

"Thank you. Your gardens are most adequate now. I am the master of celebrations, an artist, a dancer, and a singer. This event, my friend, will be one that you will never forget."

Situated within the area sectioned off for the Mejuarian living ground, he admired the fantastic array of flowers, brought with him from the kingdom on the back of dragons, now placed stunningly throughout the gardens. Varied colors sat upon the outstretched wings of convincingly carved dragon statues made of wood. Seated atop two pedestals in a rock opening that delivered falling water forming a stream that ran around the Mejuarian village, they appeared as protective deities ready to defend the villagers from any hostility. Alejandro also hurriedly created a bed of flowers in the Mejuarian Crest's design in the garden's center to add to its splendor.

"What more needs to be done in this area? It is for the guests."

"More tables, I will need more tables," said Alejandro, running over to a small clearing to the right of the stone circle. "Here, more tables for the feast and such a feast we will have. Fruits, berries, melons, bread, cakes, and of course, wines that will grace your tongue." Dragonors hurried in with more wooden tables and chairs, "Put them there," he ordered. "Tell me, Tinzadri, do you know why we celebrate today and why this day is the most important to us?" The two of them entered the center of the stone circle, and Alejandro grinned broadly.

"Today, your king will have his first mewling."

"Exactly, but not just his first. It will be the birth of a new generation for the Mejuarian. I, Alejandro, see this tragedy as hope. It will bring us to Thire-los again. I am sure of it."

"We have no gods anymore. Deserted by our warlords many long times ago. This has harmed us none."

"Much is said in those few words, my friend. In hope beyond hope, only there resided the seed of life." Tinzadri's statement was exactly what he expected from the brash Dragonors' spiritual nature. Like many Mejuarian, it was dead; he believed based upon stories he heard about them. "Yes, my friend. But Thire-los was no warlord. They were great in one." Alejandro felt like other Mejuarian that Thire-los observed them and gave them unique talents and gifts. Nevertheless, he did not necessarily agree with their old-fashioned ideas and belief in love.

"Alejandro, I heard of your energy and enthusiasm, and they were right. I do feel that you will give a celebration that we will remember."

"The ships are coming," someone yelled.

Alejandro gleefully peered up to see the Mejuarian King airship growing closer in the distance. "Come, my friend. Let us go meet my king."

The Royal Fleet Arrives

King Teloby and the others sat below the galley's deck, listening to the musicians gaily play their instruments. Mejuarian danced, sung, and had a festive time the entire trip; some never slept on the journey, continuing with the festivities. His villagers' overindulgence was not worrisome because his race was a resilient, hardworking group with exceptional abilities.

Two crucial things bothered the king, though: relocating his village to the region of the Dragonors, and the destruction of his kingdom by a meteor. They were much different than his own Mejuarian, and their lands were harsh compared to the soft tropical lands in their kingdom. Along the trip, he recognized two meteors. Raczis, his learned friend, did not predict what happened and the mere fact that he was wrong caused doubt within the king. If the brilliant scientist and his staff missed the second meteor, was it possible he too should not have moved his village? An explosion in the skies between the two meteors, everything was all wrong, and he reconsidered his decision. In his last conversation with the observatory director, the scientist concluded that his village might still be intact. King Teloby would have one of his airships return in a couple of days. Today, though, along with the rest of the Mejuarian and the Dragonors, he would celebrate the birth of his first son.

"We can see the village."

Crowds below deck whistled, clapped, and cheered at the news, and the whimsical musicians began parading the line of dancers out of the galley. Merrily, the crowd followed them out, singing to the tops of their lungs, filled with excitement and exhilaration. Perfect in pitch and tone, the musicians twirled through the tables and chairs gaily and up the hallway, entering the stairway, they pirouetted up each one until reaching the deck.

King Teloby felt less glee than his villagers that hurried out to the deck of the ship. At least they were happy, and no one grumbled too terribly, that he knew of. The villagers seemed to have accepted the move, and for that, he was grateful. As the last of the dancers bopped out of the room, Teloby raised his golden goblet to Lord Ephenio, blessing their new alliance together. "May the Dragonor flourish forever under the rule of Lord Ephenio, and may the Mejuarian be forever indebted to them," he toasted. After he finished the last of his wine, King Teloby slowly followed the others out of the galley to greet his new lands.

The cold fresh air hit him like tiny knives on his face; nevertheless, it felt good to King Teloby when stepping out on the deck. Relief washed over him when he saw the Mejuarian excitedly pointing at their new village. The king searched for the queen. Finally, he noticed her, her two friends, and ladies standing near the stern of the airship. He walked over to the queen and gently took her hand in his, wrapping his fingers between her lovely delicate digits.

At once, her sedative auras attacked his nervous tensions. Like a wave of water or drug, her closeness washed them away and comforted his mind and inner being. Usually, he fought off the fluffy emotions that came from her. A stern harshness, the elders connected to the god Thie, the king never desired bubbly feelings. However today, he badly needed them. King Teloby allowed them to dissolve away his fears.

"How are you doing, Nymeria?" Teloby bowed his head briefly at Saraphim and Syberias, and the two other ladies politely nodded back at him and smiled.

"I am quite well, Teloby," she answered, laying her head upon his shoulder. "I cannot wait to get to our new village so that we can have the birthing and I can hold my son in my arms."

"Yes, me as well," Syberias beamed. A slight smile came over her face, but King Teloby saw the stress and worry upon her face.

Typically, every time he saw her, the council lady's long wavy red locks and the hair on her J-shaped tail were always impeccably adorned. Each piece hung perfectly, but this time, though, her pretty face drained of life, it seemed.

"Where is Raczis? Is he going to miss this? He would not dare," Seraphim said, stiffly looking around for him. "There he is! Raczis, Raczis, Tyrion, here," she said, waving her arm wildly above her head. "There is that terrible bird. It is such a pain. That despicable creature better not come over and squawk in my ear, or I am throwing him overboard."

"You do know, it is a bird and will only fly back, don't you, Seraphim," King Teloby teased.

"I do not care. I don't want him around since that bird is awful and annoying," she sniveled, glaring hostility at the giant blackbird. "A bird should not speak. It is evil and foul."

"Saraphim, I would not, there is nothing evil in Yadekda." Scowling angrily, Tyrion gawked at the old Mejuarian as if she had said enough.

"Are you ready to see our new lands?" King Teloby quickly changed the conversation. There was no need for argument before landing in their new lands.

Saraphim frowned, indicating her disapproval. "No, I am not ready, and you know my feelings about this trip, Raczis."

"I really hate to be a worrier, but I have not seen the Hameau for quite a while," Syberias looked towards the back of the ship, bending over the edge of the railing. Tyrion put his arm around her waist, pulled her back into the vessel, close to his side.

"Everything is perfect, my special one. I am sure it has only fallen a bit behind the fleet. It does have its own engine to help it along. In the excitement, the collective might have hurried the journey along faster."

"He is right. We are a bit ahead of schedule, so I am sure that is what happened. Don't forget, we have Captain Jonus piloting the ship, and he can handle anything that can come against it."

Swampy wetlands came into view. The Mejuarian King circled over the planet briefly, allowing the passengers to take in the entire region's layout and the section of land set aside for their new village. The closer to the planet they came, the air began to get warmer, and the aroma of the Dragonor village wafted up, inviting the airship closer. Dragonors and the Mejuarian that arrived earlier stood around the landing area waiting while Mejuarian musicians played a jubilant song, continuing the spirit of celebration.

Alejandro walked down the wooden walkway leading along the front of the landing airship. Arms waving above his head, he frolicked around dancing merrily. "Welcome, my friends, welcome." Happily, dancing about, he led them to the ground where Dragonors were constructing tents for temporary housing for their new homes. "Come, my friends, come," he sang merrily.

Alejandro smiled at Atrurso, who strutted proudly behind the water lord, Zavalza. Discreetly his friend and loved one waved at him, supplying him with an extra burst of joy.

"Alejandro, it impresses me that you were able to accomplish what you did here," Zavalza sneered, glancing back at Atrurso.

The water lord's white eyes scowled haughtily at him. An arrogant grin upon Zavalza's bluish shiny face, Alejandro believed the water Mejuarian felt directly touched by the hands of the god Thie, himself.

"My great Lord Zavalza, I am Alejandro, the greatest artist in all of the virtuosities," he told him, politely. Zavalza was not a fan of his relationship preferences, either. The water lord was one of the elders depreciating him and his talents because of his freeness in love. Much like the others, he thought him a little too much like female Mejuarian, pampering and adoring their appearances. These old goldies, he called them, frowned upon his atypical behaviors.

Alejandro danced barefooted, prancing about, rejoicing in the arrival of the Mejuarian.

Where is the Hameau

While most of the others unloaded the ships to prepare for the ceremony, Syberias stood staring into the sky, looking for the Hameau. They were on the airships for over two days, and her body worn out from all of the packing and stress of moving the village. Nevertheless, there was no rest for her until her mewling's nest landed safely on the ground. The Mejuarian King landed over two hours ago, and the Hameau left at the same time. Still, the Hameau had not arrived, and there was something wrong. Syberias knew it in her heart. Her last reading told her that something would happen to her mewling on the ship. No one believed her.

Tyrion worked with the others, organizing the livestock, and helping the Mejuarian settle within their new land. Syberias knew she should have been helping him and she had so much work awaiting her after the birthing ceremony. Concern over her welfare, offering to wait with her, she only wished he could share her agony. This was her burden, not his, and she was the only one who could hold it. Drenched in worry, she did not care if she had a bed to sleep in or how lovely the gardens were, only the delightful sight of her nest. "What is taking Captain Jonus so long," she asked, pacing back and forth.

"Syberias, dear, you must relax. Your endless worrying is causing a tizzy in me. Now please stop that pacing," Saraphim told her.

Again, someone told her what to do. Syberias' opposing personas of the goddesses Ireania and Lotus and the god Os' brash temperament, lost in confusion and anxiety, irritation grew within her. Angrily she answered, "I will not stop pacing, Saraphim, and don't tell me what to do."

Saraphim looked shocked at her sudden outburst of anger. "There is no need to be rude, Syberias."

"I am sorry, but I am so worried." Syberias stared into the sky. An enormous red dragon soared by, belching out flames of fire while traveling along. "That dragon is beautiful."

"I never thought that I might see so many of those dreadful creatures." Saraphim glared back at the Mejuarian busily working, creating a place for their new habitat. "I cannot allow myself to enter those dreadful canvas homes they have built."

"Yes, life will be different for us, Saraphim."

"At least Nymeria is happy," the snobbish older Mejuarian scowled bitterly.

"Why do you mock our friend's happiness? She is the queen and has many duties."

"Syberias, you know as well as I do, moving the village was a mistake."

"Yes, I do. That does not help us now, though, does it?" Syberias retorted, "So, I kindly ask you not mention it again." Saraphim huffed loudly.

While the two of them waited, other Mejuarian females with nests on the Hameau began gathering around the landing area, hoping that the ship would arrive soon. After twenty more minutes had passed and the ship still had not arrived, tension began increasing in the frightened mothers.

"Where is the Hameau?"

Nymeria walked up, taking her arm in hers, she held Syberias closely. "The Hameau should have arrived by now, I would think."

"Yes, I agree," commented Syberias.

"There must be something wrong," Ukla said. "We must go and get the king."

"Most certainly," agreed Nymeria. "Please, Ukla, can you go and find him?"

"Certainly, my queen."

Syberias gazed at Ukla while she ran off, but it was too late. They should have listened to her because she tried warning them about the horrors in her visions. The Hameau was out there now, lost. She only prayed her nest was with it when they found the missing ship. After the passing of another ten minutes, King Teloby, Sidor, and Tyrion came back to the landing area.

Teloby took Nymeria in his arms. "I am sorry, I had to meet with the council. We planned to meet as soon as we arrived, and it was necessary to do it right away. When I heard that the Hameau did not arrive, I came immediately." He pulled her close.

"Syberias, my love, are you alright?"

Syberias wanted to yell *No!* A warning was given to her. She tried telling them all, they ignored her instead, including Tyrion. "It is not here, Tyrion. I am afraid I am not alright, and neither is the Hameau."

"I am sure there is nothing wrong. Lord Ephenio is sending out dragon riders to look. Captain Jonus is probably just taking it slow."

Syberias yelled, "Your words are nonsense, and you know it. I tried to tell you. I tried to tell you all!"

"Calm down, my love. I am taking Yadekda, and I will go search for it as well."

"Please find them, Tyrion." Others standing around gaped at her; some of them had their mouths hanging open. For sure, she just now confirmed all of their judgments that she was a bit peculiar. Reassuring herself through inward strength, she said, "King Teloby, please forgive me for my flareup."

"You have been doing that lot lately, Syberias," Saraphim lectured. "You must remember your place, my dear."

"I understand my place."

"Our nests are missing, and for anyone here to try and disregard her concerns is truly horrible," Nymeria agreed. "I want my nest. I want my son, Teloby."

"Nymeria, my love, we are not trying to slight Syberias in any way. There is no need to worry until we find out what has happened. I do not want to upset the villagers for nothing."

Syberias shrugged her shoulders. "It does not matter if anyone believes me. Just find the Hameau and the nests."

"Please do not worry, my love," Tyrion told her, trying to comfort her.

Syberias snatched herself from her mate's embrace. "Hurry, send them out as soon as possible."

"We will," King Teloby pronounced.

"Will you be alright while I am gone?"

"Yes, Tyrion, just go."

"We will find the ship, I swear."

Syberias tried to smile. "Hurry back, my love, and be careful. I love you so much, Tyrion. I am sorry for my anger earlier." Syberias was almost in tears; however, she would not let them flow, not in front of the others. These were not tears of sadness but droplets of grief as they fell from her eyes, softening her doubts and insecurities. Forces she tried to shroud all her life to be a proper Mejuarian female grew stronger. If they were of the god Os, then so be it. Syberias knew a battle was upon the Mejuarian, possibly one not seen since she saw it in her reading.

Chapter Six

The Worst is to Come

Arvunglies Come Out of Hiding

Zacharias stood on the banks of the Mi-lo River. A wooden spear in its sheath, its silver arrowhead gleamed brightly at his feet. While he fished, he waited for his captain so that he might lead his army on the long trek into the hills. Commander of the Arvunglies, spear guard for Queen Marina, Zacharias was responsible for surveying any damage done by the dragon that lived within the mountains near the big river. A few days ago, a ruckus was heard in the south end of their lands. Zacharias suspected that the dastardly black dragon attacked one of their outposts.

Since the dragon came into the region, he worried little about it attacking the queen's village and spoiling the queen's treasure vault. The large scaly monster often flew across their tiny floating homes and pole buildings along the side of the waterways and their outposts. Shrewd and spritely movements, they ran from his fire, and quickly they hide; the tiny folk knew how to keep out of sight and avoid injury from its deadly flames. Still, its deadly fire destroyed their wooden stilt homes and towers.

A bamboo fishing pole in his hands, its line cast into the Mi-lo River, a runoff of water from the great river that ran across the lands of Ercutis, he watched the fish nibble at his bait. Only enough water to wet the high boots of the Dragonor or Mejuarian, the small Arvunglies called it a river. Zacharias hoped to catch a rare river bottom Koke—a minnow of a large fish, whose eggs sometimes drifted away from the currents. This rare treat, papaya-glazed Koke eyes, he might present to the queen at tonight's river food parade in hopes to gain favor.

A day of food consumption and drink, this weekly event held in the queen's tiny village, the villagers shared their unique foods made from jungle herbs, plants, and anything small that moved upon the land. Minnows in their rivers, bugs upon the ground, and flying creatures from the air they caught in their small nets, Arvunglies prepared them in stews and curries for the feast. The little people housed along the river had started to arrive at the queen's village since last night, ready for the delicious smorgasbord.

Zacharias gazed down the stream. Cone-shaped straw hats upon their captains' heads, their brown bodies looked like specks in the distance. Scantily dressed, in loincloths and leaves, barefoot they patrolled the waterways. Spears braced upon cubbies at the back of their vessels, standing on their bare feet, they maneuvered the boats down the streamflow with a single oar attached to the stern center. They held onto the blades with their feet and busied them to steer the boat while the small folk cleaned fish or arranged bundles with their hands.

Vessels made of wood, their hulls decayed in places, and repaired with tough brown bug skins, the little people pasted the gooey substances against their ramshackle keels keeping the unworthy sea vessels afloat. Houseboats, workboats, the latter having cubbies in their rears, to protect their captains from the rain, carried bundles of chipped grass, other herbs, dried baby minnows, rat, skewers, and sweet ants their owners bartered. Some of the more prosperous owners painted images of owl eyes on the bows of their basket-shaped boats. These wealthy merchants sold along the channel as well; only they peddled the best, dried spider legs, coconut wine, and caramelized flea eggs. When these floating demons coasted in between torchlit quarters, the boats' fronts looked like glowing eyes watching over the township at night.

Boats smashed into each other regularly along the waterway. Captains of small shabby ships sometimes became victims of pirates with larger vessels; the raggedy boats fell apart like weakly glued sticks when callously rammed by hurried skippers. Pieces of broken board scraps, fabric, furs, and housewares scattered along its banks so often, it was usual practice every day for the tribe to gather up salvage. Debris, allotted on a first-come basis, if the owners were slow to recover their goods, the finder got to keep the treasure. This was the law of the waters. In fact, while he stood there fishing, one captain ran another's vessel aground. The poor Arvunglie now floated in the mess of debris while scavengers waited on the banks to grab what they saw and wanted. Given only two hours to collect what he could, the poor captain needed to hurry.

"For pete's sake, it is Phil, you all know him. Give him a break," Zacharias said, frowning at the scavengers. With Phil struggling in the water, they frightened the fish. Zacharias sighed. "Get out of there, Phil. You're scaring the fish away."

"I must collect my sacks, Zacharias."

Zacharias had a bite before the ruckus began in the water; the low capsized boat was fortunate for fish.

"Captain, the others are ready," Zelldah reported.

It was too late, and he could not get another bite. Dropping his fishing pole, he left the line dangling in the water and Zacharias picked up his spear and walked through the jungle to meet up with his men. Hopefully, he might still have a fish hanging on when he returned.

Arvunglies were ancient people and inhabited the waterways along the rivers' runoffs. They were tiny and much too little to safely occupy the actual riverside's borders, but they made their homes among the shallow runoffs. The little folk inhabited the lands long before some of the new beings that now roamed their lands showed up and brought in their dragons and the colorful animal/men that trampled through their lands.

Tiny Arvunglies appeared as small humans that might have been lost in the capsule of time. Long straggly hair, or curls so tight, they looked like knots upon their heads. Complexion as light as pure cream to dark as the night, the tiny folk carried pouches around the waist holding their small knives, fishing twine, and other tools. Feet as tough as leather, they wore no shoes, and they hung from the branches of trees by their curved toes when hiding or hunting for bird eggs. They were a resilient people, proud, tough, and carried spears to protect themselves from attack. Fear of nothing within their little hearts, they hunted snakes that loomed over them.

Furiously, the little folk attacked their prey like an army of locus ferociously destroying a wheat crop; blackbirds, some smaller creatures, and jungle dwellers, they captured food bigger than themselves. Brutally they pursued their prey, hiding like an unseen enemy, and except for the dragon roaming their lands, other jungle creatures feared the nasty little folk.

***

Zacharias reached the wreck sight, and it was a disaster. Someone lay unconscious upon the ground among debris littered upon the Earth and down the mountains; possibly one of the spaceships he saw flying through the skies, he imagined. "That black demon is at it again. Poor guy."

The creature was one of the brightly colored men with a tail and big ears. Distress filled his heart, and he wanted to help him, but he did not have the power to save the suffering being. Even if he took him back to the village, their shaman might not have the mixtures to cure him. Arvunglies only lived short lives, died from the smallest of wounds, most survived no more than thirty years. Their medicines only healed minor scrapes. Zacharias knew this creature suffered from far more than a little cut. With the tip of his spear, he pricked the metal against the being's face, and he moaned softly. The creature's eyes stayed closed, though.

Anyhow, he did not come out to save a foreigner. Zacharias trekked through the jungle to see if there was trouble in one of his outposts. Now that he saw the amount of destruction and bounty around him, he mourned for the poor creature, but this abundance was worth his army's time to scavenge. Metal, wires, and wood. Excellent shining wood that would make great boats, not to mention the colorful round treasures strewn around. Brightly colored, strings of tinsel draped off some of them, his big eyes bulged from the precious booty around them. Sparkling treasures caught his eye. Zacharias hunted for one with a lot of twinkling sparkles on it. The army could only take one; this would make the gift ever more valuable when he gave it to Queen Marina, personally.

"This is the perfect gift for our queen," one of his soldiers cried out.

Zacharias walked over and surveyed the bright object. It was perfect. Green leaves on its outside, coated in a rainbow of glittering sparkles, the glow of the thing was magnificent. "Yes, I do believe this will do. I will handle this," he commanded, shoving him away from the object. "Take what you can back to the village. We will come back for more if need be." When he looked down at the treasure, the spectral of twinkles glittering around it seemed to change its colors. Hypnotized by its beauty, staring in awe for a moment, Zacharias was unable to take his eyes off of the fancy prize. "It is perfect. I need help here."

Several of the Arvunglies gathering around him, he saw that the bright object mesmerized them. "Bring it," he commanded. A group of the tiny Arvunglies gathered the nest on their shoulders and carried the prize towards the jungle, back to their little village.

"Hooray," the group cried out in unison.

Zacharias stared at the broken creature and wished him well. "Zelldah, see to the others. Send word if you need more to help."

A Promotion as a matter of fact

Fires burning along the waterway for long distances, their stilt homes illuminated brightly. The dark waters littered by sparkling lanterns from the small boats, their images cast across the dark waters and made the streams appear busier than they were. It was a lovely warm night, and Zacharias was happy for himself. Everyone was out and bartered with each other, holding out for a tedious tidbit. The queen was on the way, which he concerned himself with; it was a grand time in the Yeloknif lands. Everyone sat along the banks ate and enjoyed the river parade's delicacies of bistro delights. The sharp sounds of reed flutes added to the roar of water and loud chatter; the village was a roar with excitement and carousing,

Aromas of decadent jungle flavors filling the air, the spicy smells of barbecues and greens made him hungry. Zacharias could not leave, though. His queen was on her way with others in the royal guard since he chose to cook and give her the precious gift he found today in the mountains. Although others helped him bring in the valuable package, claiming the sparkling object as his own, he followed the village norms. *Finders, Keepers.*

Since he was the commander, he was the finder of all. Zacharias was generous to his men and their families; then again, any precious treasures were his finds to give to the queen. The little commander also stopped his men from taking any more bobbles since he believed that the giants might not miss one of the treasures, though two missing might be easily noticed. It was he who would present the treasure to her majesty tonight, and tonight the queen would place it in her treasure vault under his name.

Zacharias dipped one of the eyes into the jelly. The glaze's tangy/sweet taste was perfect for his eye recipe, so he placed the skewer across metal rods across the firepit. When he returned to his fishing pole, a fish swam, attached by the hook on the end of his line. It was not a Koke; the hook grasped onto a blood shrimp. Their eyes were just as good as the Koke, but not as rare. Jam-packed with coals in the pit, the meat sizzled. It smelled wonderful, and he could not wait to give it to the queen. One of the eyes was already done; he cut it into four pieces. With each piece of the eye garnished in spider eggs and wrapped in a stringy leaf, Zacharias placed the four packets back on the grill to seal in their flavors. His stomach gurgled, but he refused to go on the food parade until she had arrived.

Zacharias gazed at the sparkly object sitting upon the ground next to his two-level stilt home. Built of planks of wood and bamboo stalks, he realized his roof needed replacing. Large leaves, green now weather-worn, brown and wilted, tears in the mummified leaves would soon let in the heavy rains. Each level had an excellent waterfront view and a porch extending over the water. His house was one of the more affluent in the lands. Torn and water spotted, pieces of fabrics strewn across a clothesline on both levels, the mantles protected the hut home from further intense jungle sun coming in through the windows. Hammocks on both porches, and near water on the ground, he snoozed and lazed around when the queen did not require him.

The object glittered under the fire torches that lit up the front of his home and the stream embankment he sat on while he waited for the queen and prepared her delightful treat. Zacharias wondered what it was. Indeed, some type of adornment belonging to the ones riding the dragons or the ships' colorful people. Often, they found jewels. Or should he be honest and say, many times, the tiny folk confiscated jewels, pieces of metal, arrowheads, scraps of cloth, and everything else they thought was of some use to them from the giants.

A roar of a shell in the distance, the queen was arriving. Her carriage boat, rowed by several of his guards, was getting close, and the fanfare of its arrival was exciting to everyone. The queen's quarters, covered in red and gold fabrics, the vessel appeared as a luxurious gondola traveling down the streams. Royal in appearance, it was the best vessel in the lands, and Zacharias claimed responsibility for that as well; he found the shiny red and gold cloth near or in the Dragonor village. Also, the only boat with more than one oar, his guards stood on their feet along its sides rowing in order of their heights. Jando, the least of them in size, stood at the front and waved a lantern as the horn blew.

At last, she arrived. "My Queen. I am most honored to present to you my delight this wonderful parade evening." The queen stepped out of her cubby. Ushered by his soldiers, she sauntered down the gondola's length and sat upon the paddled seat arranged at its front, made to hold her pleasantly plump body securely on the moving boat.

When Queen Marina sat down upon her seat, the boat leaned to its side. Guards assigned to her moved to her left and attempted to keep the boat balanced.

"Zacharias, I do look forward to what you have for me every parade. What do you have for me tonight?"

A slender leaf draped over her round body, and a string of twine wrapped around it at her waist, the queen's back and fronts were hidden. Bare flesh on the sides of her body exposed, she actually covered very little and was quite a bewitchingly little Arvunglie. She was lovely, and her yellow skin was fresh and glowed under the firelight. Although she was a bit plump, this increased her appeal to Zacharias. Pieces of tiny flowers made into a crown, the orange and yellow florets locked around her golden yellow matted dreadlocks.

"Tonight. I got two things for you, my queen." Zacharias stepped over to her and handed her one of the steaming packets of the glazed eye on a piece of wood he used for a plate.

In proper fashion, the queen put the plate to her nose; big nostrils upon her round face widened when she breathed in the aroma of the wrapped meat. Poking her fingernail in it, she remarked, "This smells wonderful."

"You will like it, my queen. It is glazed shrimp eye."

"Oh, you do know how much I love my shrimp," she giggled. "By the way, Zacharias, I sometimes get lonely. I would like a roommate, and I want it to be you."

She had just proposed to him as if she were dealing with a typical day-to-day business opportunity. Of course, this was what he always wanted. Although, he figured it might him doing the asking, and maybe it might not be in front of all of his guards.

"This so good, Zacharias. Save them all for me."

"Of course, my queen. I will bring them to you when I bring you my next gift." Zacharias pointed to the object sitting on the blanket next to his home. When the queen saw it, her eyes lit up, and an expression of pure delight came over her face. Quickly she stood up, almost causing the little gondola to nearly capsize. Hurriedly Zacharias steadied her while the other guards helped her out of the boat onto the mushy embankment.

"It is magnificent. What is it, Zacharias?"

"It is a gift for my queen," he said proudly. Queen Marina grinned at him, showing her pretty white teeth. Her plump pink lips curled at their sides cutely, and Zacharias wanted to kiss her. He dared not to, even though at this moment, she was his fiancée.

Queen Marina reached out and touched the object. "Umm, it feels warm."

"Yes. Nothing to worry about. That is from the hot sun earlier."

"It is just great. What I always wanted and what value will it add to my treasures." She took Zacharias' hand in hers and held it in her small fingers. "From you. My loyal servant, I can always expect something that taps my fancy, like this," she giggled, kissing his cheek lightly.

"For my queen. This whole big world," he replied. "When I saw how it sparkled, I thought of your sweet brown eyes." Marina again giggled like a little girl, and her round tummy bounced around. Too much of a pampered life, and not very energetic was the queen. Traits that were not very favorable in the Arvunglie community. Nevertheless, Zacharias loved Queen Marina. A soft body appealed to him more than the bones of the other skinny women in the lands.

"Did it come from the giants?"

"Yes. I found it on my dragon hunting party today. One of the animal/men was there, but he was too badly injured for our medicines."

"I am sure you did your best, Zacharias."

"All that I could." Within moments, the stranger's injuries forgotten, the queen grabbed another eye off of the plate.

"Come parade with me. I have asked you to partner with me. Why not let the villagers know of our love right away?"

Zacharias was not ready to tell the others, but she was his queen, and nothing more could be said. "Of course, my queen."

" Don't forget those delicious, glazed eyes," she said greedily before attempting to get back into the boat. "There is lots of room and privacy in my tent, Zacharias," the little queen said, smiling. She glared at him like she gazed at her food hungrily. This disturbed him, but at the same time, he found her openly free passions very flattering.

Chapter Seven

The Search

If the journey to the Dragonor's region had gone as the Mejuarian wanted, Tyrion would be celebrating with the others now, resting in the garden, waiting for the birth of his first child. Syberias was upset because she blamed him and the king for the missing nests, even though she did not say those precise words. Tyrion held on to his confidence that he or the others would find the lost vessel and the captain. Jonus was a great pilot, and the worse he could think of was he had to land the ship somewhere along the way, and the searchers needed to find out where.

Lord Ephenio sent out six dragon hunters, Tyrion, and Vincentru, to locate the absent Hameau. Shortly after they left the village, they broke off into groups. Tyrion, who stood on the back of the big black bird, Yadekda, tagged along, riding next to Shanara, who rode her giant dragon, Buderous.

"Do not worry, my little Tyrion. We will find the nests," she told him. "Vincentru and I fly across these lands always, and I know them. And of course, there is Buderous; my companion can see anything from way up here." As if understanding her, the giant red dragon let out a scream, and Shanara patted its massive head.

Shanara was dressed in black, and her long silver hair waved behind her as she flew along. Tyrion realized that Vincentru loved the Dragonor; however, he found her much too bold and her stance a little too brash, not to mention the ability to ride a dragon. Like himself, she was good at what she did, and for this reason, he might not expect a better partner to help him find his daughter.

Tyrion was not particularly fond of dragons, though he had to admit their interaction with the Dragonors was quite interesting. At first, he and his large black friend Yadekda shied away from the dragon. One of the shorter Mejuarian, the great beast, towered over Tyrion, which made him seem runtish. His abilities gave him the freedom to be fearless of all creatures, and soon he realized that Buderous was only a big awkward cat, grouchy and mean, but tender to those who mattered. Then he understood why Vincentru loves Xochitl. Tyrion knew for sure that he did not want to ride on the back of one like his friend; though, he did like soaring through the heavens on the back of his own friend, Yadekda.

Tyrion sought any chance to leave the ground and investigate the airy nothingness around him. Since his gifts, elders prophesied came from the goddess Ireania, made him long for extremely high altitudes. As a mewling, he climbed the tallest trees he found in the village. Nimbly Tyrion moved through treetops and soared from tree to tree as the wind and his own will held him up. Tyrion could not fly; no Mejuarian flew, but when he dived between the trees, if he fell from the great heights, he effortlessly landed on his feet, then steadied himself with his thick muscular tail.

Tyrion owned a close harmony with nature and all its elements, and he sensed changes in the land and environment. This made him a good farmer. If Tyrion heard a tiny bug gnawing, keen hearing and an acute sense of disturbance within his crops, he detected the bug's location. He did not believe in harm to any creature, so Tyrion ushered the little creature out of his produce to better lands. Like Buderous, his eyesight was excellent, as well.

As most Mejuarian, he possessed an Ercutian build, and his animal nature was noticeable by the thin yellow furs upon his body, ears, tail, and a peculiar Mejuarian marking. From the tops of his small, pointed ears to the bottoms of his feet, he was only six feet, short for a Mejuarian. With a very light layer of yellow fur over his metallic cream skin, he radiated a sunshine color. Upon his head was layers of curly yellow and creamy hair with something of a kinky nature. His mane looked like an outrageous afro when not braided or bound by an elastic. Syberias loved running her fingers through it and rolling his curly strands into several braids during the hotter times. A short, curved tail, coated with fur like that of his head, Tyrion was simple in appearance as he was in his demeanor. Quite fine-looking as well, barely noticeable yellow whiskers extended from his rounded muzzle.

Tyrion steadied himself as Yadekda flew forward. The bird's large black eyes scanned the ground, searching for anything familiar. Usually, his friend's antics left the two of them talking throughout the entire journey. At this time, though, Yadekda understood Tyrion's concern, and his trusted friend remained quiet, allowing him time to digest everything that happened the last few days.

How is this possible? Tyrion thought to himself. Even when they found the nests and Captain Jonus, the joyous event that the

Mejuarian planned would not occur. Tyrion thought about the days leading up to the terrible news. These were happy days, and all was great within the village because on this Day of Dodekatheon, not only would he become a father, but the King was honoring him for his new wine. Tyrion wished he could rewind the days. No Mejuarian had that gift, though.

A Wonderful Life

With a red glow in the sky, Tyrion felt troubled all that day; nevertheless, he had no idea of the devastation heading towards the Mejuarian village. The day was warmer than usual. His crops needed watering more than once, so he launched the drenching contraption, and waves of waters spurted from the ground saturating the roots, within moments. After dousing them, the waters then disappeared back into the soil, leaving fertilized, moist black soil behind. All day, he repeated this process, which was very strange; Tyrion went on with his day with his friend, unaware of the disaster to come.

Tyrion remembered the joy he felt that day. The frightful squawks of Yadekda caught his attention, and tiresome watering his crops, he peered up to see the massive bird soaring through the sky. Seconds later, descending from his great heights, thunderous sounds from his great wingspan and muscular landing body caused him to fold his small ears down, wearisome of the maddening noise. Crazy winds from the swooping of his wings, Tyrion felt the chilly winds upon his body, enjoying the force of the strong wind pushing against him.

Mirror-like, razor sharp talons spread out as if they were preparing to swoop him up off of the ground and tear him apart. Yadekda squawked loudly and landed next to him.

"What's up, Bro?"

"Could you get any closer? You almost knocked me over." Tyrion chuckled.

"It's not my fault. Bro, I just don't know how much awesome power I have." The great bird shoved Tyrion gently with his outstretched wing, and he stumbled backward. "See, I told you, Bro, too much sway," he laughed.

"Okay, I got it, you are awesome," Tyrion replied in a sarcastic tone, mocking his friend's adoration of himself. At first glance, for some of the less spirited Mejuarian and mewlings, his terrible figure frightened them. It took time for many of the villagers to accept him.

Tyrion knew, however, that he had the temperament of nothing more than an oversized sparrow.

"Hey, Bro, just cruising along and checking out your crops. Lots on the menu today, mmmmm baby, it's making me hungry just remembering the sight of your scrumptious delectable," Yadekda stuck his long thick tongue out of his beak and squawked loudly. "You don't mind if I sneak on over and try a bit, do you?"

Tyrion chuckled, "When have you ever asked permission? Anyway, before you bed down in the greens, give me a ride."

"Well now, since you gonna be feeding two soon, I just want to make sure you could spare enough to give your old buddy a handout," Yadekda laughed. "You know it starts out good, then them mewlings gets to crying. You won't be able to hang out with little old me no more."

"I know you think I am crazy for wanting a mewling because you don't want a family. You, my friend, will never experience how happy I am today."

Yadekda skipped around Tyrion. "That is a happiness that I don't want. No birdie is gonna tie me down, Bro." He flew upward and hovered over his head, blocking out the intense heat and clowning around. "You see the sun in the heavens. It don't quit shining. I figure when it quits, then old Yadekda might just then settle down."

Tyrion thought about his statement. "That makes no sense. What does the sun dying out have to do with you having a family? Your agreement is pure garbage. You do realize that if the sun dies out, so will you."

"Bro, don't you get it? It's deep mind thinking, man. Deep."

"What is deep mind thinking?" Tyrion chuckled. "Get down here."

"Bro. See, even you asking that is proof enough to me that your mewling is already changing you." Friend and flying mate, the big bird balanced his massive body on his tail feathers impressively.

"I am pretty sure I have not changed in such a short time. Besides, I am not a father yet. I am sure you are insane, though."

"Pause. Stop, Bro, you are just not seeing. I will say it slow. Get it this time 'cause you are hurting me."

Tyrion laughed. "Explain away then."

"If the sun quits, then I settle down and have a family. Make sense now, Bro."

"You know you will die? Right?"

"Yes," Yadekda replied.

Yadekda was famous for his peculiar sayings and too stubborn in his ways, therefore debating with him any further was pointless. "You are one of a kind, my winged friend. Who would settle down with you, anyway?" Tyrion chuckled.

"That's what you say, Bro. There this cute birdie been flapping her wings in front of old Yadekda," he replied, standing back up, lifting his massive head proudly upward, he blinked a black marble eye at him. "Anyway, Bro, all I am saying is some males eat their young." Tyrion gazed at him in horror. "Hey, Bro, just messing with you, man."

"Do not talk anymore," Tyrion told him. This statement was too much, even for Yadekda's dumbfounding comments. "Give me a ride, then go eat."

"A short one man, my back is really sore, and I gots to go get me some food."

"Well, thank you for taking a minute out of your time to fly me around. Oh, wait, just before you eat out of my crops," Tyrion told him playfully.

"Chill Bro, I will take you," Yadekda' laughed.

"With the celebration near, I want to check on the Tysmelon. It won't take long, and then you can eat as much as you like."

"The new melon, it's been a while since I came to your gardens Bro, I have not had a chance to eat any. I see you got some of them red beets over there too. Don't mind if I try a few of those. I never tasted any from this new crop."

Tyrion watched him eat of the beets yesterday. His funny friend's obvious bending the truth was a common tactic of Yadekda, which Tyrion assumed he used to try and hide his healthy appetite. Deliberate deception must have been an unconscious response from the big bird because he had waved at Tyrion, too, while he stuffed his beak.

"Let's go," Tyrion said, sprinting forward, preparing to leap on the back of the bird as he took off. As in the usual practice, he ran next to him, pounced forward, and landed upon Yadekda's back. Firmly he planted his feet near the bird's neck, folded his arms in front of him, and stood tall while he balanced himself securely. A fusion of movements, mimicking his friend's steady movement. Eyes closed, recognizing Yadekda's glide, he became one with the great bird. Yadekda felt his buddy's mind invading link connecting with his own thoughts, which allowed Tyrion to expertly ride upon his back. This removed any of his fears the giant bird had that he might hurt him.

Tyrion's excitement nourishing his friend, he climbed upward high into the sky and soared among the soft trails of clouds. At last, he circled the village. The castle looked like a miniature model of the king's marvelous home. As the two of them sailed through the sky, enjoying the cool breeze, Tyrion wanted to never return to the ground; he had forgotten about the crops.

"I never asked what your name meant," Tyrion asked, hoping to get some glimpse into his friend since they had such a close connection at this moment, and he might read his mind for secrets within it.

"Yadekda. Chancellor of the Skies," he replied. "I guess I never told you about myself, huh, Bro."

"I guess not," Tyrion chuckled.

"Well, I guess it is not a good time to go over that now. Long story."

"Chancellor of the Skies. Some fancy name," Tyrion chuckled, but Yadekda stayed quiet, so he decided to drop the conversation. "The sky is red today, have any idea why?"

"Nope, Bro, I have not seen anything out there."

"Let's go to Tysmelon. I truly love to keep flying, but Syb will call me soon for the last meal, then we are going to visit our nest."

When the two of them reached the melons, Yadekda circled the crop while Tyrion stared down at the fruit; several neat rows of it spread across the area, which he might make into wine. If Vincentru negotiated a trade with the Dragonors, he would barter for beautiful fabrics for Syberias to design pretty dresses for herself and Harmonia.

"Is that it? The most magnificent fruit I am ever going to eat?" Yadekda asked. "I gotta tell you, Bro, your melons don't look that good."

Tyrion chuckled," Not all of them are ripe." A moment later, he released his mental connection to Yadekda and prepared himself to jump off his back. Without warning, Yadekda angled his body awkwardly. Tyrion lost his balance and toppled headfirst to the ground, tumbling into the overripe Tysmelon. Mushy rinds squashed beneath him, and the wet sloppy mush from the melon was all over his clothing and face.

"Hey, Bro, I knew when you made that fancy move back there that I needed to be careful. It was a good thing I was looking out for the two of us." Yadekda, who also lost his balance because of Tyrion's quick disconnect, which left him in a state of momentary confusion, too tumbled down to the ground. Luckily, he missed the crop and did not destroy them all but landed in an empty patch of soil.

"What do you mean, what did I do? I did the same thing I do all the time, I tried to jump off your back, and it was you who was not paying attention."

"No, Bro, it was you. Do you need an instant replay?" A hint of sorrow coming from his big black eyes, he said, "Now, I have to go and wash in the springs. This will be my second bath this year, and I was not planning on taking two."

Tyrion laughed and said, "I thought I smelled something up there."

"Ya, funny. Bro, look at yourself. When Syberias sees you, there is going to be trouble, man. We can run now and never look back."

Slime on his face, he wiped it with his hand and looked down; his clothing was filthy. Black rind smeared everywhere; he looked like he purposely tie-dyed it in black paint. His tail, matted in the rind, he was fearful to look at himself. "Syberias will not be happy when she sees me. She only last night brushed out my tail," he laughed.

"I don't blame her. Look at yourself," Yadekda roared out in laughter again.

"I am sure it is not that funny."

"You don't see what I do, Bro. We should just leave now. Heh…he."

"The only place I am going is home." A broken feather dangling from his friend's wing, Tyrion quickly grabbed it and stashed it beneath his shirt, hoping to keep it clean.

"Ouch. Hey, Bro, that is personal property. Intrusion into my space."

"Thank you. Hopefully, this will give me some type of absolution with Syb when she sees my clothing," he chuckled, walking away.

***

Tyrion never gave Syberias the feather, and he was not sure what actually happened to it. Never negotiated for the wine, and now his daughter, too, was missing as well. A bit of sorrow rushed upon him and he did not allow it to take him over. "How is it going, my friend?"

"Bro, don't you worry, ole Yadekda gonna find them."

"I know you will." Tyrion gazed over at Shanara. Lost in his thoughts, he did not notice the Dragonor move from along beside him.

"There, Bro," Yadekda squawked widely.

Suddenly, Buderous let out a large puff of smoke mingled with particles of fire. The dragon swooped down quickly and began to dive, and Yadekda followed him down. Tyrion held on. At last, his keen eyesight focused upon something laying upon the grown. "There. It's the ship."

Pieces of the ship were everywhere, and he saw the wreck of the Hameau. The sight of the white sails and fragments of the hand-carved wooden hull made his heart sink. *Syberias was right.* Concern for her welfare overflowed within him; his mate told him she saw things the others did not. *Maybe they could have stopped all of this if he would have just listened.* Slowly Yadekda approached, and Tyrion gasped in disbelief at the sight of the wreckage. "The entire ship is nothing but pieces," he said aloud and peered at the intact altar, resting on its side, and the scattered nests. "Do you see Captain Jonus?"

"No, Bro." Yadekda circled over the wreck once more, and Tyrion surveyed the nests. So far, he did not see his daughter. The baby mewlings scattered everywhere; he was sure she was here somewhere. His link broken, springing off his back, he landed on the ground next to debris. Searching around the area, Tyrion looked for Captain Jonus.

All the nests he saw looked a bit beaten, although he saw no punctures or holes in them. "Are you checking the nests?"

"They look okay," Shanara yelled, frantically inspecting the debris. "Did you find the captain?

"No. Where could Jonus be?" With only the desire to find Captain Jonus, and too, his own nest, Tyrion rifled through the wreckage desperately. "Captain Jonus, Captain Jonus."

A weak voice called to him, "Here, here, Tyrion."

"Where are you?" he asked, struggling to pinpoint his location. Beneath the sails, Captain Jonus laid trapped under the control panel.

"I'm pinned," he said to him weakly.

"I will try to remove it." Tyrion tried but he was not strong enough to move the massive panel off Captain Jonus. Never before had he seen a Mejuarian hurt so severely, and Tyrion found it difficult to look at him. For sure, his friend's wounds were extensive since the panel was heavy, and broken bones were injuries that Tyrion's abilities were useless to cure. There was blood, yellow stains of liquid darkened his eyes, and hair, which was as well matted from sweat leaking from his destroyed body. It was clearly evident he suffered. "Help me."

Shanara ran over, and the two of them attempted lifting the massive control panel. Much too heavy still, Tyrion cried out for Yadekda. Often the large bird helped him around the farm, removing large boulders and trees. "Yadekda will move it. Let's find some rope."

"There is plenty of rope here," she told him, snapping her blade from its sheath. The blade's metal gleamed brightly; it was made of some type of Dragonor steel that he did not know the name of. Most Mejuarian had no use for weapons, especially farmers. Hurriedly, she cut away the rope attached to the sail, and the two of them tied it around the control panel.

"Yo, Bro. I am here."

"Thank you, Yadekda."

"Don't you go getting all emotional on me. That's what buds do for each other." Yadekda shoved Tyrion with his wing, grabbed the rope from Shanara's hand in his beak, and lifted the control panel off of the ailing captain.

Captain Jonus moaned loudly, even though he did not appear to move or flinch when the massive weight was lifted from him.

"Are you well?" he asked, falling down to his side upon the ground.

"Better now that I have that box off of me," he responded weakly. "I think I lost my legs, Tyrion."

With the control panel off of his friend, injuries to his body were apparent. "Don't worry. You will be out of here before you know it. You will be all right." Tyrion looked at Shanara. "Please, can you take him back on Buderous?"

"Of course."

"I am going to stay with Yadekda and collect the mast. Have the king send back an airship."

Captain's Jonus' body, stilted and strapped down to a piece of the hull, the two of them tied him on the back of the mighty dragon.

"Don't worry, little Tyrion. I return with them as soon as possible." An instant later, the female Dragonor sat on the back of her companion. Buderous stretched out his gigantic wings and flew off, leaving a gust of wind behind him.

"Woah, that is a big guy," Yadekda commented.

"Yes, he is."

"I can take him down, though." Tyrion gazed at him and shook his head. "Hey, I am just saying in case you wanted to know."

"Great, that is nice to know," he chuckled.

"The hard part's over with now, Bro. We just collect these little babies and take them to their daddies and mommies. Then the fun begins." Yadekda laughed. "No sleep, grouchy mate, dirty bottoms."

"Shut up, just collect them," he laughed.

"Duu de duu. Duu de...." Yadekda strutted off on thin, black, bird legs whistling, and moving debris out of his way with his giant feet.

Tyrion decided on a clear grassy area not too far from the crash site to begin gathering nests and taking them back to the area to wait for the airship's rescue. Yadekda was his friend, however now, his main priority was finding his daughter. Therefore, working on the opposite end of the field of his friend, relief occupied his thoughts. There would be good news for Syberias when he returned.

The Mysterious Black Bird

Yadekda walked through the debris. Everything was a mess, and the nests were everywhere. Wanting desperately to help his friend, he loaded the colorful cocoons under his wing. In all honesty, he wanted to eat more, and there was nothing around to eat. All day long was his eating habits, and there was no set time for him to enjoy a delicious meal. Tyrion told him he ate dayzers and not meals because he ate for hours at a time, rested for moments, then repeated his feast.

Several nests clutched in one of his wings and talons, skipping on one foot, Yadekda returned to the pile to neatly line up the nest he carried across the ground. Although Tyrion said the nests were indestructible, he was gentle with them, wanting to make sure he did not harm any of their precious insides. Most of the nests were collected now, but still a few were missing. At last count, with this latest batch in his claw, five were left to find. Hopefully, the two of them found them soon. The humidity from the dense watery area was bothering him. They had yet to enter into the caves; if Tyrion had not collected them, that might be the next location to search.

With the mountains surrounding the bushy lands, it seemed that all of the moisture remained in the ground; this dampness plugged his nostrils. Yadekda would rather stay away from stinky marshland. Nothing lived in these lands, but mindless creatures living off each other for survival. Not that he was not afraid of the big wild cats and other vicious four-legged animals that hunted the grounds preying on birds, he just would prefer to avoid the confrontation—a vicious consumer's cycle. A self-proclaimed vegetarian, the thought of eating something weaker than himself revolted Yadekda.

Often, he flew over the lands and stopped a couple of times, but now, he never bothered to stop. It was spooky. In the darkness, close to ground lights sprinted about, and when he looked closer, they disappeared. Yadekda believed them spirits from those lost in the jungle.

In his youth, beautiful cinnamon-colored wings, gleaming white feathers upon his regal head, he remembered roaming the skies in an awesome presence. Crystal blue eyes, able to spot the smallest movement from great distances, a golden beak, sharp as refined metal, and fatal golden claws, Yadekda mastered the skies and ruled over his vast territory.

Loved by many creatures but hated by even more, those that found him threatening betrayed him. Captured by them, they delivered him to the terrible Guardian of Darkness: a punitive, brutal guard, for one of the lords of the lands far away from Ercutis.

An unyielding pleasure to see sorrow, the terrible man, inflicted torture on those sent to the blackened dark caves by the great warlord. Yadekda vowed never to say his name and refused to mention it, even in his thoughts. He was a ruthless and terrible warlord, or which he later found out, dreadful Ercutian.

In the beginning, Yadekda was called Pama. This name was not suited for his master's fierce image. The guard made him Yadekda, Warden of the Darkness. In his heart, he enjoyed his master's attention and performed for the giant brutish guard happily. Magical potions given to him, he soared through the fire-lit caves, revealed his expansive wingspread, and graceful audacious flight. Also, given the ability to speak, his glorious tongue and quick wit entertained his master for hours upon end. For his own solace, he flew through the caves and sang delightful songs, endeavored to brighten the morbid sadness.

Since the guard treasured his trophy prize, he gave Yadekda life. What type or how long he might live, the great bird was not advised. Was he immortal? Yadekda did not know, however, many, many, many cen-cycles, what the Mejuarian called years, he knew he still lived. A curse the vicious guard put upon him, he soon came to believe, after every year, that he was still alive in the dark caves.

On one particular day, his master's fierce anger lashed out at a resident. Ruthless and not a bone of pity within him, the guardian decided to use him as a terrible weapon against the poor human. The guardian delighted in the screams of pain, and to this day, Yadekda will not remember his crimes. Him, who the great bird loved, made the once king of the skies shameful and hated. Like the slaves, there was no choice except to follow the commands given to him. So he hurt those weaker than himself. As if the torture of those sent as captives were not bad enough, he took Yadekda out of the caves unto the land above; there, he made him torture innocents with his powerful beak and claws. And finally, the warlord's command the great bird placed a painful symbol of submission upon the king or queen of the lands with his sharp talon.

Yadekda could no longer take the horror, and one day refused to harm anyone else. Punished due to his disobedience, the guardian locked him in his dungeon and chained him to the wall. Time passed, and he lived on and on; anger and hate immersed him. Worse than his master's betrayal was the fact that his beautiful feathers turned an ominous black, his gleaming talons, beak, and claws and nails, too, grew dark, and his lovely blue eyes lost their light. They grew black.

Jailers of the guardian of darkness changed from time to time. Yadekda understood that the days, weeks, months, and years passed. One after another, the jailers that came to torment him turned crueler. Yadekda continued to live, although, for months at a time, he had nothing to eat. His wicked master never visited him; however, now and then, the horrible wardens told him that the guardian sent scraps of raw flesh. There was no light or torches near his cage and left in complete darkness, the jailer unkindly threw meat to him, as if he were nothing more than a wild animal. Yadekda searched the dirt ground for the piece of morsel; this insult only helped strengthen his already acute eyesight. Now he saw as well in the darkness as in the light. He never wanted to eat the dirty raw meat, but hunger pains attacked him, and when he tasted the raw flesh, Yadekda could not help himself.

Yadekda mourned his situation; he never wanted to commit such acts, and he did not understand why his master treated him in such a terrible way. Enslaved in the darkness too long, broken in spirit, he grew furious and only wanted to confront the evil guardian to kill him. One day, the jailer for the guardian stopped coming, and he never received even the scrap of meat he was used to. Sounds from the captives' moans, which once gave him hope that he was not alone, stopped as well. Still, he was captive, and whatever crept across the ground or wall became his meal. Over the terrible long years, the underground walls grew moist, and his chains loosened. With all of his might, Yadekda pulled forward, and the chains popped from the wall; he was free.

Deep in the darkness, he searched for the ruthless guardian and broke the chains from his chest, arms, and legs angrily while he hunted. For days, he wandered through the dark, dank underground cavern, furious with the taste of blood in his beak. No one was there, and with freedom in his grasp, after so long of a time of imprisonment, he felt the skies call to him. He left the underground world forever.

Outside of the caves were different, and he did not know where he was, frankly. Structures were different, and places that were once only burnt villages and parched forests now had clean, fancy buildings resting upon them. Cleared paths with some type of vehicles moving across the long winding paths frightened him. Yadekda did not want to be there as this was no longer his home; it was a place that made him dark and ugly. Black glossy wings outspread, he soared high into the sky, so high the sun made his darkness glimmer almost white. Upward he flew, never stopping to enjoy its warmth. While he passed through the light, then darkness, light, darkness, then, at last, he reached another beautiful illumination, so he decided to rest. Weary from his journey, in places where he resisted the pull against him and tried to drag him back down to the ground, he hovered above the beautiful land and searched for a place to rest. A growl in his stomach made him realize he starved from food; however, he needed rest now and would fill his stomach later.

The great bird slept in a shallow nook within the high mountains for days and refused to go underground again. High above the ground, this gave Yadekda a view of everything around him. Hunger called out to him, and Yadekda left the mountains; he had hoped to find berries or leaves he could eat. Everything was different in this world. It was peaceful, no loud noise, and nature like he remembered before his capture; he wanted to stay. Over the years, he stole from the Mejuarian gardens at night, though he soon realized that they were amicable beings. Yadekda and Tyrion were friends for many cycles now. Once again, he felt honored to be friends with a deity.

The wet bushy area called his name since three nests were still missing, Tyrion's included, which pained Yadekda. Tyrion was his bro and best bud. One day, he might pass on and leave him alone again. Until then, he would find his daughter, whatever it took.

***

Tyrion anxiously waited for the Mejuarian to return. "Yadekda, search over the mountains again. The three nests have to be somewhere." *Why was this going so wrong?* No longer would he have good news to give Syberias when he returned. So far, they located Captain Jonus, the Hameau, and most of the nests; however, still missing was his daughter, the king's son, and another. Tyrion thought of the other couple whose nest was not recovered. He did not know who it belonged to, since, in truth, he was too busy governing his sector and cared not for the courtesies of who was birthing a mewling.

Only one place left to check; he climbed upward, heading farther into the mountain. The terrain began growing dark and bleaker, the further traveled from the crash site up the mountains. Brush and the trees appeared dead as if burnt, and Tyrion noticed the smell of burning. There were no Dragonors in these lands, at least that is what Shanara told him; stepping softly, he cautiously crept forward, unsure what awaited him ahead. A step away, all the brush and tree were absent. Tyrion entered an empty field; kneeling down on the dark, dry ground, he felt the soil. The parched ground, definitely cleared away by tremendous heat, was thirsty and scorched. *Nothing will grow here again,* he said to himself. Proud of his excellent farming abilities, he knew land and soil, and this was no good. In the distance, the open mountains split into dark caverns. Unsure what to expect or what caused this damage, suspecting a rogue dragon might have burned the ground, Tyrion stepped up to the crossroads.

A foul smell began to assault his nose as anxiety began to rise within him, "There is nothing here that will hurt me," he whispered. A moment later, stepping up to the cavern, he peered into it. The smell was dreadful wafting out of it. Warm, damp, rotten odors assailing his sensitive orifice; his stomach felt nauseous. Tyrion stepped back to avoid being sick. Dragons were dreadful, and he was sure this beast was in no way similar to those the Dragonors had as companions. Tyrion turned and quickly jogging back down to the crash site to wait for Yadekda, yet failed to see the little man following him.

Tyrion's heart hurt. A pain he never had before, and he knew this would devastate Syberias. A memory of her standing upon the ladder, caressing their daughter, came into his mind. It was difficult for him to convince her to come down so that they could finish their packing. Then it struck him, their nest was sitting on the corner of the altar. His heart began to beat faster; he had to find the piece of the broken altar.

"What up, Bro?"

"A piece of the altar is missing as well as three nests. The end holding my daughter."

"Calm down, man. They are all here somewhere."

"Are they? The ship was struck by a meteor."

"Hold on, Bro, this is not all your responsibility. You have got me, all of the other Mejuarian, and those guys with the dragons." Yadekda skipped over to him and looked down.

His friend towered over him, and his black glossy eyes considered him with an awesome gaze of hunger; nevertheless, Tyrion felt the sensitive nature behind them.

***

Zacharias followed the colorful man up the mountain pathway. Intent on searching the grounds, never once did he have to hide from the stranger. The creatures were indeed strange to him. Ears on top of their heads, and tails on their butts, he found them odd, and this one's little, yellow, curly-cue tail was just plain dreadful. It did not move like the other creatures' tails and was motionless behind him as if it were an ornament glued on. Laughter burst from him. The stranger stopped and turned around. As quick as lightning, he ducked under a fallen leaf and became very still. *The big lug probably wouldn't have noticed me anyway.*

The stranger was heading toward the dragon, so he followed. Arvunglies, tiny in size and agile in feats, they were able to sneak through the caverns overlooked; the stranger was too big to hide from the great beast, though. His loud footsteps announced his approach to the dragon, who was probably sleeping right now. Which was the best for the stranger since, without notice, a stream of intense fire could come from the cave, burning him to a crisp. And he would suffer a fate just like his destroyed outposts, which they were continually rebuilding along the banks of their rivers.

Zacharias understood why the animal/man was willing to go into the dragon's caverns; he assumed he hunted for the glittery object he gave to the queen, who announced their union to the rest of the villagers. Now he earned even greater respect. With certain authorities directly upon his shoulders, an idea surfaced into his head. Who was better to get rid of the dragon than the colorful creatures and their riders? A trade was in order, removal of the dragon for the valuable treasure.

Finally, coming to his senses, Zacharias presumed the stranger, turned, and started running from the dragon's lair. There were plans to be made, and when the strangers came back to pick up the rest of the objects, he would have a meeting with them.

Chapter Eight

Room for More Trouble

His father left for the veterinary office, and Mrs. Cheazemina watched over Brooklyn, so Ren sneaked out of the house and spent most of the day with Mark. The two of them lazed the hot day away on a swing chair, drinking lemonade. The day was beautiful, and since neither of them was in trouble for theft of the taffy, he freed his mind to think about the UFO. The strange objects were not from Earth, and Ren was very sure of that, regardless of what his father told him. Ren just hoped his father was careful with the pods while at the hospital, and they did not do a body snatch on him. Thorough knowledge of his father and his ways, he would know, though, and the aliens would not fool him.

"Did I tell you we found a couple of UF0s?"

"No. Dweeb, stop your lying."

"I am serious, turd. Listen, I found two pods yesterday when my dad made me go to the lake."

"UFO's, huh. What did they look like?"

"I don't know, nests or something like that. Oblong cocoons."

"How do you know they are UFOs," Mark chuckled and punched Ren in the shoulder. "You have watched too many space movies."

"Whatever, whiteboy. Like you don't believe in ghosts and goblins. Is the old man in the dale still a warlock?"

"You bet he is. Probably in the dale casting one of his spells right now. Anyway, show me these UFOs."

"My dad took them to his office."

"Like I thought. You are liar, turd."

"If you don't believe me, come on. Let's ride to my dad's office, and you will see. He's there anyway and will probably be glad we came by."

"Sweet, we can head out to Franklin afterward and get some cider. You know Jamie Lee has the hots for me."

"Franklin's sister does *not* have the hots for you, and you better not tell Franklin that," replied Ren, standing to his feet.

"All in the charm. No girl or woman on Earth can resist these charms." Mark stood up and did a strong man pose. His bronzed, tanned chest gleamed from sweat, seeming to increase the size of the football champ.

"Put your shirt back on. You stink, wheezer."

Thirty minutes later, the two of them stood at the back door of his father's veterinary clinic. Hubert's car was not in the parking lot, and only the emergency lights burned throughout the reception area. His father was no longer there. Ren thought he might return home since he was on temporary house lockdown, except for school. Another thought got the better of him, however. Surely, his dad knew he had left the house by now, so he might as well show Mark the UFOs. Mark searched for a way to enter the building. His father never left his keys outside anymore. Since the incident with the drugs, neither did he trust Ren with his keys.

"Let's go around to the front. We can get in through there. The door is not like this steel." The steel back door of his father's office was already installed when he bought the building. There were always plans to change it. Mom died, though.

"You watch out for anyone coming. I am going to pick the lock. I got pretty good at picking my father's liquor cabinet." Mark grinned cheekily.

Ren stood on the side of the road, watching for cars to make sure no one saw Mark picking the lock. "Hurry, there is a car coming. "

"Hold on, I almost got it."

"How do you expect me to hold the car, dumbo?" As the vehicle approached, Ren waved and smiled at the passing motorist, hoping to draw their attention away from Mark.

"I got it," Mark yelled, trotting back. Ren opened the door, and Mark followed him into the dark office.

Dusty ran up to Ren, crying as if he were irritated by something. "What's got into Dusty," he laughed. The aggravated cat ran off, and Ren followed him. "Come on, Mark, they are probably in his lab."

The poor cat's screeches were very disturbing, and Ren soon found out why when he saw him scratching wildly at the incubator holding the pods. "There they are. I knew it. Those are UFOs. Look how Dusty is acting. Mad Kitty," Ren chuckled and tapped on the glass door.

"What is he doing?"

"Yeah, watch out for those claws. They can tear through metal. Super Dusty," Ren laughed; reaching down, he picked up the chubby kitty. For a moment, Dusty quieted down and began purring softly. "Weird, huh Dusty?"

"What the…" Mark walked up and gazed at the objects. "Freaking weird, dude."

"Yeah, I know." Like he found them, the pods had only a small charring upon them. Other than that, Ren believed that they were perfect as when the aliens created them. Like in the movies, the two of them sat in the warming chambers, appearing as designer bobbles waiting for their host. "Touch one. I dare you."

"What did your dad say they were?" Mark gazed at the object then tapped on the screen.

"He does not know. He thinks they are something man-made. I believe they are UFO's that dropped from that meteor the night we snagged the candy."

"Unreal, man."

Ren stepped in front of Mark, opened the incubator hatch, and felt one of the objects. Warmth continued to radiate from the pods. The intensity of the alien inside it felt much more potent than it did the day he found them, which he found odd. "Touch it, doofus. It won't hurt you."

Mark reluctantly touched the object and jerked his hand back quickly. "What is that? I felt something."

Ren laughed, "I know, right? An alien, and it's getting stronger," he replied in a spooky tone. "We better split before they hatch. Sorry Dusty, but I think it should take your body over mine."

"Stop the crap, Ren," Mark told him, hurriedly walking away.

The two of them left the building, and Ren ensured that the door was locked behind him so that his father might not realize he did a B & E into his clinic. Along the almost deserted highway, he felt peace. Ren enjoyed riding the two-speed bike down the road to Franklin's farm because he used the second speed the entire trip and the bike seemed as if moved along by itself. There was nothing much to see when he left the town, but riding on the asphalt road, through the fields and overgrown, aromatic crops was peaceful. Thoughts of his mother surfaced mostly when he biked through the quiet and also what direction he wanted to go.

The shrill sound of a police cruiser's alarm went off behind him for a moment. Ren looked back to see Lt. Dwight coming up behind them. "Not that dufus."

"Ignore him. We are riding our bikes. How can he arrest us for doing that?" Mark chuckled.

A moment later, the police cruiser pulled up alongside of the two of them. "Youz boyz riding on the wrongz sidez of the road."

"Yep, Lt. Dwight. We know we are, but you have to understand that we can see the traffic coming when we ride on this side."

"It feels safer," Mark agreed.

"We aren't hurting anybody."

"Youz isz breaking myz laws, thatz who youz twoz are hurting. But I guess youz boyz are right aboutz that. Anywayz I aint gonna harass youz twoz aboutz that today."

91

"Thank god for miracles," Ren said under his breath.

"Whatz that youz said, boy?"

"Nothing, Lt. Dwight, just thank you."

"Youz daddy tells me youz gonna doz better Ren. Iz that right?"

"Yes, sir. In fact, we are on our way to help Franklin's dad with his crops. Right Mark?"

"Um-hum."

"Thatz some good newz. Keepz upz the good workz," he told them and drove off.

"He is such a spaz and thinks he knows everything."

"A spaz-it-all," Ren chuckled.

***

Ren watch Mark put on the charm with Jamie Lee, Franklin's sister, while waiting for Franklin to come out of the house. They had plans to go out to the dale and look for the old man. She, too, just like Mark, both having narcissistic tendencies; Ren chuckled to himself as he listened to each of them brag about their accomplishments. Mark of speaking of his football swagger, and Jamie boasted about some debutante duties. Ren did not care.

Jamie Lee's lightly toned pecan complexion was a mixture of her mother and father's heritage, Afro-Mexican. She wore no makeup today, which was quite a shock because although she was younger than Ren, her face was usually caked in the heavy goo. Wavy black mane, the prissy girl's hair shined from all of the hair grease packed within its strands. Her short skirt showed all of her long brown legs; too skinny, the little sticks reminded Ren of bird legs. Playfully, she twisted one of her black and white oxford-covered feet, which made her look as if she were ready for a cheerleading competition. Ren thought she was ok, but not as pretty as Susie. Two years younger than Sam, who was the youngest of the four of them, he thought she was a baby.

A few minutes later, Franklin's mother stepped out of the house with glasses and a pitcher of apple cider. "Hello, everyone. Please have some cider. Franklin is out back. He will be here in a minute."

"He is washing the dishes," Jamie Lee giggled.

"That's enough, Jamie. You go inside and finish your own chores. I will be right with you." Franklin's mother, Sally Mae, poured the cider into each glass halfway full, precisely measuring the amounts in each one. "I am so glad to see you both. Where is Sam?"

"Oh, he could not make it this time," Ren answered.

"He's probably home stuffing his face." Jamie Lee giggled playfully while still flirting with Mark.

"That is not nice. Now you go into the house, girl."

"Bye Mark, bye Ren." Jamie turned and prancing off. A moment later, she looked back and waved goodbye at Mark.

Sally Mae seemed to sing as her bubbly personality came out in over-exaggerated long words that reeked of cheerfulness. Picking up two glasses, handed one to Mark, and hugged him warmly. She gave Ren the next drink, pulling him into her arms; her warm body smelled of rose. It did not smell bad; however, it was not his favorite smell, either. Ren felt uncomfortable; holding his breath, he kept out her motherly scent and avoided not hurting her feelings by abruptly shoving her back.

Finally, Franklin came out of the house. The lanky brown boy wore a t-shirt covering his upper body, worn overalls, with one of the straps hanging loosely, and a baseball cap over his dark hair. Beat up tennis shoes on his feet; the tongues and laces were missing. Ren knew these were his work clothing, but his school clothing might have been newer and cleaner; nevertheless, his wardrobe always looked the same. Franklin was not flashy, and overalls and cheap sneakers were his typical choice of fashion.

"Hey," he said, sat down, and picking up a glass of cider, he took a drink.

"What's going on, Franklin?"

"Nothing much," he said. Franklin was not much of a talker. Ren knew he was one of the hardest workers, though smart and wrote poems in his spare time.

"Riding over to the dale. Want to go?" Mark asked.

"Sure. I'm up with that."

"Franklin, can you please drop off Mr. Bill's cider," Sally Mae asked, who was now standing behind the front door screen eavesdropping.

"Later, mom. It's in the wrong direction."

"It won't take you that long, Franklin."

Ren thought about old Bill, the night watchman. The old man needed payback for ratting them out to the police. "Hey, we can do that for you, Mrs. Sally Mae."

Mark and Franklin stared at him. As if Mark understood what Ren was doing, he agreed. "Yes, we can. Come on, Franklin, we can do that for your mom."

"I'm not bringing the money right back."

"Ok, but don't lose it," she said, stepping outside with two jugs of cider in her hands.

Franklin shrugged his shoulders. "Let me carry those. You are going to hurt yourself."

***

Franklin walked out of the house. Work clothing thrown in the corner of the room, sneakers with laces and tongues were on his feet. On his blue Schwinn bike, he rode over to join Ren and Mark. Franklin had built a small rack across the back tire that held an old plastic milk crate that he carried his books, apples, cider he had for sale, or items he had picked up for the farm. Today, the carton carried two jugs of cider and a brown paper bag that held some hot sauce and a small, fermented prune juice container—the latter Franklin's father used for the pigs to keep them regular.

"Are you sure you want to do this?" Franklin asked.

"Yeah, we are. Old Bill needs to get his due," Mark chuckled.

"Well maybe if the two of you weren't thieves, you wouldn't have to worry about that old man."

"He called the cops on us, Franklin. Yes, I want to do this." Ren rode on. His plan was perfect if only Franklin helped. "Come on. You brought the stuff; we might as well use it."

"Ok, but I am not going down for this."

"You won't. Just give old Bill the new cider. Get his attention, and Ren and I will handle the rest of it."

"How are you two going to get in the house," Franklin asked.

"I can do that. We broke into the vet's office earlier," Mark boasted.

"Into your father's office? Ren, you are asking for it," Franklin chuckled. The most conservative of the three of them, Franklin preferred not to play practical jokes. His friend was, nevertheless, a willing culprit most of the time.

"He won't know. I wanted to show Mark the UFO. Anyway, you get Bill to drink the stuff, and Mark and I will sneak in and cover his toilet seat with this invisible hot chili sauce. Then we wait."

"What UFO?" Franklin asked.

"Never mind, we will tell you later. Let's just stick to the plan right now," Ren told him.

"You in Franklin?"

"I guess so."

Twenty minutes later, the three of them had finally reached old man Bill's home. While Mark and Ren snuck around the back of the house, Franklin stepped up to the door carrying the two jugs of cider and a free sample of his father's latest pig brew.

Franklin knocked loudly, "Mr. Bill, I have your cider."

The old man lumbered to the door slowly—"Franklin boy. Good, I have been waiting for that. One second, let me get your money."

Franklin looked through the house while the old man searched his jacket pocket hanging in the corner. To make sure the two of them could get in secretly, he looked into the living room. Mrs. Bill was sitting on the settee reading a ladies' journal; he signaled Ren and Mark to keep going. Like most of the old homes in Parryville, there was a direct passage to the rear door from the front door. Franklin peered through the old frame house and watched Mark and Ren sneak through the kitchen's back door. "Mr. Bill, my dad wants you to try his new brew," he yelled, keeping the old man's attention upon himself.

"Certainly, boy. That dad of yours makes some pretty fine stuff." With two dollars in his hand, he shoved the money at Franklin and released the cash before the young boy could grasp it. The bill fell to the porch.

"Here you are. Drink it fast. My dad says it's better that way," he said, reaching down to pick up the money while old Bill gulped down the laxative.

"Now that is some good shine. You tell your daddy I said so, boy, and tell him to send me over a jug."

"I will do that," Franklin answered, stepping off of the porch before he burst out in laughter.

Ten minutes later, the three boys hid in the hedges around the house's side, which gave them an excellent view of old Bill's bathroom. The small window was open, and the curtains pulled wide open as well.

"He's gonna go all over himself." The UFO's forgotten for the moment; he needed to get back at the old man for his betrayal. Ren held the mini spy camera that fit in the palm of his hand, aiming at the window to get the perfect photo of old Bill. Only one dollar and ninety-nine cents in the Superman Comic book. Although he was unsure what type of pictures the James Bond knockoff camera took, it was a great deal.

"Yeppers. I can't wait to teach pig boy to mess with me. My dad wanted to go out to the factory and punch Bill in the face," Mark agreed. "Old pops was not too happy about Dwight either."

"I saw your dad. I thought he was going to blow a fuse," Ren chuckled, enjoying the thought of revenge.

While the three stood outside of the bathroom discussing old Bill going all over himself, the old man rushed into the bathroom, shoved down his pants, and sat on the stool.

"Close that door, Bill. I don't want to smell you," his wife cried out. The three boys chuckled softly.

"I don't know what was in the shine the boy gave me. It aint working too good with my stomach."

Horrible sounds coming from the bathroom, the three of them peered on as old Bill made himself comfortable on the toilet. Within seconds, he dived off the seat and screamed, rubbing his butt cheeks with his hands.

"Ida, what cleaning supplied di.... ouch, it's stinging me. Get it off." The more the old man wiped at his bum, the louder he screamed from the pain.

Already, Ren found a mistake in the ad; the camera was supposed to take shots quicker than a regular camera. It took forever for the camera to process the photo, and he might not have enough time to use the ten shots on the film roll he ordered extra. Nevertheless, Franklin and Mark were almost rolling upon the ground within the hedges with laughter from watching the old man suffering from the hot sauce coating his bottom.

"What is going on in here, Bill," Ida asked. "What on heavens are you doing?"

"Something is on that toilet. What did you put on it? I told you to stop trying all those cheap cleaners," he screamed. "Get it off!"

"There aint nothing on that toilet seat, Bill. It's only your imagination," his wife told him.

Underpants down to his ankles, old Bill ran out of the bathroom screaming from the hot sauce marinating his hind part. Ida looked down at the toilet, shook her head, and walked away.

"Bill..."

The prank was worth the time it took for the finale. Three boys burst into hysterical laughter when the two of them left the bathroom. Moments later, cutting through the field behind old

Bill's home, they found the highway. The boys rode along, reminiscing the discomfort of old Bill.

"Serves him right," Ren chuckled.

"That moonbeam threw the money at me today."

"No way. The pig, you guys want to hit old Bill again?" Mark chuckled.

"I am game," Ren replied, however, he needed to return home after the ride the dale. His father was going to be furious that he had left the house, anyway.

On the Lookout

Lt. Dwight sat behind the Sarah Beauty Story sign sitting on the highway. The officer thought of Ren and Mark, riding along like normal boys going to work in the fields to make a little cash. This small venture was doubtful; he knew the two boys and believed that the two bad boys were probably up to no good. Young juvenile delinquents and their polite Lt. Dwight schmoozing did not fool him. Although it was quite evident, Mark and Ren pushed the sweet potato pie in their own father's eyes, hiding their sins, there was a cell waiting for the two of them in his jail. Regardless of how much his county Commissioner father complained to the Mayor. The law was on his side.

A lot of dirt could be hidden on this long road, he thought to himself, then gazed forward. Whatever the two of them were up to might be secret to him now, but he believed the old saying, 'What was done in the dark will come to light.' Dwight lived by the words. That's why, at all times, he was on his best behavior. Even in his own home, he wore creases in his jeans and t-shirts. Lt. Dwight, too, prided himself in the fact that he did not smoke cigarettes; he did have a cigar once in a while with the chief. Neither did the officer drink alcohol or beer, eat pork or shellfish, and made sure he took his wife out to dinner once a month. At this moment, he did not have his own kids, but he and Cecilia planned on having a big family. The force took his attention now, and frankly, he did not have time to throw baseballs with his son or attend the ROTC functions. One day, maybe, when he was Police Commissioner, he would have children.

"Dwight, are you there? Over." Mary Lee announced on the radio.

"Yesz, Imz here. What youz got? It's not aboutz that Mark and Ren isz it, Overz?"

"Not right now, but it has been two days. I suspect we will hear something shortly. Over."

Static, once again buzzed, before speaking, remembering Mark and Ren earlier. "I sawz them outz here onz the highway. Godz knows what they couldz be upz too, over."

"Maybe we can wait them out," the sound of laughter came over the radio. "Sorry to be the one to tell you this, but you need to go over to Frank's. He is putting up a fuss over there, over."

"Not that foolz. Onz myz way, over."

***

Testimony of Joseph Killian written by Office Dwight Strong.

Frank Thompson, the local bully and town alcoholic, in keeping to his normal behavior, drank too much homemade moonshine and became belligerent with his neighbor Joseph. Under the booze's influence, he threatened to fight Joseph and kill his dog if he ever came into his yard again. Frank followed the dog back into Joseph's yard and kicked the poor little poodle. Frank, who was ten pounds heavier than Joseph, who was 150 pounds soaking wet, grabbed Joseph and threw him to the ground while he grabbed his dog and attempted to flee. Joseph picked up a tire iron that he was using to change the tire on his 1935 pickup. The two of them ended up in a physical altercation in which Frank had been injured by the tire iron.

Lt. Dwight summarized the statement he took from the two warring men before he sat in the seat of the police cruiser. "So, yous kicked the dogz first. That's just tooz lowz Frank."

Glaring at the convict for his obvious cruelty to animals, he shook his head.

Dog beaters, were worse than thieves and tonight his passenger was going to spend the night in his accommodations. The Lt. glared back at Frank, adjusted the sunglasses on his face and proceeded to drive back to the station.

"Mary Leez, Iz bringing inz Frank. Hez stinking toz. Over."

"Don't tell me that, Dwight. I just had Howard clean those cells from the batch you brought in yesterday."

Frank slept soundly in the back of the cruiser while a passenger in the car's back seat. A metal cage separated the criminals from himself. Lt. Dwight carried Frank back to the station for arrest and processing to spend the next few nights in a cell. The drunk man would be there until the state judge from the Lalahasi County showed up to hold trials in Parryville. Shackled at his feet and cuffs on his hands, his arms and legs dangled from the roof of the vehicle as he lay hogtied to a latch Dwight installed on the ceiling of his police cruiser. Those that committed crimes deserved no comfort, the Lt. believed, and he treated them in ways he felt warranted; like pigs that return to the muck, he had no pity for their cries of innocence. Loud snores came from Frank, his mouth hung oven and spittle dribbled from the sides of his mouth. Truthfully, Lt. Dwight only had repulsion for the condition that the drunken bumbler had put himself in, and not so much for Frank.

Old Luke

Old Luke from the dale was walking down the road. Dwight liked the old man, even though he was quite odd and did not socialize with the townsfolk. Often during his patrol, on the hunt for speeders, the old bent man piqued his curiosity while he hobbled down the highway. The Lt. wondered where the man was going. Sometimes he asked, and the hermit only said, "Just here and there, Lieutenant." This aggravated Dwight, but everyone was entitled to their privacy, unless they were up to no good.

Old Luke was a good man, though, and it never entered his mind to arrest the hermit. Many folks in town believed him to be a demon that fought against the good God-fearing people of Parryville. "A house divided cannot stand," was his motto. Also, to those that insisted that he arrest the unsocial man, the Lt. always answered, "The pot cannot call the kettle black." The people of his town drank, smoked, fought, beat their wives, and caused all types of ruckus in Parryville. In his opinion, there were demons everywhere, and the actions of one lonely man living in isolation was not the cause of the sins they committed.

Dressed as always, in a white cotton shirt and brown corduroy pants that might have fit at one time, however, now were too big for his thin bend body. High legged Indian moccasins with the flopping tassels, he was an anomaly among the others. Long stringy grey hair, braided in two, very neat plaits, fell down along his pasty white, wrinkled face. Too white for the sunny region's tanned-toned complexions, his appearance was as if he walked in darkness only. Even old Luke tried to reside among the town citizens, Dwight believed the man's simple ways still might isolate him. The people of Parryville wore the latest fashions, fancy Elvis hairdos, and drove the best cars. Nevertheless, for one that stayed in the woods, he was always clean. A small black pouch, like a purse, hung from his shoulder; Dwight believed he carried his meager pennies in the little sack because it was a little too feminine for the bent old hermit.

Dwight peered at Frank through the rearview mirror; he was still sound asleep, so he stopped the car.

Old Luke also sold the most beautiful jewelry, which he loved to buy for Cecelia. Silver and golden polished chain bracelets, and rings, adorned with dark jewels, unlike the stones sold at Tallahassee's Kay's Jewelry store. Obviously, his stones were fake glass, because Dwight knew because the old man did not have a penny to his name. An old shack in the swampy dale made out of rotted logs and rope, he too was a squatter on state lands. Even if he wanted to, the Lt. could not arrest Luke since Deedli County grandfathered 'Right of Squatter' to him. The old man might live in the swampy lands till his death.

Dwight pulled the cruiser along the side of the road. "Hey, Lukez. Howz youz?"

Luke bent over and looked through the window. "Good day, Lieutenant. I hope that these lovely days find you well." He smelled like trees, which was not a lousy odor, but nature and the outdoors was not Dwight's thing.

"Iz, doing good, Lukez. Surez isz a hot onez today," he replied, wiping the sweat growing upon his face from the hot air pouring in through the open window.

"Yes, it is. We will see rain tonight, however," old Lucas answered and gazed up at the skies. "The leaves on the trees are hiding themselves."

"Isz that right?" No clouds were in the sky, and the and the sun hoovered brightly over the town. "Where youz get thatz from? Themz skyz isz beautiful."

"Yes, they are, Lieutenant, at this moment. Soon the heavens are going to release their cleansing waters."

"Cleanings waters. Whatz are youz talking about, Lukez?" he asked. Odd speech as well, it was no way he could live an everyday life in Parryville. "Anyway, what youz gotz today?"

"Something perfect, Lieutenant. I was thinking about Cecilia when making it. The color will match her eyes." Old Luke smiled. White pearly perfect teeth gleamed in his mouth, and his wrinkled pink lips turned upward. Odd, green, or blue, or even sometimes yellow, depending upon how the sun hit them, his stare was wise and yet intrusive. "Here, take this."

Dwight took the red velvet cloth from the old hermit. The smooth material was soft in his hands; it held something heavy. Excitedly, he unwrapped the cloth and saw the loveliest bracelet. Cecilia would love it. Delicate strands of darkened gold wrapped together, there were hundreds of tiny green jewels embedded throughout the metal. As faultless as Dwight believed possible, the strands of golds appeared to weave in and out of the gems; however, they did not. "This isz just fine, Lukez. What youz wantz for itz?"

Lukez closed his man purse and said, "Nothing. Dwight. Return the favor sometime."

This did not shock Lt. Dwight since most of the trinkets he got from the old hermit were free. Sometimes, feeling sorry for him, he tipped him a couple of dollars. Luke just dropped the money in his bag as if it were loose coins. "Well, Iz tell youz, this isz just lovely and Cecilia'z gonna love itz."

"It is my pleasure to give you something she will adore, Lieutenant."

"And I doez."

"Have a good day, Lieutenant. I should move on before I am trapped in the rain."

"Yes, youz doz that." Lt. Dwight peered again up into the sky. The sun was bright and shiny today, and the weatherman did not say anything about rain. He shook his head in disbelief at the odd man.

When the Lt. returned to the station, uncuffing the man, he helped him out of the car. Just as he closed the car door, water flooding from the sky started to fall down upon him. Strong winds picking him from the ground, he and Frank fell backward onto the wet parking lot blacktop. *Soon the heavens are going to release their cleansing waters*. The words of the old hermit came back to him.

"Getz up, Frank," he cried, straining to get to his feet, fighting against the heavy winds. Lt. Dwight laughed.

Chapter Nine

Lost May Not Be Found

On Ercutis, in the Dragonor's region, everyone knew the Hameau had not arrived, and King Teloby postponed the ceremony until Captain Jonus and the nests made it to the village. Still, some of the Mejuarian and Dragonors sat comfortably and waited at tables, and upon blankets thrown across the grassy ground, Alejandro stood in front of the onlookers. Although most of the Mejuarian soothing talents of the others, they too, challenged in their supernatural abilities by the dreadful event, could no longer rely upon their neighbors or mate's assistance in these times. The end result was Mejuarian lived lives of utopia, and this unexpected disaster left most disconcerted. Those that relied upon Thire-los' given gifts suffered.

A silver box at his feet, removing The Mejuarian Star from the protective case, he released the gem from his grip. The star floated upward, levitating in front of him for a few seconds. The bright object arose above the garden, resting above the place the altar would stand when it and the nests arrived. A brilliant light bursting from its core, a rainbow of reflecting particles radiated out, jammed the air and overlaid those below it in shimmering twinkles. Tiny multicolored glittering particles falling from the star disappeared when they hit any surfaces and secreted an aura of merriment.

This unique item was discovered amongst the other treasures in the temple that the elders gave away to helpful villagers that assisted in the cleanup. Alejandro aided with this clear-out and confiscated the precious relic in return for his hard work. The dancing Mejuarian realized, when released from its protective case, the star provided an essence that soothed him; clearing his head, he concentrated on nothing but his movements. Like many other strange relics located around the

Kingdom, the Mejuarian could not explain its anomalous properties. Of course, many believed that Thire-los left the item with ancients, along with the other peculiar things many of them held sacred and carried with them as tokens of cultural pride.

Tables draped in elegant silver linens brought the gardens alive that early day, giving it a festive appearance. These seats, just for the expecting parents, decorated under Alejandro's instruction, had a cloth hand-embroidered upon its face, the symbol representing the god of their parents' unique abilities: Rose of Lotus, Sword of Os, Staff of Thie, and Feathers of Ireania. Shimmering flowery white plates, golden goblets and cutlery sat atop of the tables as well, along with tall thin blue candles poised in perfectly rounded golden candleholders.

The blue candles were birth torches. Mejuarian only used these candles at the Blessing of the Dodekatheon because their burning wicks directed its heat towards the nests. The altar, found within the parents' tables, the blue candles were strategically around the birthing pillar and caused its marble surface to grow warm. These candles never burned down, nor did their flame die out until the last new mewling left the celebration. Elder Mejuarian, too, noted that Thire-lose left these valuable treasures with the village as well. Still, others believed magnetic energy in the altar pulled the heat from their flames into itself and created a pocket of warmth for the nests.

Within a few hours of being swathed in the heat, the nests birthed into little mewlings that crawled around like puppies, kittens, or resembled Ireania's offspring, and hopped around on birdie legs with bodies like the Ercutians. Each new mewling owned its own unique characteristics, talents, and gifts from the god Thire-los, but only at the beginning of their long life. When the mewlings became young Mejuarian, their bodies underwent a metamorphosis. They walked upright and took on the appearance of one of their parents.

"My friends, please enjoy the pleasures of the evening until our King returns." Mejuarian and Dragonors cheered gaily. Most were making the best of the situation, and he intended to help them enjoy themselves during the somber time. Music from the Mejuarian band played jazzy tunes on their string and wood instruments accompanied by the sharp sounds of the reed flutes played by the Dragonors.

"Only you can create a celebration when such sadness is around you, my friend."

Alejandro turned to see Atrurso standing behind him with a grin on the short muzzle upon his golden face. Long yellow curls pulled atop of his head between two stunted ears, tumbled behind his back, and his green eyes reflected pure compassion, that of Ireania and Lotus.

"Atrurso, why are you here? Undoubtedly, your sector must need their fabulous leader."

"I heard Zavalza speak to you earlier. I wanted to come to you." His adored-one moved over and discreetly touched his paw and nudged his body against him briefly. "Are you well? You must not let him take away your peace."

"And how can I allow such a horrible person to spoil this beauty?" Alejandro danced around Atrurso spiritedly and stopped to face him. "When I know that you are there."

"Always."

Atrurso said no words of endearment, and most never soft, even when they were alone. Practical always in his attitudes and ways, his frosty demeanor seemed distant; nevertheless, his presence by itself assured Alejandro of his love and gave him confidence in his talents. "Please, my dearest one, tell me, what new news is there?"

"Nothing more than we knew before. We must wait."

Alejandro walked away from the gardens and stood amidst a bunch of trees in the shadows. Safely away from the prying eyes of others, he took Atrurso's paw in his. "I feel such fear."

"There is fear in the village, yes. There is hope too, Alejandro."

"Yes. I know. I have spoken to our dear Syberias, and she does not believe her nest will return with the Mejuarian King."

"I have heard this sentiment from others as well."

"Do you feel that it is true, Atrurso?" With the sound of these words, his body grew numb. Alejandro felt as if his heart collapsed; all of his inward resolutions vanished. "Where are they then?"

"We will know when the ship returns."

"Syberias is such a sensitive, and her visions are true."

"The faith in such abilities is lost among us, Alejandro," Atrurso sighed. "Relocation to the Dragonors region is only a band aid."

"What is this, you say, my dearest?"

With a gentle touch upon his face by his loved one, his fears disappeared for the moment. "There is more to us as Mejuarian than science."

Alejandro understood his opinion. The two of them often spoke of the Mejuarian no longer using their inward sensitivities that he, like others, believed Thire-los gave them. Because of this, the village was losing its identity. "There are others, too, that believe."

"The days to come will tell." Atrurso smiled. "I must go."

"We will meet later."

***

King Teloby, now one of the anxious parents, waited for the Hameau or Vincentru, one of the Dragon Riders. Before he saw the great beast, he heard the loud roars of one of the dragons coming in. It was Magnus, and upon his bareback, sat Lord Ephenio's granddaughter, Shanara. His heart beat faster. *Where is the Hameau?*

"Where is Tyrion?" he asked.

"He is with the airship. It crashed in the mountains near the jungle," Shanara told them and began unraveling something laying upon the dragon. "Here, help me. Captain Jonus is hurt."

King Teloby and the others lingering around anxiously ran over the large dragon. Captain Jonus lay upon the middle back of the massive creature. "He needs Qusdyr; he is hurt badly."

"Bring him to the healer's home, and have your Mediatrician meet him there," a Dragonor in the crowd yelled. "Tell our healer as well that your captain is hurt."

"Tyrion said to bring The Mejuarian King."

The Mejuarian King was his fastest airship, and if Tyrion requested this vessel, he needed to get going as soon as possible. "Have Sidor ready my airship. Now!"

"What about the nests?" an anxious voice from the crowd asked.

"The nests are fine. Tyrion is with them," Shanara said, in an effort to calm the crowd.

King Teloby followed healer Buren into a small room within his large floating home. A place of medicines, which the Mejuarian did not use, the king surveyed all of the herbs around the room. For a brief second, curiosity over the different herbs and medicines took his mind off the situation. Jars and ceramic pots occupied with leaves, twigs, crushed powders, and all sorts of strange concoctions sat around the room in cabinets and on wooden shelves placed against the wall. Mejuarian only had a couple of potions and elixirs that Qusdyr used to treat them. Their Mediatrician would use touch and the Mejuarian link, which released his healing talents into the body of the injured Mejuarian.

Captain Jonus let out a small groan regaining the king's attention. "How are you, my friend? What happened?"

"My deepest apologies, my King. I tried to save them. I tried my best, but the ship lost power after the meteor hi…" Captain Jonas spoke weakly. He could not finish his sentence and closed his eyes.

"All is well, Jonus. Please do not concern yourself with this travesty. Tyrion is collecting the nests, and we will have the celebration tonight. You rest. Qusdyr will come soon."

King Teloby patted him on the shoulder and left the house. On his way to the airship, he ran into Tovar, making his way through the crowd.

"My King, is everything alright with the mewlings? I have heard Captain Jonus crashed the Hameau."

"The Hameau did crash, but we are not sure why yet, Tovar. Can you have everyone meet in the gardens in ten minutes? I would like to talk to them and let them know what is happening."

***

Syberias stood in the crowd holding onto the Queen's arm and listening to the King's message. Tyrion had not returned with their daughter, and now she was lost to her; she knew her mate was not coming back with her nest. Although she had tried to warn them before the crash, no one listened. They would find the nests and celebrate tonight, but she would not hold her daughter in her arms.

Her ambrosia leaves were dark this morning, and although they had no pictures for her to decipher, their darkness confirmed her worst fears. At this moment, though, she knew one thing. With all of her might, she would hunt for her daughter. Wherever they searched from now on, she was going to be there. Syberias intended to learn how to ride a dragon, if she needed it to find her daughter. One day she would find her, she knew that. But for now, Harmonia would not be in her arms tonight.

For days she agonized in her loneliness and pleaded for their help. Now that she knew for sure her mewling was gone; she could not cry. All her sadness and tears vanished this morning, and all she had left was her determination. Syberias smiled at the queen, released her grip, and left to go home and wait for Tyrion.

The Mejuarian King Arrives

"Thank you, Tyrion, for staying here and gathering the nests," King Teloby told Tyrion.

"There are still three nests that I can't find. Yadekda and I have looked everywhere, except for in those mountains there." Tyrion pointed to the caverns with the awful smell leaking from them.

"That's right, Bro. Don't worry, King Teloby, we will find them," Yadekda agreed.

A talking bird was bizarre to King Teloby, but he realized the massive creature was not from the Mejuarian lands. Many strange beings existed on Ercutis and the surrounding planets, and that was why he hoped to increase the kingdom allies by finding them. Teloby did not always appreciate the outsiders' talents and natures, like riding on dragons and eating flesh. Still, all were welcome in his Kingdom, except for the dark phantoms since they were hostile to the Mejuarian.

Even though he could tell Tyrion was trying to hide it, he saw the concern and worry in his face. The King waved for the others in the party to disband and collect the nests. "Is there a problem, Tyrion? The worst is over now. We will get the nests back to the Dragonor's village and have the ceremony. You and Syberias, and Nymeria, and I will hold our mewlings. Alejandro planned a great event."

"I cannot find my nest," Tyrion blurted out. "It was on the part of the altar that is broken."

King Teloby stopped talking and concern came across his face. Yellow strands of hair falling in his face, the King gathered them up and tucked them behind one of his upright ears.

"We can't find the broken piece of altar either."

"Tyrion, you have done a lot of work here today. The whole moving of the village has taken its toll on everyone." King Teloby patted Tyrion on the shoulder. "The day is still young." King Teloby walked over and gazed down at a yellow decorated nest and considered it carefully. When he arrived, he had quickly scanned the collection of nests, looking for his. Since he did not see it, now that the others were out looking, he decided to slowly walk from nest to nest to look for the purple silk that Nymeria had used to tenderly drape over their mewling nest. The king walked over to Atrurso, scrutinized each of the nests, ensuring they were all still intact and suffered no injuries from the crash.

"Have you found any problems, Atrurso?"

"No. I don't expect to either, King Teloby. We believed the paste used to create the nests was indestructible. Now we know. Since the birthing cycle starts tonight, I don't think we have anything to worry about."

"Thank you. Have the nests taken to the ship, please." Anxiously he walked along, carefully studying each one. Still, three were missing, he knew when he came to the end of the line of baby mewlings. King Teloby exhaled deeply. His nest was missing as well.

***

Zacharias and the rest of his army hid beneath the wreckage of the spaceship waiting for the time he felt it appropriate to approach one of the colorful beings. Finally, the one he figured must be the commander walked over to the wreckage and began sifting through the pile of valuable wood and debris.

"Arm yourselves," Zacharias ordered.

Tiny Arvunglie soldiers held their small spears upward with their tips at the sky. Shells of stink bugs held out in front of them; they stood behind an unbreakable barrier. Bamboo cone hats upon their heads, leafed loincloths and brassieres their armor, the tiny jungle army might have been a formidable force if they were fighting others their own size.

"Halt, who goes there," Zacharias ordered. The big blue and white colorful being stopped and looked around. Long strands of yellow hair fell down into his face, across his pointed nose, and his tail swung about, almost hitting Zacharias. Quickly he moved out of the way. "Down here."

The animal/man looked down; his army held their swords forward, pointing them out through their shields as if they prepared for battle.

"Oh, there you are," the animal/man said. "Well, hello."

"Your spaceship crashed on my lands," Zacharias said gruffly. Although he was small and the creature towered over him, Zacharias needed him to know that he had no fear. "Now my lands are scattered with debris."

"Yes, I see. I do apologize for that. I will certainly make sure that it is removed."

Zacharias thought for a moment. There were so many pieces of good wood they could use to rebuild their outpost; however, most of it was too large for even the whole tribe of Arvunglies to move it. Another deal came to his mind. "I am afraid I am going to have to make you pay a litter charge."

The small army of Arvunglies agreed, "Whuh," they cried out.

"A litt...er cha..rge," he stuttered. "I don't know what that is."

"It is simple. You have to pay me," Zacharias told him.

"Pay you for what? Who are you?"

"I am Zacharias. Betrothed to Queen Marina, Lady of these Lands. Second-in-command to the leader of the Arvunglies. Commander of the Arvunglie army, and Chef."

"Oh," the animal/man replied, quite taken back by Zacharias impressive stature, he believed. "I am King Teloby. King of the Mejuarian."

Zacharias nodded his head, held his spear up, and said, "I think we can settle this charge quite easily, though. My village needs that wood. So, to clear up your debt, you cut into smaller pieces, and I will take that as payment."

King Teloby chuckled at him. "I think I can agree to that without much argument from my council."

Things were going smooth in this meeting, and the animal/man, although sort of slow and dimwitted, was going to be cooperative. "Stand down," he told his soldiers, and the battalion of Arvunglies lowered their shields and held their spears along their sides.

"No one has spoken of the Arvunglies before."

"That's because no one knows we are here. We are quick and smart. The Arvunglies have been here since the beginning of time."

"That long. That's impressive," King Teloby replied. "Where do you live?"

Now the questions of the king were intruding upon the safety of the villagers. No one knew the village's location, and since most of the big ones never looked beneath the bush along their streams running from the river, they remained hidden from outsiders. "We are jungle folk."

King Teloby looked around. Zacharias saw two of the other animal/men walking toward him. And one was notably large and dark, almost like the bears in their lands. "Weapons up," he commanded, and the Arvunglies took to their battle stance.

"King Teloby, we have gathered all of the nests we can find," the big one said.

"Then there are still three missing," the king said sadly.

"Yes." The huge animal/man saw them and moved in front of the king and said, "What in Ercutis are those?" He laughed, bent over, and gazed down at them.

"Stand firm," Zacharias commanded, stepping back to join in on the battle arrangement. The big one laughed and stood straight. "You laugh, sir?"

"These are the Arvunglies; he is their leader, Zacharias," King Teloby responded, motioning the big one to step back. "Zacharias, this is the commander of my Legionnaires, Tovar."

Stepping out from among the army once again, he said, "I am Zacharias. Betrothed to Queen Marina, Lady of these Lands. Second-in-command to the leader of the Arvunglies. Commander of the Arvunglie army, and Chef. And I don't see anything that's so funny. Do you, my warrior army?"

Loud roars erupted from the Arvunglie army. They cried out, "No. Fight," and took on the next stance, one to which the little army prepared to attack the big one.

"We might be small, but we are invincible."

"Brother, I think I might disagree with you on that one," the big burly one chuckled.

"Tovar," the king warned, then looked at Zacharias, "Zacharias, we are not here to attack you. We have lost some of our property here, and I need to get it back urgently."

"I know," Zacharias answered. "I have one of your bobbles, and I am pretty sure I know where the other two are."

"Where is it?"

"It was a gift to my queen. A precious shining treasure," he replied proudly.

"They are no bobbles. Those are our mewlings," the third animal/man said.

"Tyrion is right, Zacharias. Those treasures you have taken are our babies."

Zacharias stared at the three of them. Anger in the eyes of the big one, he did not command his army to stand down; Nevertheless, there was anguish in the eyes of the other two that he believed was sorrow. "My people meant no harm. Of course, we will return your children to you."

"You are truly a leader, Zacharias."

"And I am pretty sure the dragon has the other two. He likes shiny treasures, you know."

"What dragon? Where is he?"

"The one in the caverns," he replied and looked at the animal/man with the curly tail. "The caverns you were at earlier. You know, the ones with the smell."

Tyrion looked down at him, "You were there?" Zacharias nodded his head. "Hmm. I thought I saw something."

"Right behind you all the way. Anyway, back to the dragon, this beast is destroying my outposts. The way I see it since you know the dragon riders, you can go and get your babies and kill the dragon as well."

"Kill a dragon? What is he talking about? My King, I say we smash his village and take the nests."

"You will never find it," Zacharias snarled. "We were here long before the dragon riders and yourselves. When you came, it came."

"If the mewlings are with the dragons, we have to go and get them."

"I agree, Tyrion, but this must be thought out carefully," King Teloby replied. "We are fortunate that there is still a couple of days left before they need to birth."

"Is that little imp sure that the dragon has the nests? Or is he only lying?" Tovar scowled.

"My honor is my honor. I have one of your bobbles. The dragon, I presume, has the other two. I know that the beast roamed the lands the night of the crash."

"What do you think, my King?"

"Zacharias has proved himself to be honorable so far. I have no reason to doubt him."

"Then we go into the caverns," the big one grumped angrily. He had a bad attitude, all the time, Zacharias reasoned.

"Yes. We will return to the Dragonors region first, have the celebration for those nests we have tonight. The other Mejuarian should not have to suffer because of some of our misfortunes. I and others will return in the morning."

"My King Teloby, I will be honored for you to meet my Queen Marina."

"It will be my pleasure to meet your queen," he said.

"He cannot come, though," Zacharias ordered, pointing at the big bear-man.

"My King, you will go nowhere with him," Tovar growled; with squinted eyes, he balled his fists.

"Tovar, I want you to take The Mejuarian King back. Inform the council I want to meet with them when I return and have Alejandro prepare to start the celebration at the ninth hour."

"Yes, my king." The big man looked down at Zacharias, scowled, and walk away.

Zacharias handed the King and the other curly tail Mejuarian a sheet of cloth. They stared blankly at him. "Put it on your eyes. We will guide you to the village."

Chapter Ten

Right in Wrong

King Teloby's heart dropped when he found out the other two nests were with the dragon. His palms began to burn; peering under the cloth, supposedly blocking his eyesight, he saw a brilliant fire grow within his palms. This was no good; he had to keep it under control, especially in front of their new allies. Droplets of water began to drench out the tiny flames of his Mejuarian marking.

To avoid walking into the branches, he concentrated all of his energies on sensing obstacles before stepping forward. A rope tied to his waistline, dragging him along, two tiny soldiers directed him towards the village. Sounds coming from the flowing water and the ground turning mushy beneath his feet, the king realized he was near the river. King Teloby was not exactly sure where, however. A few steps later, stopping, he judged they did not walk any longer than a mile. So, the village was not that far away from the crash.

"You may take off your blinders," Zacharias told him.

King Teloby looked down, and before him was a line of tiny beings that reminded him of wild, unkept Ercutians. Zacharias stood before them; his small tan face was covered in spots of mud. A little female dressed as the others, strutting up to him, a group of what Teloby felt might have been her guards, surrounded her. She was very precious, a crown of tied branches on her head, she would make a lovely gift for any female mewling if he believed in servitude.

"King Teloby. Queen Marina and my betrothed."

"My queen," he said to her politely, bowing respectfully to the little Arvunglie.

Marina sat down upon her throne, placed on a red piece of fabric in front of him. "Please have a seat, and we will discuss our little dilemma," she waved for him to sit down. "It is such a pleasure to meet you."

Teloby looked around at the mushy ground while the queen spoke on. Several of the soldiers pulled a large, braided matt towards him and Tyrion.

"Please. This is our village cover for times of heavy rain. I am sure it will work quite well for you as a chair."

At least the moisture on the ground was not soaking into his clothing, he thought to himself, and said, "Thank you."

"I know that my Zacharias has told you about that dragon."

"Yes, he has."

"Well, we want you to kill it, make it go away. I don't care what happens to it."

"That is what Zacharias has informed me. This is no minor thing you ask of us."

"King Teloby, I really do not mean to get any of you killed. That dragon has to go, though. The dragon riders brought that dreadful creature into my lands. Besides, that terrible thing probably has your babies."

"We are aware of that, my queen." Teloby gazed at the perfectly plump little person that was so small even with his keen eyesight, he had to attune his eyes to see the color and delightful beauty of her eyes. "Mejuarian are peaceful villagers, and I do sympathize with you. I am not sure we can defeat the dragon."

"Of course, you can. I believe it. Your babies, though." Marina popped a piece of something unappealing in her tiny mouth.

"And why is that?" There was the issue of the missing nests, and she was right. They were going to have to go into the caves. Marina's knowledge about the Mejuarian bothered him.

"Such colorful delightful creatures. We watched you for many years, and I know you fancy ones can do anything," Queen Marina laughed jovially and threw her hands in the air.

"And how have you watched us?" Teloby asked cautiously. Walls around the village were protected by forces, which only permitted entry to Mejuarian or those they allowed to move across the barrier. Mejuarian believed these electrical energies naturally came from the ground surface of Ercutis. However, it was once thought that the god Thire-los placed the protection around the village. King Teloby did not believe in the latter, like many others. "Have you been to my village?"

"I am not going to lie to you, King Teloby. I did command my army to try, but soldiers couldn't get in. Maybe one day we may come into your glorious kingdom."

"My kingdom is under threat at this time; however, I hope one day to return. You, my queen, are welcome to visit at any time."

"What threat is that? I know of no threat, Zacharias." Her fiancée shook his head no.

"No, that is not it," the king replied and went on to tell the queen about the Mejuarian problems.

"How good it is to be friends," she said. "We might be small. My army is mighty, though, and when you return to your village, we will help you with your repairs."

"My gratitude to you, my queen, and I accept your offer of friendship." These tiny people were offering the Mejuarian friendship, which pleased King Teloby, enforcing his belief that he was a good king after such a tragedy. This was another allegiance from unknown allies; nevertheless, he doubted they could be of much help because of their size. "I will speak with the Dragonors about the dragon."

"That is all I will ask, then. Zacharias, Hunny, please have the army bring the king's beautiful baby. Please have some stewed jungle leaves and shrimp eyes. Zacharias, my betrothed, made them. Very scrumptious," she said greedily and popped something in her mouth, which made an awful crunching sound. "Mmmm."

King Teloby took the wooden plate, not much bigger than the thumb on his paw. It took ten royal Arvunglies to bring the dish, garnished in balls of round burnt leaves. "Of course," he said and looked up at Tyrion, who stood over him with a smirking grin on his face. "Tyrion, please sit. You must try this delicious dish," he winked. "Perhaps you would like to attend our celebration tonight, my queen."

"Oh, a party? Will there be lots of wonderful food?"

"There will be," Tyrion responded. "I also have a nice wine you need to try."

"Yes, I do love celebrations and eating," the queen gaily replied. "Zacharias, it sounds like so much fun."

"Um, huh."

Queen Marina was much more enthused about the event than Zacharias, it appeared to the king. "You can return with us on the airship."

The Mejuarian King Returns

In the meantime, heading back to the Dragonor's village, King Teloby sat on the airship alone in his quarters, uneasy about informing the villagers of the missing nests. Only two were left they were unable to locate now, and one was his since the nest the Arvunglies returned to them did not belong to him or Tyrion.

He encouraged the relocation that affected everyone, much worse than he anticipated. At this moment, he could not help but feel hopeless in this situation. Teloby questioned himself repeatedly and every answer to the question what happened to his son and Tyrion's daughter was dreadful. *If they searched the caves, would they discover that the dragon hoarded them or, worse, ate them? What if the altar broke while the airship was still in flight, and the nests fell from the ship before it crashed? What if the meteor burned the mewlings to a crisp?* The nests could then be anywhere. His first-born would never be born and might pass over before him. *"This should never be,"* he spoke to himself. King Teloby never mentioned his apprehensions to anyone since he was sure the others, especially Tyrion, experienced the same fears and emotions.

Mejuarian were strong and proud, and this too would pass; nevertheless, the question was, could he pass through this hardship? As the king, he could not appear to lose control. King Teloby believed that today, he felt the mad king Dactyl's distress when he searched desperately to find the lost god. Would he fall into madness over the loss of his son? In his head, a voice he heard had given him confidence before he boarded the Mejuarian King to leave for the

Dragonor's village. He wanted to have confidence in this voice, which was himself. With the ship's soft thump, The Mejuarian King landed, so King Teloby prepared himself to meet the others.

Several mothers and fathers of the missing nests still waited at the landing area with nervous expressions of excitement pasted on their faces. When the airship's captain laid down the walkway, parents of the missing nests began to board, making sure their mewlings were safe aboard The Mejuarian King. Qusdyr stood in their path and halted them. "Please do not remove the nests. Only come aboard and see that your nest is safe. Do not touch it!" Qusdyr's authoritative, snobbish tone halted the distressed parents. "Go to the gardens for the birthing after that. The temple elders will see after the nests."

"Where is the altar," a voice yelled from the audience.

"The altar is here," Qusdyr told them. Their questions no longer his concern, he turned and scrutinized the parents on board the airship.

King Teloby peered down from the airship and saw Nymeria standing with Syberias waiting. Still, he could not remove the situation's stress; typically, Nymeria was his shield, and the uplifting auras she released gave him the ease he needed. Her own peaceful conscious would be destroyed when he told her about their mewling; he would receive no relief from her today. This had to be the worst day of his life, even compared to that of his father's passing, who meant everything to him.

King Teloby decided to discuss the missing nests with Nymeria and Syberias away from the crowd to stop from bringing any further gloom to the reunion of the joyous parents with their nests. Close behind Tyrion, he weaved through the mothers and fathers flooding onto The Mejuarian King, while many of them thanked him. The appreciative group reached out paws of gratitude at him, which made the journey down the six-foot plank longer and more difficult than he wanted. Nymeria smiled happily, her Mejuarian marking, the sparkle in her eye, lit up brilliantly while she held onto Syberias as if two of them were joined together. *Nymeria does not know,* he thought. Syberias, on the other hand, displayed no joy; stiffly, she hung onto the queen, as if waiting for her turn for the 'Seasoning'. A ritual required by all mewlings to undergo at age five, not very pleasant for the males.

Nymeria rushed over to him and threw her arms around his neck. "My love, I am so glad you are back." Her stare not at him but at the deck of the airship. "We are ready for the birthing."

So much glee exploding from Nymeria, King Teloby did not have the heart to take it away; quickly, the nervous father blurted out, "We have some of the nests. Two are still missing."

Syberias gaped loudly, and Tyrion held her close. "It is my nest? Isn't it?"

"Syberias, ca…"

"Tyrion, do not tell me to calm down!" Syberias jerked her arm from Tyrion's grasp. "Answer my question, please."

Other Mejuarian being together around them, the King did not want to alarm them. "Syberias, please lower your voice. And yes, Tyrion and our nests are missing as well."

"Teloby?" Horror filled his queen's beautiful face, and the once lovely grin on her face was no longer present; her plump golden lips turned flat. If only brief, a respite from his own momentary suffering in her happiness, he held her close. "Our nest is missing as well, my love." Nymeria's legs gave out beneath her, and he had to hold her up.

"Teloby. Tell me this is not so."

"It is so. I told you. I told you all, but no one listened to me."

"I know, Syberias, but this is not the time for that. We are sure the nests are out there."

"Out there. What is *that* supposed to mean? *Where* out there?"

"We found others willing to help us. We will find them." Syberias turned her head from him and fell into Tyrion's arms.

"What do you think happened," Queen Nymeria cried. Tears streaked down her face gluing the fine, sparse hairs down upon her coppery face. The stress of the last few days, the glowing aura around her, dissipated, and with his last bit of news, he saw it disappear. Teloby squeezed her hand.

"We do not know, my love," he told her, trying to speak with confidence, but he sensed they all knew of his own uncertainty. "I will speak with Captain Jonus later. He might know what happened to the altar. All I know is that a piece is missing, as well as our nests."

"Our nests sat on the corner. If you remember, they were side by side. I stood and watched them both on that corner for what seemed like an eternity before I could leave," Syberias said softly.

121

"Are you sure?" King Teloby asked.

Tyrion agreed with Syberias. "My special one, you are right. I remember seeing the two of them side by side."

"Yes, I too remember. Tyrion and Syberias are right, Teloby," Queen Nymeria said, and once again, she stiffened. Teloby grabbed his dear mate before she fell and held her again.

Syberias lifted her head, and tears began to fall from her already dull eyes. "This is what I have known ever since we heard of the meteor. I did not understand it, but now I see clearly and realize why I woke up this morning, and I knew I would lose my mewling." Syberias gazed sadly at the queen, "I did not know your nest would also be lost; I am so sorry, Nymeria, my dear friend and queen."

"Like the king says, we will find them," Tyrion said to her with worry in his eyes.

"We will help," a tiny voice said from below. Careful to avoid the stampeding feet of the Mejuarian boarding the airship, the Arvunglies waited until they could, without harm, escort the Queen from the ship. King Teloby watched as the soldiers, dressed in shreds of golden fabrics for their loincloths, and furs jackets on their chests. Also, the little queen wore a golden belted toga with fur around the neck of its collar. "The spirits will help us find them."

"Queen Marina, my mate, Queen Nymeria, and Tyrion's mate, Syberias."

Nymeria's perfect hosting talents overtook her sorrow as King Teloby hoped it would; releasing him, she peered down, and a bit of a shock came over her face. She did not stare but politely in manners and ways, nodding her head respectfully. "Queen Marina."

"Queen Nymeria, the king has told me so much about you. It is a pleasure to meet you."

"You are welcome here."

"We are here for the birth of the babies. I cannot wait to see the colorful little babies run around. It will be so much fun," Marina giggled, taking Zacharias's hand in hers, who was standing next to her.

"Thank you for coming," Nymeria told the queen. "And if there is anything I can do for you, please let me know."

"That I will do, but for now, just lead us to the food."

Teloby grinned at the little queen's lust for food. "Sidor, please escort our guests."

Before she left, the queen said, "Queen Nymeria..." As if she forgot what she was saying, she paused for a moment then continued. "Nymeria, that is such a pretty name. Zacharias, we must name our daughter Nymeria," she grinned, and it looked as if the two of them shared a secret that King Teloby did not care to know. The king looked away.

Nymeria smiled sweetly, "I would be honored to be your daughter's namesake."

"Then it is so. Let's go eat."

"They are lovely, Teloby," the queen told him. A gentle smile coming across her face, the joy gave him pleasure, although her Mejuarian marking was still lifeless.

"Not only that, the Arvunglies believe they know where the other two nests are."

"Where, my love?"

"In the dragon's den," Tyrion answered, and Syberias held him tight.

"The dragon, they want us to rid their lands of," King Teloby finishing Tyrion's comment, scanned the eyes of the others, searching for their feelings.

"A dragon. How?" Syberias asked.

"We will find a way, my special one. Do not lose faith."

"I have not lost my faith, Tyrion. It is to be for now," she responded. "I know you two must be tired; you must come and eat."

"There is a council meeting early, Syberias," King Teloby told her as she pulled Tyrion away.

"Yes, I know. I will be there, my king."

"Syberias is right, you have to eat, and we have a celebration immediately because we cannot hold back the others from their joy."

King Teloby breathed in deeply. "You are right, my love. We must not give in to our own sorrow."

Chapter Eleven

Something Happens Over Night on Earth

Dusty, the chubby kitty office attendant, watched with curious attention as something began happening to one of Hubert's objects brought into his home. After the vet left, he was able to resume his typical responsibilities, a leisurely strut around the building, inspecting the tops of the desks and cabinets, and lazing on the chairs in the warm sun. Dusty watched passersby out of the window, and more often than he wanted, meowing at the prisoners. He had to stop their whines, and the latter took too much time from his precious naps.

Today, he had another job to do: standing watch all day and now late into the night, over the weird-smelling creatures. Now, something within one of them was coming out. Fierce growls erupted from the orange cat. Dusty, earlier, hoped Hubert heeded his warning about the lodgers of the pods he had; the doctor ignored his counsel, though. It was out now, and it was too late. Dusty pounced up on his back legs, up and down, attempting to get a peek at the creature. On his up jumps, he pawed at the incubator glass, threatening the beast and letting him know that he was on the lookout. "Go away," he hissed.

***

Heat in the warm incubator near the temperatures of their beginnings, and the moon's cycle in its exact position, the protective casing of one of the objects dissolved from its inside to its outer. The unknown substance soaked into the small baby within it, giving the embryo the essence of its creator. Magical in its defensive characteristics, but simultaneously, the paste gave the little one life. Knowledge of itself, supernatural abilities, and intelligence, which the baby needed to become one of its own. In essence, the goo was as necessary as the seed within it. As the creature's shelter doused its body, the little one grew larger, becoming the being it was meant to be. Finally, none of its refuge remaining, all that was left were small dark debris littered upon its colorful fur. And in the end, a puppy with unique colors lay curled up next to its companion, which had not come out of its home.

It stirred, opened its eyes, and lifted its head. Although just born, its senses were acute, and its eyes were fully open, and it thought with reason and logic. Slowly untangling its legs from beneath its body, it pushed itself up and stood on its wobbly four legs, inspecting its surroundings. Unfamiliar with its new body, the little creature fell back down within a few seconds upon the towel because its legs were not strong enough to hold its weight yet.

Something made an awful annoying sound, piercing its heightened hearing, and it scampered around below it, screeching, jumping up, and hitting at his protective barrier. Determined in its mind to find out what was going on, the little one was intent to stand and see what that thing was below, making all of that noise. After a few tries, its persistence won over, and its frail limbs held the little creature up. It took a few wobbly steps, came closer to the transparent casing, and looked down. Its nasty sounds were not very pleasant, causing it to step back. Unsure what the angry monster was below, the little creature was leery of its hostility, and it moved back to the rear of the incubator. Its immature body was still adjusting to its new environment; the warmth gave it a bit of well-being.

Free from the home it spent such a long time in, it waited for its companion to come out. Loneliness in its heart, the little one waited excitedly to greet the other with warm smiles. *I am very happy; I am not alone.* Still, its companion took its time. The creature missed the peaceful sounds it had heard for so long. Warm voices that it heard for so long, which pacified him and made him want to come out, was absent. Only the thunderous scowls from that thing below welcomed it; fear crept within its tiny body.

The little one tried remembering the recent voices it heard. 'Ren' was a name it recalled. If it waited long enough, Ren might return. *Where am I?* it asked itself, listening for anything in the distance, beyond the horrific sounds below. The creature only heard knocks, ticks, hums, and other annoying yelps. No sounds of love he heard anywhere.

Finally, its companion began stirring, and a friend was coming. *Did it know where the two were at now?* Gradually its surface dissipated, revealing another small creature similar to itself but unlike it in many ways. Golden eyes and pink fur, its companion was so different; the little one sensed it was not going to be much fun. There was something else odd about it as well; the little one did not know what it was right now, but it would find out. Its companion's eyes glazed frightfully. The little one spoke to its companion, *Do you know where we are?* It said nothing, and the little one sensed fear in its companion, so it moved closer to comfort his little pink pal.

What? Who are you? Do not touch me! it finally responded. *Go away.*

As it expected when it saw its fluffy yucky color, the other creature was going to be difficult. It was scared, though, and only being difficult, so it ignored its companion's commands and snuggled against it and nudged it against the side of their new home. *Something is not right here.* It said to its companion.

A Surprise Awaits Hubert

Before he could enter the clinic's heavy iron back door, Hortence ran excitedly to meet him, with Dusty following near behind. At first, Hubert worried because he was a few minutes late, which was so unlike him. However, before he could say anything, she cried, "Hubert, what are they? The two babies are just so adorable. When I got here this morning, poor Dusty was beside himself." Hubert stood still for a moment, struggling to figure out what his overly excited administrator was carrying on about. Had she lost her mind? No new patients checked in this weekend that he was aware of.

"Hor…" Hubert could not get a word in as Hortence carried on and on.

"Poor Dusty was purring and scratching and climbing the cages to get to the incubator. Of course, I had to find out what was happening. Then I saw them. They are so adorable." Hortence did not take a breath during her recital of how adorable the babies were. Her ability to cease talking amazed Hubert; his administrator, at last, took a deep breath and took his hand. Hortence pulled him through the hallway between the cages of barking and whining dogs.

Prissy little Prema, a sickly little poodle suffering from too much coddling, yapped happily at him. "I will return, Prema," he said to the panicky little puppy.

When the two of them arrived at the incubator, stopping, Hortence, his strong-willed, professional administrator, bounced up and down on her high heel pumps, like a child receiving their cone from the ice cream truck circulating around the neighborhood. Expecting to see the cocoons he placed there only yesterday, peering in dumbfoundedly, Hubert gazed amazed. Unsure, what to say, he stuttered, "They've hatched."

"Hatched. What has hatched? Hubert, what in heaven's are you talking about?" Overly thin red lips turned into a big grin, and eyes covered in light blue eyeshadow and heavy eyeliner shined with curiosity. "I have never seen anything like them before. Where in heavens did you get them? Who brought them in?" She asked, bombarding him with a series of questions impatiently.

For an older woman in her seventies, the thin shapely woman barely looked like she was forty years of age. Full of energy, she sprang around the office, helping him out more than she actually really understood since his wife passed away. Hortence bent over; Hubert thought she might topple forward since she wore heels that had to be at least six inches tall, causing her to lean forward awkwardly. Nevertheless, like a skilled artist, she easily lifted the chubby kitty in her fashionable stilts.

All Hubert could do was stare into the cage at the small creatures peering back at him. One of them only appeared as an odd-pink ball of fur. Hubert was unsure of the color. The two of them huddled together, their odd-colored eyes, one set of purple, and the other a pure golden tone, gazed at him, filled with fright. Hubert chuckled inside, not at their fear but at his discovery. "Hortence, what color is that, do you think? The one that is just fur."

"Hmm. Tango Pink, I believe. Such a lovely color."

"Um, hmm." If anyone knew what the color was, it would be Hortence. Vogue, a bible to her of sorts, the administrator studied the magazine intensely in her spare time.

"They look so afraid. Let's take them out." Quickly, she grabbed at the latch.

Hubert caught her hand, "Hold on, don't. I have too many questions about these two."

The two little ones had similar coats. A bit larger than the other, one of them stood up and walked over to the door and peered out. The majority of its body cream, vibrant blue strands of straight hair blended into the cream and fell from its prick ears and tail. A butter-yellow stick mohawk ran down the center front of its head between its ears. Hubert chuckled. Its eyes of purple were like no other eyes Hubert ever saw or studied. Head of his class, in Veterinary College, he knew about every creature discovered so far, and this was no ordinary house pet. Strangely, too, its eyes were round, identical to that of a human child glaring at him, curiously probing his presence. A freak of sorts, but much too adorable to dislike.

"Hubert, you are not making any sense. First, you say they hatched. Then you have so many questions for yourself. Explain this to me." Hortence threw her hand in the air and sighed. "Are they not puppies?"

"Hortence. Do you actually think that is a puppy?" Tango-pink, the smaller of the two, had only two colors of curled ringlets over its body. Golden strands of dangling tight curls mingled with its primary shade of pink fell from its head, and small round ears tumbling down its face like Shirley Temple locks. As far as Hubert could see, since it lay in a ball, the hair on its tail was long but curled as well. Its golden eyes were also human but had more of a curve in them, like that of a cat. Deep black lines around her eyes, and long dark lashes on the top and bottom, they were faultless, much prettier than Hortence's expensive, carefully applied eyeliner and mascara. Upturned lips on her small muzzle, Hubert, frankly, had to say she was animal/human as well. The two creatures were amazing. *Was Ren right?* Were these two from some UFOs or the result of some bizarre experiment he was unaware of?

"Hmm. First of all, I don't know what these two are. Ren found them Saturday when we were picnicking at the lake." Hubert gazed at the little purple creature now gazing up at him. "When I left yesterday, neither looked like this. They were just pods, nest, coc...s," he stuttered. "They certainly did not look like this."

Nothing was in the bottom of the incubator. No leaves or goo that held it together remained, not even on the towels, which were just as fluffy as they were when Hubert left. Something should have been left behind, but small shards of dark rock littered the towel. The debris he tried prying away from the cocoon when he examined it. "There's no birth material." Hortence must have thought him insane since he believed this about himself. At least Ren and Brooklyn saw them also.

"Heavens," she said, looking at him confused. "Do you think they are dangerous?"

"I am not sure," he replied slowly.

Hortence poked the glass with her bright pink nail and called out, "Hi little ones, we will not hurt you."

"I was going to break into their cocoons today when I came into work. I started it yesterday, but Brooklyn needed me home." Hortence stared scornfully at him.

"Good heavens, Hubert, it is a good thing you didn't," she cried. "Look at those delightful little faces. Get them out. If you won't, then I will." Hortence was his administrator; nevertheless, she only worked because she wanted to and did not need the money. Pampered from her birth, her porcelain skin gleamed as bright as her strong personality.

Relieved that he never cut the cocoon open, he said, "Let me look at this little blue guy. It does not appear as timid as the other." Hubert shoved Hortence aside; gently opening the latch, he wished not to scare the little one. The small blue creature bounced out of the cage and jumped into his outstretched hands without any encouragement, to Hubert's astonishment. Never once did it exhibit any fear of him, and the same strange warming energy he felt the other day immersed his hand. Hubert moved his pinky finger. "Look at this, Hortence."

"My goodness, Hubert. What is going on?" Hortence was aware of his lack of movement in his hand, and her shocking look only copied the way he felt.

Its body was basically canine in appearance, but its paws were longer than dog feet, and its digits were similar to fingers. The little blue pup was definitely male; he was confident that when he turned him over. "Take this one," he said, handing the pup to Hortence. She giggled happily and held it to her face. Hubert reached for the other. A little more cautious than the first, this one primly stood up, gazed at Hortence, and eventually stepped up to his hand. *Can I have the girl, Daddy?* Indeed, Brooklyn was right; one of the creatures was for sure female. How did she know that they were different?

"Know what," Hortence asked, handed Hubert the little male pup, and took the female from him. "She is just so adorable."

"Brooklyn said one of the cocoons was a female."

"She is perfect for your precious angel. Oh, Hubert, you should take them to the children."

"These two are not going anywhere until I find out what they are."

"Well, yes, I agree. But look at them, Hubert, there's nothing harmful in any of these two." Hortence held the pink one to her face and snuggled it. "Oh my."

"What happened?" he asked, concerned by the expression on her face.

"My toothache. It was disturbing me most of the morning. I don't have it anymore."

"That's strange."

"Yes, it's strange. In a good way," she giggled, walking away, snuggling the pink pup in her arms. Dusty followed her, no longer upset or agitated, but purring gently.

Well, the only way to find out what they are is to examine them."

The Examination

Hubert eagerly examined the little blue pup while Hortence, always serious and proper, now she giggled; he felt too similar in elation, and for a moment, Hubert thought that he could believe in the tooth fairy. Ears which stood upright, like those of a shepherd dog, however not as tall, Hubert noticed it moved to the slightest sound in the room. Turning to its direction, his tail stood erect; when he sat down, the straight appendage still remained upright.

"What are you, little fellow?" he asked, and its deep purple eyes gazed into his. If he did not know any better, Hubert would almost expect the little one was trying to communicate with him. A stiff mohawk of yellow hair, the thick patch of stiff hairs ran between his ears like spikes, making him quite hilarious in appearance. Nothing really odd about its body, besides narrow openings along the side of its neck, buried under the fur, its body looked like a puppy from at a distance. Gently he examined its paw; the hair upon its foot was soft, like twines of silk, and its digits reminded him of hairy fingers instead of those of an animal. "I am pretty sure this little guy can hold something in his hands," he chuckled. At his side during the examination, the administrator played with the pink pup and took notes from his analysis.

Both pups, definitely from the same place he believed, were not from the same litter of animals or experimental batch. The two of them walked about on all four limbs; nevertheless, there was something about the male that made Hubert think of royalty by the way he explored and moved about in his environment. Its small head always lifted up, and sharp stubby muzzle pointed upward as well, he searched proudly with no fear or hesitation. As if he were a king, was all he could say. Then again, the pup was only a couple of hours old. Why wouldn't Hubert expect the creature to be up and navigating flawlessly around its environment?

On the other hand, the female was graceful, and she moved about, not fearfully, but delicately and cutely, as if she were born for others to pamper. Her prissy ways seeming as if she feared any stain upon her little feet, Hubert saw her inspecting them as if she felt something unpleasant on their bottoms. Which, of course, she did not lick as he knew other canine creatures would; this little one used one of her front paws as a hand to brush it off.

Thin fur protected both of their skins, which was the same color as their primary coloring. The little female was precious, though; tango pink skin complexion, wavy strands of silky pink and golden hair tumbled down her body. She had the sort of eyes that Irene, his wife, had. The ones that lured men into their web of submission, though at the same time promising soft kindness and joy. The little girl's eyes were beautiful and exotic. Brilliant golden irises, the same color as the gold strands in her hair, the two orbs were solid. An examination with his slit light, Hubert still could not recognize their fibers' shape but saw what looked like a tiny jewel embed within the corner of her right eye. The little diamond sparkled at times, and in that instance, Hubert felt a wave of contentment and optimism overshadow him that he had not experienced since Irene's passing.

A tiny nose pad was barely noticeable on her upturned muzzle, which gave her an almost arrogance in her appearance. Dark red lips, a few barely noticeable whiskers, Hubert felt the price of her makeup job would cost more than yearly wages.

"Such a darling. I want to debut her on the debutante stage," Hortence exclaimed gleefully, picking the little girl back up. Hubert shook his head at her. "What on earth do you think they could be?"

"Nothing that I know of. Maybe the two of them have been genetically reproduced," Hubert responded. The thought of finding a new species thrilled him, and something deep within him said that these two little ones would change his life. At this point, he dared to think of the horrid experiments done in a secret laboratory to them. One thing was for sure, he sensed no danger from these precious creatures.

"The little guy has no whiskers. That is odd."

"Yes, I have noticed that too," he replied. "Hortence, I don't know what they are, but I am sure they are valuable to someone or something. We need to keep them safe and secret for now."

"Most assuredly, Hubert," she replied, leaving the room and taking the girl with her. At last, she went back to work. Hubert let the little male pup explore the space he felt was his kingdom while the veterinarian searched the manuals for anything similar to the creatures. He might have been missing something.

Later that morning, he suspected the pups might have been hungry. So, he set up a feeding system as he did with most newborns needing help to eat. Hubert set out to nurse the male pup and Hortence, the female, with a bottle in their hands. However, neither took to the bottle or the milk and resisted as if the liquid were foul. Hubert tried warm milk, cold milk, condensed puppy formula milk, dog food, cat food, a piece of his baloney sandwich, and a whole arsenal of Dusty's favorites. The two of them only peered at him, snubbed their cute little noses back into the air, and walked away as if saying, *how dare you to give me that to eat.*

Hubert tried something else, not sure if they even knew how to eat. The eccentric vet cleaned a bowl, filling it with water; he bent down in front of the little pups and lapped out of the water. The small pup gazed at him; submerging its entire face into the bowl, he lifted up his dripping head, which had an expression of "oh so much fun" on his face. The pup dunked his head again, splashing water everywhere.

"Look at that, Hubert. He is making a mess." Hortence took the bowl of water. "For heaven's sake," she said, strolling off. Too, not pleased with the little male's behavior, the little pink pup left behind her, stepping away in disgust. Dusty, evidently deciding to be friends for the moment, sat staring at the male, as if the two of them were talking.

"Hubert, your two o'clock is here." Hortence placed the pink pup in a makeshift bed and left the room.

"Mrs. Nalley and Toby. Get room two ready for me, please. Dusty come," Dusty didn't budge, seeming content with his new pal. Hubert closed the door.

Pup Finds Food

This was not where he belonged, the little pup knew. Neither Hubert nor Hortence possessed the pleasing tones in their voices that comforted him earlier, but they were both warm. Heartfelt and exuberant liveliness emanated from the two of them, which the pup found delightful; indeed, he wanted to know more about them. Still, he missed the comfort of the voice that the little pup knew from his beginning; however, he sensed wellbeing as well in the arms of Hubert and Hortence.

This was his kingdom, and those around him now, one day he would rule over and protect them because he was their king, just like the voices told him so many times. Hopefully, at some point, he might actually meet those that told him the stories of his destiny; those he grew to love and look forward to meeting one day. Though for now, the little pup was intent to learn in his new world so that he might be a good ruler.

The sounds they made, he copied in his thoughts, developed, and understood their words. For hours he heard the two of them call out to each other, and the pup began to understand their language, which he found similar to the words that he heard while still within his sanctuary. The more the two of them chatted to each other, him, or the other pup, the more he understood. When the two of them questioned each other about himself or the little pink pup, he tried to tell them, but they only ignored his answers. When he wanted to inquire of them about where he was, too, they only ignored him. Overall, for the beginning of his life, he has really enjoyed it so far.

The little pup's mind was much more alert than a newborn earthling; he became almost one with everything he studied or gave his attention, even things that did not move. New smells, sounds, sights, feelings, absorbed into his psyche and thrilled him. Too, words which Hubert and Hortence said to themselves, and not out loud, he heard, which confused him. So, the little ones started to disregard their inner thoughts. *What was a blue camisole?* The little pup asked himself. This confused him, although Hortence planned on wearing it.

Later that day, the two of them wanted to feed the little creature again.

"Hubert, what on earth are we going to feed them?"

"They don't appear to be hungry, Hortence. It is possible that their bodies don't require nourishment right away."

The man called Hubert was gentle, and the pup felt or sensed no harm from him; his natural temperament, he treated the two of them with care and made the little grow to like him. On the other hand, Hortence was too loud, and her energy discomforted him. Overly excited in all her ways, the high pitch of her sounds stabbed at his ears, and if possible, he moved out of her way when she went to grab him. Sometimes she clutched at him too quickly, and he was unable to avoid her mushy affections. The annoying gurgles that came from her when she pushed her face into his was plain unacceptable. Childish coddles were alright for his companion, who still acted snobbish towards him, though there was no time for these idle indulges for the little male. One day he was to be king.

While Hubert and Hortence examined again, so the little pup crawled into a cabinet near the office floor, the door closed behind him. Darkness, a blackness around him, he could not see; this thrilled him though since he never knew such isolation from everything around him. A sensation of coolness in the cabinet and the awareness of seclusion, the crisp bleakness possessed an excitement because he could see nothing. As a game, slowly, he maneuvered his small body in between the items and attempted not to make a noise to warn Hubert or Hortence of his escape. Moments later, surprised by his own abilities, the little pup's unique talents adjusted to the darkness. As if a light came on in the small cubby, he saw bottles filled with liquids, fluffy white towels, and boxes jam-packed his dark sanctuary. Something new was happening in his body; he sighed, missing the dark.

Nevertheless, everything captured his attention, and he needed to explore it; touch it all. Like some outside in the room, these objects were cold, soulless, and they owned a lack of intimacy, unlike Hubert, Hortence, and even Dusty. None of them gave him any particular interest but the discovery of them intrigued the little pup.

After leaving the cabinet, the pup sat chatting with his new pal Dusty. At first, a menacing annoyance to him, when the pesky orange creature finally settled down, the pup found out his new friend was a cat, and the two of them had many things in common. Like Dusty, he and his companion were animals, and he was probably a dog, the lowest of all creatures on earth. The two of them had no families, and neither did Dusty. Hubert would take the little pup and his companion to another hospital where they might murder them both. Dusty was special, though, and the vet would never take him away. The vet, simply put as Dusty called him, needed his particular stalker, and eating abilities, which he was a professional at. Too, his new friend made it quite clear that he was unwilling to give up this luxurious job, and if Hubert did not find families for them, they would end up at the other hospital. The little pup hoped Hubert found them homes because he did not want to be murdered, even though he did not know what that was.

Dusty was a bit weird, the little pup thought. Sometimes he said things out loud, but then other thoughts in his head said something else. His new friend spoke about the life he knew being a loner and the adventures he had.

"Big and black. I tell you. I thought I was a goner until I bared one of my paws in the face of the brute and said, 'Make my Day.'" Dusty scowled and showed his paw less claws. "The big louse ran and ran," *What a moron. He will believe anything,* Dusty said and burst out in laughter. The little pup heard it coming from the inside of the cat while he scowled angrily, demonstrating how ruthless he was with the big bad dog.

"Dusty, what is a moron?"

"What?"

"You said it. *He will believe anything.* Are you referring to me?"

Dusty grinned and glared at him. "No way, man. You are way too cool," the slightly confused cat chuckled and waved off the comment.

"What is a moron?"

His friend leaned in close, "Shh. Don't say anything, but dogs are morons," he whispered and winked at him.

"Yes, I get it now. That is why you called me a moron."

"So, how did you know I said that, man?"

"I heard you. I can hear words from the inside and out," the little pup announced.

"Right on, man. But if you hear any stuff from my inside, man, just know that it is really not me. I mean, that guy is a really bad dude and likely to say anything. Anything," he repeated. "So, don't listen to him, man. I'm telling you now."

"But you said you were bad on the outside too. You tell me these stories."

"Naw, not like that. It's different. Sometimes you just have to get your point across."

The little pup did not trust Dusty's explanation between his inside and outside man. Touching his paw to his face, he hoped he never faced this dilemma. Then again, Dusty was a bit of a showoff, and he knew some of the things he said might not be accurate.

A peculiarity in his mouth or stomach, he needed something. "Dusty, my stomach is off."

"Well, you probably need to eat," Dusty told him. "Hubert gave you food, but you did not want it. Food is good, dude."

The little pup remembered all of the strange things Hubert put up to his mouth, and at that moment, he realized that he needed to eat. "Oh, that is what I eat. I don't want it then." Dusty was right; Hubert tried giving him some food, but he did not want any of it, and most of the time, the smell was enough to keep him from putting it in his mouth. There was the smell of something though, sweet and tart, and the little one sniffed the air attempting to find what was enticing him. Soon the pup found it. Hubert just popped one of those captivating balls into his mouth, a gift he and Hortence never offered him. That was what he longed for, though. "Hubert has it. I want one."

"Go for it, dude," Dusty encouraged.

It was such a long way up to where Hubert was sitting; nevertheless, he intended to get there. Quickly, he jumped from the floor with all of his strength, landing upon the Formica countertop on his back feet. The little pup braced himself to keep from falling back down. The impact of his padded feet made a small thud, so peering around to make sure no one was looking, he saw only Dusty, who winked at him. Cold to his paws, the stainless-steel counter was gleaming, and the little pup stared at himself in the mirrored surface. *So, I am a dog,* he said to himself, frowning at his colorful body and intense eyes. Not particularly interested in himself, the pup moved across the top until coming to a hole in the center of the counter. Hopping down, he walked across the bottom of the sink. Droplets of water fell from the water top upon his head, dribbling into his face. The pup wiped the moisture out of his face with one of his paws, resuming his trek to reach the sweet things. Nothing interesting in the cavity of the sink, the little pup jumped back out. Finally, at the edge of the counter, the desks and treats were only a leap away. Without thought of the distance, leaping forward, and as if wings grew upon his back, he soared to his destination. Papers scattered all across Hubert's desk and onto the floor when the little pup landed. Catching his attention, Hubert quickly grabbed the little pup, stopping him from sliding off of the desk.

"Where did you come from, little guy?" Hubert looked around and gazed at the countertop. "Did you jump from the countertop?" Pure shock coming upon him, he judged the distance and said, "That is quite a distance. At least ten feet."

No time for the vet at the moment, the pup searched through the brown bag looking for what Hubert popped in his mouth. There they were, round, plump, and smelled delicious; picking up the clear bag holding them, he opened it and went to grab one in his paws. The soft wet things were too big for one of his little paws to get one out of the enclosure, so the little one used his two front paws and pulled one out. The pup was excited, the smell so enticing he could hardly wait as he put the object up to his mouth. When he bit into it, juices from the food dibbling down the corners of his muzzle, the pup took another bite that burst in his mouth.

How did you know about my grapes?" Hubert gazed sweetly at him. The little one wanted to tell the vet how he found the grapes but knew he would not understand him, so the pup just grinned. "Come in here, Hortence," he yelled.

"What is it, Hubert? You scared me half to death."

"He is eating a grape and smiling at me."

Hortence looked into his face; the little pup knew she was about to explode in her annoying behavior. He braced himself.

"For heaven's sake, Hubert. He is just a darling," she screamed and reached for him. The remainder of grape wedged between his teeth, he leaped across the desk out of her way. "Well, would you look at that?"

Hubert laughed, "At least now we know what they like to eat. No meat; how odd." The vet gazed curiously at him, studying him. "Well, you are just full of surprises, little fellow," he said, turning to Hortence. "I have a feeling these little pups have a lot more surprises in store for us."

Come over here, try this, he cried out to his companion; nevertheless, she ignored him. Irritated at her, he threw one of the grapes at her and grinned.

Why did you do that? she asked. She was going to be a pain to be around, the little pup believed. Don't you want it? he asked.

Why should I? You throw it at me and expect me to take it from you? Once again, she snubbed him.

Suit yourself then. I do not care, the pup told its companion, then took another bite from the grape. How dare she treat him in such a way? The king wanted to hit her with another one, but they were too good to throw away; he licked the juices from the bottom of his paw.

Chapter Twelve

A New Home

That night, convinced by Hortence not to leave the two pups alone since they were only newborn, Hubert agreed to take the adorable pups to his home. Both behaved very maturely for their only one day of life, and he hummed happily while preparing to close up the clinic for the night. Since the two were unknown species, Hubert was reluctant at first but reconsidered the decision carefully. There was no aggressive behavior or physical detriment, which he felt might harm Ren or Brooklyn. They quickly grew comfortable with their surroundings, and even Dusty got along with the male nicely. Hubert searched for the two pups or any creatures similar to them in the scientific journals and the VM; he found nothing. The only thing he was sure of was that they were male and female and ate berries. The female's personality was prissy and reserved; the male was proud, curious, and friendly.

He is a curious little fellow, Hubert thought, watching him try to get inside of the closed cabinet doors, which Hortence locked to make sure he did not get in. Hubert laughed at the sneaky little pup.

Early in the day, regardless of how careful he was, when the little guy suspected Hortence was coming down the hallway, he bolted through it at the exact instance that the door opened. Although just newborn, the small male was too quick, and Hubert swore to his heart, he was evilly cunning. He and Hortence chased the pup around the clinic; outwitted by the clever little pup, they stumbled over each, like clowns, when they went to grab for him. The vet hated to admit it, the only reason they caught the pup was the little creature strutted back into the room when he was good and ready.

Hubert noticed the peculiar interactions between the pups during the incident when the male offered a grape to the female. Two things he found rather curious: the male actually held the piece of fruit with his front paws, then threw it at her. The little girl pup whipped her head in another direction, a bit of snobbishness in her personality, and did not accept the grape; nevertheless, Hubert understood that the two of them communicated with each other.

"I know Ren and Brooklyn will love you and want to meet you both. One stop by the Farmer's Market on the way home to pick you something up to eat and then off to see the children." Hubert said, joy playing with his heart for the first time in a long time. The little male pup looked up at him as if he understood, and grinned, showing off a set of small white human molars.

Before leaving, Hubert said goodnight to all of his patients, including the foo-foo poodle. Both the pups safely in a cage; tenderly, the vet placed them in the back of the van. "We will be home soon." Moments later, he pulled out of the parking lot. Today the old wagon started quickly and did not sputter and spit, and he was glad of that because the road was heavy with traffic.

Finally, out of the barrage of traffic, he headed towards the Farmer's Market, located on the town's outskirts. Locals called state highway 75 *The long road* because the nearest city at its north was eighty miles away. Along the route, gators patrolled the blacktop surface and hunted for their meal, and the last gas stop was one mile away from the Farmer's Market. More often than not, the furthermost Hubert traveled on the highway was to the market to pick up the weekly vegetables and fresh meat but did not continue further north.

When he reached the market, pulling into the dirt parking lot, which added an additional coat of dust on the wagon, he turned on the wipers and water to clean his windshield. The sun was still out, and it was hot, even though it was seven at night. Summer days in Parryville were the worst, so he made sure that all of the windows were down. When he arrived at the stand, and just from the humidity, he found himself drenched in sweat from just the small trek from the van to the market.

A breeze cooled down his body when he stepped under the rickety aged wooden shelter. It smelled of fresh sweet fruit with an underlying odor of overripe or spoiled produce. Hubert was glad of the cover from the sun, even if it was nothing more than a beaten wood roof, with four poles holding it up. Only the brave dared venture under the top since it looked like the worn beams might break at any moment. Valiantly though, he headed to the organic delicacy of fresh fruits right from the fields. Grapes, cherries, oranges, apples, berries of all sorts, bittersweets, mangos, and an assortment of vegetables, and fresh meat.

"Woof, woof," old Freddie barked; tail wagging, the old hound dog, crept slowly toward him. Arthritis in his legs, they bowed a bit when he walked, but with the vitamins Hubert gave the eighteen-year-old dog, the pain in his joints did not seem to bother him too much. Grey hair disguised his long muzzle, and his lovely reddish color was almost missing from his face. Large black eyes, like those of a doe, no one feared the old watchdog, so most mornings Manuel found missing produce.

Reaching down, Hubert petted the big dog. "Freddie."

"Woof," Freddie said his goodbye, walking off, he laid back down.

"What do you have good for me today?" Hubert read the large hand-painted not so perfect letters written on a piece of board propped against the produce stand. *Manuel's Farm Market.* After he grabbed a basket and loading it with all kinds of produce, he believed the pups might eat. Hubert trotted across the dirt floor, too, covering his brown shoes in the dirt. "Manuel, how are you today?"

"I am well, Mr. Hubert. How are yous this fine day?"

"Very well. Thank you. How is Franklin? I have not seen him around lately."

"He's doing good, Mr. Hubert. Getting good grades and out delivering ciders now. If not, he would be here helping out," he replied in a broken Spanish accent. Manuel grinned; his tan complexion baked into an almost burnt red coloring from the sun; its extreme shade looked as if it pained him. Dark hair covered over by a farmer's hat, shorts strands neatly curled around his face and neck, cut nicely. Manuel was short, too, and barely stood higher than his produce stands, but his demeanor was that of a very big man. "Ren and Mark came by the other day. That Ren is really growing, Mr. Hubert."

"Yes, he is and becoming a bit of a handful."

"Yes. I know. Boys can be boys."

"I am glad that he is friends with Franklin. He has a stable head, and Ren needs that now." Hubert hung his head. What was he to do with his son?

"Don't worry, Mr. Hubert. Things will work themselves out. These things do. You must have faith in God."

These days, Hubert had to admit, he did not have too much faith. Where was God the night his wife died? "Yeah, Manuel." Manuel gazed at him and picked up the basket of produce.

"You will see, Hubert. You will see. I believe," Manuel winked at him.

"How is that heifer doing, Manuel," Hubert asked. Mary was an old milk cow that had to be as old as Franklin and more of a family member than livestock.

"Just fine, Mr. Hubert, she still gives out her milk too. Nothing but a glass; nonetheless, she gives it," Manuel laughed jovially, and Hubert could not resist joining in.

One peculiar trait about Manuel was that he used no weight scale, cash register, or calculator. Quick and accurate in check out, he was something of a local celebrity since the State Fair featured him and his mathematical talents one year. By touch alone, he determined the produce's weight and cost, then quickly added up the total in his head. Also, judged quicker and more accurately, Manuel beat those using devices to calculate the large numbers and obtain weights. A talent evidently his son Franklin inherited as well, according to Ren. "I am still amazed by that, Manuel."

The humble man grinned. "My grandfather could do it, and so can Franklin. It's nothing, Mr. Hubert."

"Which I am sure will be a great benefit to Franklin."

"I am sending my son to college, Mr. Hubert," he said proudly. Hubert felt his pride, wishing he felt the same for his own son. "Two dollars and twenty-two cents."

Manuel's prices were fair too. In town, Hubert knew he would pay over five dollars for the abundant amount of produce. Hubert gave him four dollars and motioned to keep the change because he knew Manuel always undercharged him. This mistake in cost was not because of an arithmetic error; the thin man favored their children's friendship.

"Thank you, Mr. Hubert, come back tomorrow. I have watermelons coming. Franklin and me picking them tonight. First of the season, very good then," Manuel waved as Hubert walked away.

"I just might do that, Manuel. You have a good night," Hubert said, walking out of the market and heading back to his car. Good, he was only in the shop ten minutes, the little pups were fine, and as usual, the small male pup was grinning at him.

When Hubert got home, Ren's bike lay in the center of the driveway, thrown carelessly over onto its side. There was a surprise in the rear of his van for the two kids, and if he went into the house in anger, it would spoil the moment of joy Hubert was eager to see in their faces. With a deep sigh, he pulled the car along the side of the curb, and stepping out, he grabbed the groceries. "I will return. Hold tight."

When he walked through the front door, he could hear Brooklyn in the kitchen talking to Mrs. Cheasemina, and the smell of greens and bacon wafted throughout the house. His stomach growled from the aroma of the grease, making him hungry for macaroni and cheese along with the meal. The television blaring in the living room, Hubert peered at Ren lying on the couch watching *The Mr. Ed Show.* Hubert asked nicely, desiring not to alienate Ren before he had a chance to give him the present. "You left your bicycle in the driveway. Please go and move it so I can pull the van in."

"Okay, I will move it. Right after this commercial."

"Now," Hubert commanded, walking into the kitchen. He heard Ren shuffling to his feet.

An Alien of His Own

Ren got up from the couch before the horse, Mr. Ed, finished telling off Wilber, which was always the best part of the show. A talking horse, who would believe, but it was right on the television before his eyes. Ren realized the horse really was not speaking; it was the change in technology that amazed him. For now, he saw the scowl on his father's face, although he tried hiding it. Ren was in no mood for a lecture tonight. If his father was not upset with him, he might loosen his guard, and Ren couldn't hang with Mark tomorrow after school.

When he returned inside, joining the others in the kitchen, they watched the old black lady stirring a pot of boiling greens. Ren hated greens horribly and told his father to ask her not to cook them. This was a mistake he made. Out of spite, Mrs. Cheazemina cooked a pot of them every week. On the other hand, the smell of roast beef cooking in onions made the greens bearable since the old woman made the best stew beef he ever tasted. If she made it tonight.

Brooklyn sat at the table and played with Teddy while she drank a small glass of milk. Kinky puffs of hair on her head, wrapped by two red ribbons, the balls of hair reminded Ren of mouse ears that sat atop of her cute little face. Ribbons wrapped around Teddy's small unstuffed ears lay like tattered strands across his eyes of beads. Dressed in one of her doll's frilly outfits, the teddy was just too

143

hilarious. Ren laughed, "Teddy looks like he is blitzed with the ribbons on his ears, Brooklyn."

"Ren don't laugh. Teddy does not like it when you laugh. Daddy." Brooklyn jumped out of the chair, running over to their father; she leaped in his arms. "Make Ren stop, Daddy," she said, laying her head on his shoulder and snuggled into him.

"You are such a suck up, Brooklyn," Ren remarked and sat at the table.

"You finish that milk. You asked for it, Chile," Mrs. Cheasemina told her gruffly, irritated about something as usual. At least her anger was not pointed at him this time; Ren did not think. "Albert is going up every day, Mr. Hoobert. He now selling chuck beef five cents a pound," she argued, stirring the pot while gesturing for Brooklyn to drink the milk. "Gets there and drink that milk, Gal. You chillins act like money done grown on trees…"

Mrs. Cheazemina continued her rant; tuning her out, Ren sang *My Baby Left Me,* by Elvis in his head.

"I have something for the both of you," his father said with an eagerness that Ren forgot his father owned.

"What is it, Daddy?" Brooklyn asked, screaming happily.

"I am pretty sure you both will love it."

"Yeah," she exclaimed loudly, waving Teddy in the air.

"Ren come on. I have something for you," Waiting, Hubert reached out for him to join the two of them outside. "I think you will want to see it," he pleaded.

"It's a surprise," squealed Brooklyn. Jumping from her father's arms, she ran to the van.

'What is it?" Ren asked. Frankly, he did not care about surprises from his father right now. They were usually corny and only led to more work for him in the long run. Truly disinterested, he walked up and stood next to his excited sister and made a mental note to ask him about the UFOs as soon as he pretended to be excited.

Brooklyn screamed as if someone were attacking them, which startled Ren, and he looked around. His father pulled a wooden cage in from the van's rear and set it upon the ground. His very eager sister fell down on her hands on the concrete sidewalk and stared into the cage. "Daddy, a puppy. We have puppies, Ren," she exclaimed. Unable to contain her excitement, wailing repeatedly, "I want the pink one. Can I Daddy, please, please," she began to cry happy tears, hugging the cage.

Ren glared at the two creatures in the cage and said to his little sister, "They are not puppies, silly. Have you ever seen a pink dog before?"

"Yes, they are," she responded curtly, her small arms protecting the creatures in the cage.

"What are they, Dad?"

"One second, Brooke, sweetheart," Hubert reached down to pick up the cage. "Let's take them inside. I think they will feel a bit more comfortable there."

"Wait. Are those creatures safe?" Ren asked.

Brooklyn skipped excitedly behind her father. Hubert smiled broadly and said, "Of course you can have the pink one. I think she is perfect for you. As for Ren, these little pups have more to fear from us than we from them."

Ren gazed in the cage at the two creatures. The larger of the two, the blue creature was grinning at him; he looked away, not wanting its dynamic purple eyes to bring him under his control. Of course, they were cute, but where were they from? And since they were UFO's, Ren knew they meant no good to earthlings. Well, at least that's what all the movies portrayed.

"Teddy, where is Teddy? He needs to see the new puppies." Brooklyn cried and ran off to the kitchen to get her best friend. "I will be right back, Daddy. I need to get Teddy."

"Don't run, Brooke."

Ren walked up to the cage and looked at the two strange creatures in the cage. His eyes were immediately drawn to the pink one's coat of fur and her pretty little face. "Crazy, look at the pink hair on that one. It is out of this world." The larger pup walked to the front of the cage and stood on his back legs, gazed back at him, and he had to admit, although it was an alien, he immediately liked the little creature and felt no fear of it.

Brooklyn ran back into the room, Teddy swinging back and forth in her hand, and she knelt in front of the small cage anxiously; her little boney knees hit the hardwood flooring with a bang that sounded as if she had hurt herself again. She laughed. "Hurry Daddy. I want the pink one," she cried out, exclaiming gleefully. Teddy fell on the floor in front of her.

"Calm down, spaz, you are scaring them," Ren told her, continuing to stare into the eyes of the creatures.

"I am not scaring them, and I am not a spaz. You are a spaz, double me, Ren."

Ren could not help but grin at his little sister's attempt to tell him off, and she was so happy.

"The blue pup is the male, and of course, the little pink one is the girl," Hubert told them.

"Did you find out what they are? Did they come from the meteor?"

"Ren, I hate to say it, but you might be right. I can't find anything on any animal similar to them. I have made a couple of calls to some of my colleagues, and I am expecting to hear back in a day or two. Right now, I just call them pups. That is, until you both give them names."

"Dad, are they dangerous? Did you check them out for mind control? Maybe they are body snatchers, although the pods birthed." Ren could not believe his eyes. The pods he only took Mark to see yesterday hatched into to these incredible little creatures. The whole thing was very cool in a way, his very own alien. Nevertheless, he watched too much television and was still a bit leery of the pups.

"They are not dangerous, Ren. Hortence and I spent the entire day with them. The little pink one snuggled in her lap. I am not sure where they are from, but maybe these guys are a blessing to our family."

"A blessing to our family. Yeah, Jesus," Brooklyn screamed.

"Oh, I forgot, they eat berries, bread, and fruit, and this little guy is inquisitive, quick, and smart. And not to mention, he is a thief."

"What?" Ren asked.

"He is a thief," Brooklyn coughed out through laughter.

"A thief, what did he steal?"

"He stole my lunch. Well, part of my lunch," Hubert chuckled. "The little turd-knocker figured out how to get on top of the microscope table to reach my grapes."

Laughter erupted once again in the household. Mrs. Cheazemina, evidently not used to the happy ruckus, rushing from the kitchen, called out, "What in the world is going on in here?" Uneasily, the old woman glared at the two pups; shaking her head, she left. "Dogs. That all I need, dog hair…", mumbling to herself, she slid back into the kitchen.

"How did he get that far up, Dad?"

"Ren, he can solve problems. He figured out how to jump from the stool to the sink and then over to the microscope table."

"How do you know that is what he did?" Ren asked, still unsure if his dad was serious, but then again, they were UFOs; anything was possible.

"I saw him with my own eyes," he said.

"They might be Martians, Dad; nothing makes sense in any of this," Ren exclaimed, gesturing with his hands. "It's just like in the movies. They will come and take our bodies." Ren bombarded his dad with questions, his voice filled with apprehension and a look of bewilderment on his face.

"Ren, let's not worry over that now. If you see any behavior you feel weird, odd, or Martian-like, let me know. One thing though, like you said, these two little ones belong to someone. Or if they are from Mars, we need to protect them and keep them our secret for now."

"What if the government wants them? How are we going to keep them a secret? What if the G-men are listening to us right now?"

"Let's not get carried away either. Give me some time to do some more checking and keep the two of them in the house."

"Is it possible they are some type of genetic experiment, Dad?"

"I don't know. For now, we need to keep these little guys safe, I believe."

The Little Male

A new environment about him, the little male pup stared out of the cage at his new kingdom. Frankly, it was a wonderful new land, and there were lots of objects to explore and leap around on. There was even something in the corner, which was strange indeed. Sounds of others talking, with appearances like Hubert and Hortence, the little pup marveled at the people inside of the enclosure that moved. Their presence was nowhere close that he sensed; eagerly, he waited to escape the cage to meet them all. Strange smells, not strong odors like those that made him sneeze, bothered his nose, which Hortence wore, but much more pleasant ones that calmed his anxiety. Too, no more Dusty, which made him feel bad. Hubert gave him and his companion a home, and he was happy about that. The tall structures yelled out for him to climb, soar, and leap from.

147

The little pup wanted to dart out of the cage and do one quick look around his new kingdom. Then again, to listen and wait might be the best. His ears attuned, he listened for the lovely voice that called him a king. *A sweet echo that told him to care for his villagers would make him great* resounded in his thoughts. For such a long time, every minute he could remember, the voices taught and explained to him how to be a king. That supportive voice was not here either, so the little one was prepared to learn independently if he could not find it. This was home now.

Newness of his kingdom somewhat overwhelmed him. Still, the little pup sensed no harm from them. Hubert and Hortence, loyal caretakers, the pup had no choice but to expect that Ren and the smaller version of Hortence might be the same. His eyes glued upon Ren, he gazed back at the young boy with the same curiosity he stared at him with. The little pup moved to the front of the cage and lifted his head proudly. *Ren,* he said to him. Just as Hortence and Hubert spoke to each other, the boy said nothing, so the little pup realized he did not understand him. This inability to communicate was a hindrance to the little pup, and he was intent on finding a way to talk with at least one of them. Filled with confidence, he stepped out of the cage and looked around.

Brooklyn screamed, "He's coming out of the cage."

"We can all see that, Brooklyn. Step back, so it can't use its powers on you. Did you take a look at those eyes, Dad?" When he stepped closer to Ren and Brooklyn, he quickly shoved his sister away from him.

"Stop it, Ren," she yelled and reached out for the little male happily. *Oh no,* the little pup thought to himself, this one is like Hortence. Sensing the warmth that would come from her face and the gurgling sound from her mouth, quickly darting out of her way, the pup sat next to Ren and glared at Brooklyn with displeasure.

She scowled, grabbing the red fabric that was Teddy, she held it close to her chest, and her bottom lip stuck out. Yes indeed, although she was not the same height as Hortence, the little squealy one was another assistant in disguise.

Ren laughed loudly, and the pup grinned at him, showing a mouth filled with white teeth. "Is he smiling?"

"I believe so. That little boy grins a lot," Hubert chuckled.

Obviously, not happy with him again, the pup's companion looked up at him. Golden disapproving eyes glared at him, then snatching her gaze away, she condemned him with revulsion.

Prissy pink, a name he heard Hubert call her, waited for someone to take her out of the enclosure. They really did not speak to each other; she hated him, the pup believed. Nevertheless, there was something in his head that allowed him to hear her thoughts. They were too silly, much like the words of Hortence, and now he believed Brooklyn was the same. There was no way he would let the little screeching one touch him, enough of the cuddles.

Ren was different since he gazed at him inquisitively, examining him, and wary of every movement he made. Like his own distrustful feeling at birth, the one like himself might be worthy of his attention as he now believed that Hubert, too, earned that place. It was possible the boy could teach him a lot. Dusty said he was a dog; Ren said he was not a dog, but he repeatedly called him an alien. *An alien, maybe that's what I am. What is an alien?* the pup asked himself.

***

Ren watched the pup in awe as he moved towards him, mesmerized by the colorful creature with the strange face. "Is his face human," he asked his dad. "What a spaz, his eyes look like he is trying to get into my brain." Laughter overcame him when he saw the little pup run away from Brooklyn. "At least he knows to stay away from her," he chuckled, and the little alien grinned at him.

Aliens existed; Ren was sure of that. These two just did not remind him of the spacemen, drooly creatures he saw in comic books and movies. These two had no big heads, frightening appearance, malnutrition bodies, or bulging eyes, no spaceship either. "Where are you from?" he asked the little male; the purple in his eyes lit up like twinkling stars. Ren jerked back to get away from the power of the little pup's eyes; tumbling backward, he fell onto his butt. "Did you see that? His eyes just sparkled."

Hubert noticed Ren's reaction to the little pup and burst out in laughter. "I am sure it's just the light of the sun upon them. I noticed that under that flashlight today."

"It's not funny. That alien just shot some type of ray out his eyes at me." Ren felt a bit of embarrassment since the little pup still grinned pleasantly at him. A few seconds later, the contagion of the laughter caused his shame to vanish, and he burst into laughter himself. Now he was ashamed of the way he had responded. There was no ray shot at him. It was possible that the alien slowly brought him under his control, and he would be careful of those strange eyes. Then again, maybe his father was right; it was just the sunlight.

Brooklyn giggled playfully. "Yeah," she screamed. "The pink one. The pink one." While his father took the pink alien out of the cage for Brooklyn, Ren remained mesmerized by the friendly little creature who challenged all of his previous beliefs of spacemen's hostility. The result of an evil doctor's mad experiment, as well. Ren supposed he would not call it wrong because the creature was just too cute. Of course, as a man, he would not coo over the little alien. Nevertheless, his heart softened, seized by his innocent grin. A sense of peace relaxed Ren, alien or not, dog or not, he was happy for the new pet.

"She is so soft; she tickles, Daddy." Brooklyn cradled the pup in her arms like she held a baby and the same way she had carried Teddy so many times. "I am going to call her Pinky." As if she too were in love, the little pink pup closed her eyes and fell into Brooklyn's face, and the two snuggled together, as if they were best friends.

"Put her down, Brooklyn. You're drooling all over her."

"Daddy, help me up, please," she said, motioning for to help her stand because she cradled Pinky in her left arm and Teddy was held securely by her right. Hubert reached down, lifting her small body by the arms, he pulled her up. His father smiled, and for the first time, it seemed to Ren that he was genuinely happy to be around the two of them. "Thank you, Daddy." After she was comfortable on her feet, turning, she began to run out of the room. "I have so many pretty clothes for you to wear. You will be best friends with Teddy and me."

"Brooke, be careful with her; she is still a baby, and don't run, please."

"I will be careful, Daddy," she yelled and slowly walked up the stairs, still chatting happily with her new friend.

"Dad…"

"Don't worry, Ren. Just enjoy it for just a moment."

"Brooklyn, don't yawls run," Mrs. Cheazemina scowled, stepping out of the kitchen. Something else caught her attention, other than his darting sister, she said, "No dogs. Mr. Hoobert, these chillins do not listen to yous cause yous always changing yous mind and never says no to them. I won't clean behind dogs."

Ren glared angrily at the old black woman; her gray dress, much too big, hung down to her feet, and the flat shoes on her feet scrapped as she dragged across the floor. "Shut up. No one asked you," A glare filled with anger, she scowled at him.

"You aint gonna take care of that dog. I said my word too, I aint either." Mrs. Cheazemina shoved the swing door open and disappeared behind it, still grumbling.

"Ren, don't argue with her."

"Dad, she ruins everything."

"Mrs. Cheasemina, do not worry about it. I will make sure the kids take care of them," Hubert screamed. "I will be right back."

"Why are you taking her side?" Hubert followed behind Mrs. Cheasemina, trying to appease her. "Come on, let's watch Mr. Ed. Later you can help me work on Mr. Jensen's project. By the way, stay away from that old lady. She is pure evil."

As if he understood him, the little alien gazed at him, following him into the living room. Ren watched the pup walk over to the science book, lying on the floor that he should be working on instead of watching television. "That is the solar system. But then again, I bet you know that," Ren smirked. "This is where we live now. It is Earth, and you are here." Ren pointed to the image on the picture representing the Earth. "This is Mars. This is where the Martians are from and probably where you're from." While he pointed at the image of Mars, the pup stared at him. "Are you from Mars?"

Dinner with the Pups

That night at dinner, for the first time since his mother died, laughter could be heard at the dinner table. Even though Mrs. Cheesemina had made greens, she made no macaroni, which was his and his father's favorite, and the hamburger meat was burnt. Hubert thought that the aliens might like the greens because they were not meat. Ren shot down that idea, followed by close agreement from Brooklyn. However, his father insisted, and when Hubert offered the oily vegetable to the pups, both turned their heads away in distaste at once. The reaction of the aliens caused another bout of laughter from the three of them. Hubert threw out the greens and burnt meat, and from that moment, neither of the three of them tried to contain their joy. Bologna, tuna sandwiches, and milk were their dinners and a bowl of fresh fruit salad for their alien pets.

Hubert brought down a green flowered seat highchair that Brooklyn used for her dolls and Teddy, but it had not been used in the kitchen since his mother died. Knots grew in Ren's stomach because he did not want to hear Brooklyn crying about her mother when she saw the chair. Instead, there were no tears, and Teddy did not get the honor of sitting by himself. To his surprise, his sister gently placed the female alien in the chair, who was now dressed in a blue baby doll dress with golden bows holding up the hair from her eyes. Ren chuckled because clothing on any animal was plain weird; nevertheless, his sister was happy and laughed throughout dinner. Teddy was not forsaken but given the honorary seat of sitting next to Pinky in the highchair. Two small eyes stared at Ren, and he leaned against his new pal, who munched on of a bowl fresh fruit. Like the male, she sat up on her bottom, her pretty pink tail fell from through the back opening of the chair delicately. Weird indeed, like the male, she used her front paws to pick up and hold the pieces for fruit while she ate.

The male sat in his own chair next to Ren, phone books placed in the bottom of the chair lifted the small alien up. Effortlessly he sat up and ate out of his bowl of fruit set in front of him on the table.

"What are you going to call him?" Hubert asked, taking a bite out of his sandwich.

"I think I will call him Bracket," Ren responded, petting his new pal on the head.

"Bracket. Why Bracket?"

"Yeah Ren, why Bracket?" Brooklyn agreed. "You should call him Purply."

"And you should shut up, Brooklyn. That is a sissy name."

Hubert laughed. At long last, his father was laughing with him and not yelling at him. For this moment, things were great, and Ren felt happy.

"Well, it is different for a name, and he is different. So, I think Bracket is a good name for him."

"Bracket," squealed Brooklyn, and bread and tuna flew out of her mouth. "I like it, Ren."

"Brooke, careful with your food," Hubert said as laughter erupted.

Ren watched the little male alien grin; joining in on the fun, he picked up a grape and threw it at the girl. Unable to believe what he just saw, Pinky shrugged at Bracket. His little alien looked up at him in approval, and Ren held his hand up. The little pup held his paw up, so he tapped it gently. "High-five," he told the little pup.

"Do you think they will get married and have babies, Ren?" Brooklyn laughed happily.

"I don't think so. I don't think Bracket likes Pinky. I would not," Ren responded. "She's too pink."

"Well, that is a long time down the road," Hubert said, joining in on the conversation. "This is the best tuna sandwich ever." Hubert gulped a mouth full of the sandwich, guzzled a drink of milk, and burped.

Brooklyn burped and laughed, and they all agreed it was the best meal ever.

Chapter Thirteen

Sorrows

Early the next morning, Dragonor and Mejuarian still frolicked around the gardens celebrating the new mewlings' births. Musicians still blared out tunes of celebration, and the villagers danced and sang songs of joy. Mejuarian instrumentalists, singers, and dancers, who were used to long days of revelry, continued their harmonies and did not miss a beat after almost a day of continuous celebrations.

Mewlings fortunate enough to escape the harrowing disaster, all through the night and morning, frisked around and learned the ways of the Mejuarian and who they were within the village. Littles mewlings with brightly colored coats--yellows, greens, reds, blues, and all those of the rainbow—played happily throughout the gardens. Appearances like those of strange-looking pups, cats, tiny cubs, and even oddly shaped springing fowl. With the spectacle of such differences in emerging and brilliant colors, most Dragonors stayed around simply because they were mesmerized by the amusing new mewlings.

Ambrosia juices, wines, fruits, candies, Dragornors meat delicacies, Mejuarian cakes, and even tiny frog legs and fisheyes carted in by the Arvunglies gave the celebration an abundance of foods. Smells from the garden saturated the region, and even those who had chores to do or sleep to catch up on purposely went out of their way to greet the new mewlings and made sure they took a plate of the richly decadent food.

Like a dictator that studied his battle plans to ensure all his army was in place to conquer the enemy's ills, Alejandro kept the joyous event going, and not one mishap befell the festive occasion. Mejuarian, Dragonors, even the little Arvunglies needed to keep their thoughts off their pain, if only for a short time. Nevertheless, as with all things he did, Mejuarian such as Saraphim felt the continuous celebration was inappropriate. The king, whose own mewling was missing, told him the Day of Dodekatheon should go on as usual. And he was prepared to keep it going regardless of the others' objections.

***

Sounds from the musicians playing in the gardens annoying her, Syberias lay in her bed, listening to the tunes that she should be dancing to with her mewling. She and Tyrion attended the celebration last night, and she tried with all of her heart to greet all of the mewlings gracefully and forget about her own bitterness.

Thoughts of her missing daughter shredding away any other judgments that tried to enter her mind held her captive; the bed provided more comfort than anything outside the walls of her temporary shelter. Syberias had to move, though, and although her body and mind were fighting her, something deep within her told her she had to keep going. It would be up to her to help the others find her daughter and the lost prince. Tyrion already had left, taking care of sector preparations, and she was unable to get up to help him get ready for his day.

Where are you? The words stung her heart. Host enemy forces tearing deep within her emotional being shattered every bit of joy that Syberias had known, ever. Her daughter was alive; birthing last night, she called out to her during the night. Syberias knew this because she was awakened by her daughter's soft calls, and she was not there to welcome her. *Not at the birth of my own mewling.* Tyrion told her she was dreaming.

Nevertheless, from that moment of her birth, she lay awake meditating on the cry. Syberias even tried to cry; no tears would flow, though. King Teloby, Tyrion, and the others would tell her she was mistaken just like her mate and try to load her full of herbs to make her sleep, as they usually did. This time she knew better, and she would not allow any of them to convince her that she was just overly emotional because of her inward personalities were battling.

The words of her daughter wounded her very profoundly; nevertheless, they gave her hope, too. "Where are you, my precious daughter?" No sorrow or distress in her tiny voice, she wondered where Harmonia could be. Was her daughter with the dragon, or just lost somewhere and alone? "She can't survive by herself," Syberias screamed and released herself from the grip of self-pity. This was the last time she would show emotions of weakness; She was of Os as well. The council meeting was in thirty minutes, and she had made her mind up. What could she wear to fight a dragon?

The Meeting

Four members of the Mejuarian council, the Dragonor council, Queen Marina, and Zacharias sat in the meeting chambers discussing how they should proceed in trying to locate the missing mewling. King Teloby and Lord Ephenio, both leaders with the community, sat at the front, providing the leadership and direction since it concerned both groups. Syberias gazed around the room; Nymeria was to attend, but much too ill, her poor friend lay weary upon her bed. Her nature much softer than Syberias' finicky ways, she was too weak to participate in the meeting, and King Teloby said her pains were much too burdensome for the high-spirited queen.

Little Queen Marina, along with her intended, Zacharias, both sat on the table in small chairs they had brought along with them. Confident that the Mejuarian or Dragonors would not have small enough accommodations for them, they were right since there were none. Their primitive chairs of sticks and animal hides looked out of place in the grand Dragonor chambers; nevertheless, they were official to the small clan.

Syberias spoke with the little queen last night, and if it were not for the pain in her heart, her delight might have been to spend much more time with her. Carefree, spirited, and a bit savage in her ways, Marina was so refreshing. Queen Marina was not afraid to show parts of her body; belly, deep cuts near her breasts, and even very short skirts Syberias saw her in. The little queen seemed to change her wardrobe frequently, and the clothing was what Saraphim called too risqué.

"No proper Mejuarian should show so much skin," the old Mejuarian scowled.

Syberias, on the other hand, enjoyed the liberty the little female showed in her fashion. While she sat in her gown-length garment, covering most of her arms and neck, the little queen sat in a bikini top, a very short grassy skirt, and thongs with bark bottoms. Syberias hoped she did not have to bend over because most of her chubby little bottom would be exposed, in front of the king and others in the room. What would Tyrion say if her skirt barely reached below the bum? It would save a lot of fabric, and her tail would cover most of her bottom. Syberias blushed at her thoughts.

Syberias had changed; the loss of her mewling possibly triggered something in her psyche. Os became more dominant. It was beyond her comprehension at this time. Nevertheless, when she looked at all of the significant attendees, she had no genuine affection for any of them because if they tried to stop her, they were the enemy.

"Thank you all for coming on such short notice, and of course, we all know what is happening," King Teloby spoke, breaking her thoughts. "We have two issues to discuss—the first being finding the missing nests, the second, the dragon. I have Lord Ephenio here and his council to help us." The chambers grew quiet, and everyone sat listening to the king. "Captain Jonus is recovering, and Qusdyr says he should make a full recovery in a matter of time."

"That's great news," Syberias said, seriously happy the captain was healing. It was not his fault.

"What happened? Why did he crash the airship? Has anyone asked him that?" Tovar grumped. "Did he have too much berry wine?"

"Maybe we overestimated the captain's abilities," Zavalza arrogantly stated.

"We know the old captain can guzzle down a skin of wine."

"Tovar, there was no berry wine involved. And Zavalza, I will stand behind Captain Jonus' abilities. The airship was struck by a chunk of the shattered meteor."

"Why? How is that possible? Raczis is at fault then."

Syberias listened to Tovar and the other members in the room place blame upon each other.

"It was not Raczis' fault. It was not Captain Jonus' fault. Don't place blame," King Teloby commanded loudly.

"King Teloby is right. It is not the fault of Raczis or Jonus. It is the fault of all of you that voted to move the kingdom," She cried loudly, gazing at them angrily. Their mouths hung open with the exception of Shanara and the little queen. Syberias supposed it was because of her sudden outburst condemning the village's move, which caught them all off guard since she knew they expected tears from her.

"We voted what was right to save the Mejuarian," Zavalza scowled. "Perhaps Syberias is better suited to adorning lovely clothing than sitting on this council and judgment."

"Zavalza, I am quite capable of sitting on this council. I rejected the move, and my vote was recorded. Dare not speak to me like that again." Syberias could have sworn that she saw a red tint grow upon the blue lord's face. Queen Marina burst out in laughter and almost fell off her small throne, and Zacharias struggled to keep her from falling, lifting her back into her chair.

"Sister Syb got the fire of Os. Zavalza, I think she just told you off," Tovar laughed and slapped her against the shoulder, jamming her forward into the table. A war between Tovar and Zavalza, which stemmed from histories long ago between Os and Thie, the legionnaire commander took every opportunity to belittle the water lord. Syberias did not want her comment to result in the battle of the gods; she was glad of Tovar's support, though.

"I agree with Syberias. She is capable of more than making clothing—my Lord Zavalza. I am a Dragon Fighter, and I don't make pretty clothing," Shanara sneered, taking her side.

"Shanara, your tongue," Lord Ephenio warned, glaring sternly at her. "This is a meeting and not a chamber of condemnation."

"Lord Ephenio is right. Syberias has the right to be here. And one more time, I do not want to hear the blame placed upon here or outside of this room. Raczis is not sure how it happened or what actually happened, and no one cares for our kingdom more than he. We all have our places here." Always the politician, King Teloby, tried to please everyone attending; Syberias nodded at him.

"When we have the matter at hand cleared up, we will return to the kingdom and assess the damage. For now, let's concentrate on the matter at hand."

"Have you checked the entire area?" Zavalza asked gruffly. "Is there water about? I will check beneath the waves and question my followers."

"We have, over and over. Dragon Riders, Tyrion, and Yadekda, as well have searched."

"A river runs through the caves in the distance from the jungle, Zavalza, which feeds itself from our waters," Lord Ephenio said. "And these waters eventually lead to the great waters to the west."

"Yes, but that is so far away. How could the nests have traveled that distance?" Shanara asked curiously.

"I have discussed this with Raczis, and from Captain Jonus' statement of the time the meteor struck his ship, it's possible the nest might have ricocheted into the distance anyway."

"It is settled then. I know those waters well, and I will journey to them. I have followers there as well." As always, Zavalza, the master of pride and arrogance beyond measure of any in the room, would make the journey alone. If the nests were found below the water, he would happily take all of the rescue's honor by himself.

Syberias wished for his glory; the nests were not below the waters, and she was sure of that.

"Vincentru and I also went out to search. We saw nothing from the skies," Shanara told the others; her voice soft with sorrow; her tough demeanor, at once seemed like that of a young mewling.

"And the land within twenty kilometers from the crash. We looked through the jungle but found nothing. My queen is committed to helping."

Queen Marina grabbed Zacharias's hand, puckering her lips, she kissed him on the cheek. "Yes, I am my Hunnybun." Syberias wanted to giggle at their outward display of affection, while others, not sure what to do, looked away. Only she and Shanara continued to watch the spectacle. "Like my sweet Zack has said, my people know the lands, and if your sweet little ones are in my jungle, we would know."

"Thank you, Queen Marina and Zacharias, for your help. I am sure we are all very grateful." Others in the room nodded, speaking their agreements.

"There is, however, the dragon," she piped out.

"Yes. The dragon.," Lord Ephenio repeated. A gaze upon the great lord's face, Syberias thought she saw a hint of sorrow in his eyes.

"Yes. Queen Marina thinks it is possible that the nests might have been taken by a dragon that lives in the caves in the mountains."

Syberias decided to remain quiet for now and listen in on the others talking about the dragon. If she dared tell them that she believed the mewling birthed during the night, possibly under the nose of the dragon, it might cause too much excitement. Her poor friend Nymeria might not recover from it.

"We will go into the caves and search for the nests and try and get rid of the dragon."

"Why?" Tovar scowled. "Send a Mejuarian into the cave, search for the nests, take them and let the little creatures fend for themselves. I will go."

Queen Marina scowled angrily at Tovar.

"Tovar, we made a promise, and with the help of the Arvunglies and aid of the Dragonors, we are sure we can make it leave. Or destroy it."

"Please do not be so quick. I know the damage that a dragon can do, and that particular dragon does greater than most if we are right. If he keeps his treasures near where he sleeps, it may be impossible to get close enough for you to collect them, even if you do find them."

"Lord Ephenio is right," Tinzadri agreed. "You do not know what you are up against. I cannot support entry into the cave by only a Mejuarian."

"You underestimate the Mejuarian, Dragonor."

"Tovar, the Dragonors do not underestimate us. We do not know dragons as they do. Do you have any idea who the dragon is, Lord Ephenio?"

Lord Ephenio remained quiet. It was evident the Dragonor knew who the great beast was. Syberias stared at him. "We only have rumors," he answered stiffly.

"Grandfather, you know who the Dragon is? Why do you say that?"

"We are not sure if that is the dragon."

Shanara glared at Lord Ephenio, "Grandfather, tell them."

"My granddaughter seems to think that this particular dragon is Magnus."

"And others too," Shanara interrupted.

"My granddaughter and others think the dragon attacking the Arvunglies belonged to my daughter. If this is the dragon, it will be a worthy adversary. I do not believe so; there are more dragons out there as well, however." Another worthy politician, Lord Ephenio evaded the question, giving a reason to deny what he knew was the truth. Syberias held her head down.

"Magnus left when we came to Ercutis. Some have seen him in the night. Large and red," Shanara said sadly.

"My Lord Ephenio, this might be Talulah's Magnus. Even if it is not, we cannot have dragons invading the Arvunglies village."

"That is what we have been saying all along," Queen Marina agreed.

"Grandfather, it is our fault."

"You need not convince me of the dragon's menace." with respect, his dark eyes, like black marbles, peering over at the little queen, he spoke. "My apologies, Queen Marina, Zacharias, and to the rest of your clan. We were not aware of these disasters. We will do all we can to help."

"At least that gives us a start. We know who the dragon is," King Teloby sighed. "Can we defeat it if necessary?"

"I won't let you kill him," Shanara cried out bitterly.

"We will do what needs to be done, Shanara. Magnus has made his decision. To destroy the lands of homes of the Arvunglies is against all Dragonor beliefs. We gave up on annihilation many years ago, before you or I was born." Tinzadri's stern stare was almost terrifying. Sharp Dragonor features upon his face, dark yellow eyes, thin nose, and frown upon his lips revealed a hollowness that was lost a long time ago, she believed, and the dark clothing that he wore added to his hard-hearted attitude.

"It is possible we might not have to kill it." Syberias agreed with Shanara, and she did not want the dragon to die. If Magnus stood between her and her daughter, though, she would kill him herself.

"Surely we have to go in to look for the nests. If the dragon gets in the way, we will destroy it," Tovar announced gruffly. "I still say I will go, with or without the Dragonors."

"I will go as well," Syberias announced.

Zavalza laughed. "You, Syberias? What will you do, hold its hand, and read its future?"

"My Lord Zavalza," the great water lord glared at the king, then, looking at Syberias, he grinned. "I do agree with Zavalza. I think it best if you stay here. I realize that your nest is missing. I need to make sure that everyone that goes returns."

"Entering the den of a dragon is nothing to be taken lightly as dragons can be very dangerous, if they choose to be, and we have to be very cautious," said the great lord, gazing at her.

"I will go with Tovar," Tinzadri told them.

"As well as I," King Teloby said. Syberias saw a stare of confidence and self-assurance within the king. She always had great respect for the leader because he loved her best friend so dearly and ran the kingdom well enough. His step forward impressed her, and she was glad that he ruled the Mejuarian, although she sometimes disagreed with him.

"You cannot go, my king, it is too dangerous," Tovar grouched. "You mus…"

Before he could finish, cutting in, King Teloby ordered, "Quiet," his voice was stern and with conviction. "I will go. It is my decision to make."

"I will go too, and no one will not stop me," Syberias told them.

"I will go with Syberias," Shanara answered firmly. "I know Magnus, and if you are going to kill him, I need to set it right in my own mind."

"Fair enough, Shanara," Lord Ephenio told her. "I am sure Vincentru will accompany you as well."

"He will."

"Syberias, will you reconsider this? Tyrion will not want you to go on such an adventure."

"Yes. I am sure, King Teloby. Tyrion will agree, or he will not. If only to prove my strength to myself, I need to go." Syberias was not going to be talked out of it. Commandingly, she said, "I will find my daughter."

"And it is possible, my dear Syberias, that you become a burden to the others."

"I will be no burden, Lord Zavalza and cause danger to no one."

"We both have missing nests, and no one here can persuade me not to go. I will allow the same consideration to Syberias."

Everyone gazed out in surprise at the King's decision, and the room grew quiet. Syberias was sure he understood her pain; nevertheless, she knew he did not really expect her to journey along, claiming she would be ill or something silly like that. The surprise would be on him though, she was going. King Teloby looked at her with worry in his eyes.

"I respect your decision, my king, but you are the king and..."

King Teloby cut him off again.

"No further discussion is needed regarding who is going."

"With Shanara, and Tinzadri at your side, you will have aid," Lord Ephenio said to him. "You know what you are up against, King Teloby. We will hope for the best."

"My army will accompany you. We are very good at duties requiring stealth," Queen Marina told them. "My hun Zac will lead you, as well."

"This is right, King Teloby and Lord Ephenio, and I am sure my queen wants to say we are grateful for your help."

"It is settled then; we will take the Mejuarian King along to the crash site. I would like to ask that everyone here please not discuss this meeting until we return from the dragon mission. I do not want to create excess worry and anxiety at this time for anyone." King Teloby gazed his large, uncompromising eyes at them, scanning them one by one.

"We understand my king," Tovar announced. "I will make sure the legionnaires are watching over the kingdom until our return."

After the meeting had concluded, everyone continued to sit in silence for a few minutes longer before anyone stood to leave. Syberias peered around the room, and it felt cold and tense, and she felt the discomfort coming from each of them. Typically, Mejuarian with positive auras produced calming effects, but things were different now, and now no one was calm. "Please do not worry, my friends, all will be well. We will find our nests and deal with the dragon without incident."

Chapter Fourteen

A New Discovery by Water

Zavalza strolled through the glades' thick wet brush heading to the deep waters in the Dragonor region to the great gulf leading to the kingdom of those who depend upon him for their safety. Before he reached the dense mangrove and thick vegetation covering the wet grounds, he turned to say goodbye to Essencetaria. Swamps within the marshes were no place for her. Familiar with every creature within the lands, like the crocs, large deadly snakes, eels, and other dangerous beasts sustaining the region's people. Reverence for animals upon the land and within the waters, the water lord only expected the same as the others. Unlike some Mejuarian, he believed in his supernatural abilities, seeing himself as a deity, Zavalza. None were a threat to him; he could not say the same for his cherished, though.

Essencetaria was lovely, even under the sparse lighting in the deep brush of the glades. Golden strands from her ponytail wrapped around her neck like a glimmering scarf; its flowing tail dangled down across her chest, equalling the length of the rust gown she wore. A lively coppery complexion, even under the circumstances bold, her skin almost glowed. Deep eyes, curving upward at their outside corners, their brilliant tawny coloring were mesmerizing by all that beheld them, and just like her daughter, Nymeria, the aura of her presence gave off peace. Today, however, like others, his cherished was unwell because her grandmewling was missing.

Only now, that her mate was no longer present, could the two of them spend time together? Even the moments of tenderness they shared together in their elder years were taboo in the Mejuarian eyes. The relocation of the village and fear of the meteor's destruction left Mejuarian confused. Difference of opinion and former elder Mejuarian, Zavalza believed that this was destiny, and he would take advantage of it. No longer would he hide his love for Essenceteria; they committed no offense. Zavalza took the long digits of her paws and held them in his hands. "Comfort yourself, Essencetaria. I will search the waters and send out others to explore their depths."

"Zavalza, please tell me you do not believe they are at the bottom of the ocean. Can they survive?" Her voice quaked; he took her in his arms and pulled her close to him. No words spoken between the two of them; he meditated to the beating of her heart. Zavalza counted the beats as they thudded against his chest, wanting to hold her forever, but he could not. Dark waters called his name.

"The temple elders assure us that the nests are resilient enough. We need only worry about them birthing, and we still have days before that must occur."

"I know. I will try not to worry."

"Smile for me, Essenceteria. I cannot enter the deep of the seas, knowing you feel such grief. Go to Nymeria; she needs your strength." A smile slowly crept upon her face, and her lovely burnt peach-coloured lips turned up at their corners delicately.

"I must. You are right. Safe journey, my charmed Zavalza."

"Also, my followers will need for me to check on them. I will return at my earliest with any news." Gently, kissing Essenceteria goodbye, then he watched her walk away.

After the water lord searched the waters on Ercutis for the missing nests, he decided they were nowhere beneath the waters and took off to check on his folk. A ringing in his ears, the water lord plunged into the depths of the Ercutis waters into the great abyss. For a moment, his mind and body, foreign to him, disoriented as to where he was at or who he was, so he pushed forward. It only took a few seconds for the water lord to pass through the gulf, but it felt as if he were stretched into infinity with no beginning or end.

Since most of the Mejuarian history, considered creations of Thire-los only myths now, Zavalza had no idea that many centuries ago, this very abyss he found was shaped by their god. Due to the Ercutian reign of terror, pleas of the Earthlings entered their ears through a galactic watery tunnel. Up and beyond the earthly heavens, like twinkles of light, came their wishes, and in their grand castle, high above the lands of the Ercutis, Thire-los cured the pains contained in the glimmers. Thire-los eventually stopped answering the desolate Earthlings' prayers, and as the Ercutians suffered from their own turmoils, the great gulf between Ercutis and Earth was all but forgotten.

Speedily he swam and refusing to stop, Zavalza knew that the momentary confusion would end, and when it did, he would be in a world far away from his own planet of Ercutis. The abyss' warm waters began growing cool; he passed from the familiar body of water he knew into those of a foreign sea he was unfamiliar with for a long time. The water lord swam upward quickly. Skyward he reeled, climbing to the surface from the deep depths of the Atlantic. Zavalza had no need for air; the pass through the abyss, so very unsettling, the sight of only the skies above calmed him. Like that of a fish, bobbing his head out onto the water's surface for a moment, Zavalza peered around at the endless water surrounding him. The water lord breathed in, the smell of the ocean refreshing him.

Gills along the side of his neck, small slits opened and closed, giving him life underwater like an underwater creature. His white garment, purposely designed to seal his body from the chill of the waters, wrapping around his body snuggly, at his ankles. Its hem fanned outward, creating a tail, which helped him propel himself along when he swam. Long silver strands of hair floating behind him, his pitchfork held forward, Zavalza's lean body swam through the water with the quickness of a great white and the elegance of the romantic koi. The water lord felt himself king of all the seas.

An allegiance with those in the waters, many fish and great beasts of the seas were becoming his. In these waters, he too would protect his folk and any creature needing his help, even the ancient fish that made their dwelling deep below the oceans' depths. Behemondi threatened him and his followers before the Mejuarian tragedy. He warned her not to bother his folk, so Zavalza never doubted that Behemondi might attack his residents while under the watch of the prehistoric fish he left over its protection. One thing did concern Zavalza, Behemondi never returned to the area. This was indeed odd.

Zavalza explored the oceans until he found her. In the place he left the large creature, she lay nursing her pride if not necessarily her wounds.

"Behemondi. What is this?"

"Zavalza, go away," Behemondi scowled angrily, whipping her long black snake-like body; she hid behind the beds of algae.

"I see you. You are acting very immature right now."

"Immature? Zavalza, you hurt me."

"That is true, but you did try and kill me," Zavalza chuckled, walking across the bottom of the ocean, peering down to see Behemondi's long body curled tightly as she sulked. Her red eyes, once fiery and robust, gazed sadly at him, and the great lord's anger softened; his threats to destroy her were only threats now. Behemondi was his friend, and although she tried to hurt him, the water lord knew it was out of her own pain that she lashed out at him.

"Yes, I did, and you deserved it."

"I would not say that anyone is truly deserving of passing over. I will admit, though, that perhaps I was a bit insensitive to your feelings."

"Insensitive. Is that what you call it, Zavalza?" Behemondi swam up and looked in Zavalza's face. A flare grew in her red eyes, and once again, the spark of fire that he knew of the ancient creature flared for only a moment. "Just leave me be."

Zavalza swam behind Behemondi, tracking the smoke path coming from her nose. "I have said I was sorry. Let us once again have our amicable agreement." Behemondi ignored Zavalza's pleas; however, the great water lord was not giving up so quickly. Her age and wisdom, an asset for him. If he did not destroy her, he needed her as an ally.

***

Adeline and Jimmy Grate were on their honeymoon, and the perfect way to seal their union for the many long years of togetherness they planned on sharing was turning out to be their nightmare. Both loved the water, and swimming with the dolphins, whales, and having a close encounter with a small shark was the passion of both. After many years of engagement, Jimmy finally proposed to Adeline, and the perfect Caribbean holiday also had the ideal one-day island experience. They snorkelled, dived, danced, and enjoyed fresh pork on a spit. The evening was more than both could have expected, so the two decided to explore the islands.

That morning when the two of them went back to camp, they found the others long packed up and gone. Fires no longer burned, and their camps, doused with water, were cool to the touch. Backpack, coolers, tables and chairs, and all of the evidence of a party was missing. Jimmy made a mistake at the time. The boat left at midnight instead of noon, and the two of them were abandoned on the deserted island. Jimmy decided against, or was too lazy, to look for food. Jimmy, on the other hand, blew up the small raft he carried for emergencies. And the two of them left the tiny island to paddle back to the mainland. This decision would lead to the predicament that they found themselves in at this moment.

***

"Behemondi, slow down." Zavalza swam speedily after her until he saw something quite out of the ordinary. More sharks than he had seen in one time congregated together, swimming erratically as if preparing to attack. Tigers, great white, blue, and whitetips swam around, circling something floating atop of the water. From beneath, the frenzy above he watched, then swam up closer to see what the hungry water parasites hunted.

"Help."

Zavalza heard a cry; he wondered who could be calling out in distress in the vast seas alone. Away from the shiver, he swam and emerging out of the dark foreboding water. Two earthling beings were sitting on a small raft floating atop the water, which looked to be slowly sinking. Both burnt from the sun, their bright skins were red, and the two of them huddled together, crying while the frenzy of sharks prepared to have them as a meal.

Zavalza never had contact with the beings on this planet and had no intention of letting them know of his presence. The two on the raft were going to pass over, though, if he did not help. There was always the use of his pitchfork, but its power was so dramatic that he knew he might hurt the humans or at least give himself away.

Behemondi waited below the depths for him. "What are you doing, Zavalza? You were following me."

"Yes. I called to you to wait."

"And so, I did," Behemondi told him, whipping her long body around him. This time not aggressive but playfully.

"No longer mad with me?"

"Yes. I mean, no. I will never forgive you, great water lord," she grouched, swimming away. "Stay away from me, Zavalza." This was his cue to follow her, as they did when he first ventured into the strange waters. A game they played, the two of them swam across what they called the wet Earth, exploring and making acquaintances and allies along the way.

"Behemondi, stop. We have no time for these theatrics. I need your help."

"I am no longer your friend, and I will not help you."

"It is not for me. It is for those above that need assistance."

"Those above? Zavalza, the humans hunt us with their spears, drag us from our watery home only to die because we cannot breathe. Or they just make a meal of us. I will not help them."

"That is quite a list of reasons why you should not help. What about the reasons why you should help?"

Behemondi spun around quickly; tiny fire sparks came from her nose, which dwindled into dark smoke. "Why should I help them, Zavalza?"

"I agree if what you say is true; there is no reason for you to want to save them. The Earthlings sound like the worst beings. However, I do not know this about them, and it is my nature not to let anyone perish in such a manner. You shall do it for me."

"Zavalzaaa," Behemondi whined. "You are the great water lord, and you have that pitchfork. You do it."

"I will help. I do not want humans to see me."

"Oh, I see now. The next thing you know, the fishermen will be hunting me down and having fricassee Behemondi," she turned her long black body and swam away.

"No, I have an idea. The two of them will not see either of us. We need to clear the frenzy."

"Zavalzaaa."

"Quiet Behemondi. That is so very unbecoming."

"You speak of unbecoming? How dare you! I will help you only if you promise me one thing."

"Behemondi, we have no time. The raft is sinking, and if they fall into the sharks, we might be too late."

"You swear to me, Zavalza."

"I give you my word. So, tell me what oath I have given you."

Behemondi's mouth opened, and her lips curving into a grin while her long tongue snaked out of her mouth. "Don't bring her in my waters again."

Essencetaria, his beloved, came into the waters with him. Zavalza never intended to upset Behemondi when he brought her into the waters, and her jealousy was quietly frankly a surprise to him. Right now, he needed her help, and it was a possibility he might need her later. "An agreement. Now here is my plan."

The plan was in order, the two prepared to disperse sharks' frenzy without the humans being aware of their presence; her dark body hidden beneath the black seas. Behemondi swam beneath the shiver of shark, shooting periodic flames in the water, heating the icy water above her darkened body. Temperatures in the water increasing, the frenzy of attack started swimming out of the uncomfortable waters, further away from the humans, increasing their radius.

Around the frenzy's eclipse, from the view of the frightened humans, Zavalza readied his attack. His pitchfork, a formidable weapon without using its magical powers, he pounded at the sharks with its tip, fighting with them, until one by one he encouraged them to leave the frenzy. Behemondi joined in on the battle with her long tail, attacking and batting away at the assailants with her powerful, pointed tail. Those angry enough to attack, the two of them they had no choice but to destroy, and their once partners in crime turned on them, tearing them apart. This gave Zavalza time to close in on the larger sharks, like the great whites, with such awful tempers, the strikes of he and Behemondi only bothered their tough hides. Once the blow's effect lightened, the mighty stubborn creatures pushed in closer to hopeless humans.

Growling, a noise only his ears hear, the larger fought him angrily, refusing to leave. Zavalza released an icy charge from his pitchfork, freezing parts of their bodies, and they sank to the bottom of the ocean. Here the stubborn mammal waited until thawing in the icy depths or another of their dreadful pals took a bite out of them. While battling with the group, Zavalza did not notice that the raft holding the humans was now below the water, and the two of them kicked frantically, screaming for help above the waters. The ruckus in the water, not helping their cause, their struggling only summoned the attention of two mega sharks who rose from the deep bottom. The two of them sprinted up past he and Behemondi's line of battle, alongside each other, preparing to attack the humans. No time to react, Zavalza shot missiles of ice at the two sharks, plunging the piercing projectiles deep within their tough skins. The two of them stopped, turning the water around them red.

Those hunters in the water that had given up and left returned quickly, still too close to the humans. Swooping in past Zavalza, snapping their hungry mouths at the large bodies of meat, they tore at chunks of it. The humans were within the middle of the frenzy, when Zavalza heard deadly screams of fear. Within moments, he created a whirlpool of water around the humans, shoving the attacking sharks and their meal away from the frightened people. Unfortunately, the humans witnessed this supernatural rescue.

"They saw you."

"Yes, I believe the two did, Behemondi."

"What do you want to do? Kill them."

"We definitely will not. We shall not worry about that at this time."

"Now the sharks are gone, but the humans are still in the water. What do we do now? Any plans?"

"Of course." Through the use of his underwater sonar, Zavalza called for aid. Members of his alliance within the ocean pulled a small boat they had stolen across the sea to his location. Zavalza watched the humans weakly crawl into the small boat and lay down within its bottom. Shockingly, neither of them seemed surprised that a group of dolphins rescued them. It was possible the two of them were hungry, tired, or just too frightened to notice their saviours. Who would believe them anyway? Zavalza commanded the fish to leave. With a rope around their nose, his two companions pulled the weary humans to safety.

Ally or Foe

Under the command of the queen, Zacharias decided to leave early that next morning to make sure they traveled during the daylight hours. King Teloby offered to return them back comfortably by airship. Queen Marina politely turned down the offer and told the dear king she would rather walk along the ground than fly in that darned air contraption, although the journey would take the small group of travelers more than three weeks to return to their village. Other intentions on her mind, though, she had to make one stop before returning to her own dear lands.

Within her carriage, Queen Marina sat miserably while her six pole barriers carried her along. Since they left so early, it was still cold, and although she bundled herself in a blanket of rat fur, the wet, icy air always pricked at her skin. Her long fingers were wilted and cold although the queen wrapped them in fur mitts, they felt no warmth. Even though she despised the airship trip, she hated the Dragonor region's coldness and would have rather returned by ship. The little queen could not wait to reach the warmth of her own balmy jungle. This long journey was necessary, though, and she had to take

171

the arduous trip. Vritritra's cave was out of the way. However, by the end of the day, they should reach the desolated area. None traveled through these lands if they did not have to, and the dense darkness within the trees made it very difficult to see without fire or light. As far as Marina knew, the colorful Mejuarian or Dragonors never ventured through the deadly forest, and the witch kept her home secret from outsiders.

Along the rough trip, she bobbed up and down and only peeked through the doorway to see how far they had traveled. A troupe of soldiers marched before her; another group behind her which protected her from a rear attack, though Arvunglies did not fear attack.

When enemies dared threaten them, the little fighters acrobatically stood upon their companions' shoulders and formed ladders of bodies upward, into what they called the tree stance. Deadly poisoned pricked tips on the end of their spears pointed up and outward. With a single attack, every combatant at the same time jabbed their spears at the attacker. A formidable force against anything biting or grabbing at their tiny bodies had no chance.

The ground nothing more than thick grass and bumpy terrain; the troop weaved around the tuffs of weed and beetle burrows. Unless one looked closely, they would not have noticed the little army journeying through the lands.

"We have a giant burrow here, my queen."

"We will stop. I hope there is a nice one in there." Most of the moisture burned off by the warmth of the sun. Marina stepped out of her carriage, filled with excitement. The little queen was ready and anxious to watch her fighters in the hunt.

Once in a while, it depended upon the burrow's size, the Arvunglies stopped and attacked the nest and hunted down its occupant. Its eyes, legs, and pinchers roasted on a fire pit; the squishy meat was perfect when only slightly warmed. Many purposes for the beetle shell, such as containers for holding water, roofs for some of the smaller shacks, shields, and even those with artistic talents, made pretty mosaic ground patterns out of them. Other shells less bright, their shattered pieces made clean walkways and floors hiding away the dirt and mud.

Even though the small folk lived among the dirt and grass, they were self-driven, and even within their own little village, it was common practice to hold themselves above the others in status and position. Greed and an overabundance of stuff cluttered the floors and cubbies in the shacks of the wealthy, while other homes barely had enough blankets to keep their occupants warm. Soldiers, the most prosperous villagers, sold the trinkets and materials they gathered on their patrols to those wealthy enough to purchase them. Or they traded the items for some type of work they needed on their own shack. Most of the warmer, fancier, and bigger huts belonged to them, and these Arvunglies were most respected in the village.

Arvunglies dug around the burrow with their small shovels and pickaxes that they carried in packs upon their backs, constructing a wider entrance down into the hole. Hours later, the whole troop resting from the hard work, the group of them sat upon the mounds of dirt piled around the burrow entrance waiting for their attack. These resourceful little people positioned a wall around the opening giving them room to battle with the creature and stopping it from bolting away. Not much larger than the length of the beetle themselves, several other soldiers dug another hole to intersect with the burrow, setting up to ambush for the sleeping bug on the outer side of the barrier.

Queen Marina stood atop of the dirt mound gazing down happily; she clapped her hands in excitement, watching the four trappers on the outside crawl down the hole, two abreast each other. The first set of two, then the next, the spears readied to attack. "Hurry, hurry."

Moments later, within the middle of the wall, a blue, black, and pink strange-looking beetle scampered out of the hole. Arvunglies, standing around it, poked at it with their spears, while the beetle stabbed aggressively at the little army men with two long pinchers around its mouth.

"Don't scar the shell," Zacharias yelled, shoving his spear into the beetle's mouth. Although the giant bug outweighed and outstood the Arvunglies in height, it fought valiantly but was no challenge for the spirited crew of hunters. Within moments the battle was over and, the bug lay dead upon the ground. Its long legs sprawled out around its colossal body. The tiny soldiers cut them off and wrapping them up carefully to keep their juices inside. Too, they took its pinchers and antennas, reading to remove its gleaming armor from its head, neck, and back.

"I want it." Queen Marina cried out like a little girl squealing for her favorite doll.

173

"It is a nice one, my queen."

"It will be perfect in our bedroom," the little queen remarked, puckering her lips kissing Zacharias on the cheek. "I am going back to my carriage, Hun."

"Prepare this one for the queen. Then we move on right away." Zacharias commanded.

Lovely colorful shells were more profitable, and a battle would have undoubtedly ensued so that one of the soldiers could own the rare colored surfaces. With the queen on this trip, who always made sure she took the choice stuff, the combatants did not have to fight for the ownership of the fancy ornament. Marina grinned wickedly, and she sat back, not enjoying the rough ride. "It is like riding the river rapids in here," she yelled.

Zacharias stepped up to her.

"Hun, why is it so terrible? My head is hitting the top of this thing."

"I apologize, Marina, babe. This terrain is not the best for someone as delicate as you."

"Zacharias, you do know how to make me perspire. Come sit here with me." Queen Marina patted at the spot next to her in the carriage, smiling happily.

"What a tempting offer, babe. I need to keep watch to make sure you are safe."

"Yes, you do, and that is what I like about you." Marina popped a piece of the sweet fruit she brought back with her that the colorful Mejuarian gave her. So, she allied with them, or was it that she made them believe she was their allies? Whatever case it was, the queen was in their clique now. The valuable information she had on them, she would share with Vritritra.

"Zacharias, what do you think about the Mejuarian?"

"They're alright, I guess."

"Both they and the Dragonors have a lot of valuables. We could get a lot from them, and they might prove to be good allies for us."

"I am with you, Hun, on that one. That is why I have to be careful."

"You are going to need to cleverly handle this situation. I am here with you. Just listen to me."

"That I will do, Hun." Queen Marina trusted Zacharias' council on all matters concerning the village. Frankly, he was old enough to be her father, but she loved him dearly. The brave fighter commanded the army under her father's reign as well, and she had great trust in his wisdom. Shrewd in his negotiations, she had no doubt he could help but give her good advice in dealing with the old woman.

No one in the village knew anything about the witch. For as long as the queen remembered, she was there, and the villagers feared her. Even more than the deadly dragon. Vritritra, a comrade of the Arvunglies for many centuries, could do worse damage to them. She was now the representative for her people, and it was her responsibility to keep the old witch happy. Queen Marina hated the liaison position, and she hated the old woman even more. A long time ago, it was said that she executed twenty of the village fighters because the queen's great, great, great, grandfather, or one way back in her ancestry, stood up and said no to Vritritra. After the murder of their soldiers, they agreed to supply information about the lands or act as spies on the Dragonor or colorful Mejuarian. Rarely she ventured out, no farther than the ground around her bleak cave in the black forest, and when anything new happened, the Arvunglies reported the facts to her.

Vritritra was no normal old lady either. Supernatural and evil, malicious powers of illusion, she possessed a stare that caused even the fiercest beasts in the lands to cower at her form. Everything and everyone she knew that was aware of the witch was afraid of her. Marina believed she could conquer the dragon by herself. She left it in their lands to remind them how easily she might destroy them and refused to evict the beast. It was their burden to bear, Vritritra told them. When the witch dared leave the dark forest to spy on the Arvunglies, sometimes her appearance was of an old, wilted witch. Marina never knew when she might show up like an oil spill that floated atop the river and listened to the village secrets. Other times, like a wisp of black smoke or a heap of black goo, she spilled out upon the dirt ground in the isolation of her dark, dingy cave. In a bodily sense, Queen Marina believed she had no proper form and copied the appearance of whatever was horrible and frightening.

The deadliest secret of all was, she hated the Mejuarian, and this too, the queen knew of no reason why. She shuttered to think if Vritritra found the missing nests, and honestly, Marina hoped that she was right and that they had been discovered by the dragon and not the old witch.

Marina heard the sound of the army's footsteps walking across the dying leaves in the forest. Dead and dried, they crunched beneath their feet, and the darkness growing within the tent on her litter, she knew they were only minutes from Vritritra's cave. Her heart dropped; she was thankful Zacharias was with her.

"We are here, baby," Zacharias told her, opening the doorway of her cover. Marina took his hand, stepping down from the litter. A terrible stink odor came from the dark cave; standing at the small opening of the witch's lair, her feet felt as if they were rooted to the ground, just like the rest of the dead, unmoving ground around her.

It was no cave made of dirt or deep within the mountains. Large old grandfather trees whose dried vine-like branches bound tightly together shaped a hollow that hid behind the tangled mess of foliage. Decayed leaves covered their curled dry branches and provided a warm nook, free from the intrusion and the nasty weather. Brush grown across its faces as well; it was perfect for Vritritra's long periods of hibernation.

No birds chirped in the trees because there were no birds in the forest, and no creatures scampered or ran across the grounds. Brush, once covered in leaf, now only stalks of wilted bare branches, dead leaf and stick protected the floor from any moisture. Seclusion and desolation were in the dark forest, and it was evident once she stepped into the anguished woods. No being or creature with a precious pride of life dared inhabit Vritritra's habitat if they wished to keep it.

"It smells so bad," she whispered to Zacharias.

"It does."

Queen Marina stepped further into the cave; most of the debris and brush within the cave not nearly as decaying as that on its outside with pieces of jagged stick and leaf protruding upwards. For her size, the floor was not easily treaded across. Zacharias stepped in front of her, moving the fragments of brush out of her way. Casually, walking in the light of the torch her fiancée carried, she hoped she did not step in anything gooey or nasty that might muddy her sandals. Something squished under her feet; the queen was too afraid to look down. Queen Marina closed her eyes for a moment, lifting her feet out of the slime, she kept moving forward.

"News for me?" Her voice rang out loud, commanding an answer.

Marina jumped, startled from its sound, moving closer behind Zacharias.

"Close."

"Lady of the Dark, we have news of the colorful ones."

"Why, speak me," she scowled angrily. "Where imp queen?" The old witch sat naked in the corner on the ground. Her legs, flexibly tucked beneath her frail sagging body; her awkward pose, seemed comfortable to the witch. Nothing more than bones, the skin on her neck and chest seemed to melt into her lower section when she stood up and walked towards the two of them.

"I am right here," she told her, stepping out from behind Zacharias. Marina breathed deeply; gaining her composure, she walked up to the old witch. Long thin hair on her gaunt face, sparse grey strands fell down to the ground dragging in the dirt behind her. *She is hideous,* Marina thought to herself. White eyes with no pupil, the old witch gazed down at the queen; her cold, heartless eyes gave no evidence that she saw her.

"Me am?" Marina looked at her; she was unsure what the old witch was asking. "Hideous?" she said to the queen.

Spittle from between the witch's thin drooping lips fell from her mouth. Queen Marina moved out of the way, escaping from the shower of liquid. Marina stood speechless.

"I thoughts know. Besides point. What you have?"

Relieved that the old witch did not concern herself with the incidental slip in her thoughts, Marina replied, "The colorful Mejuarian."

The old witch stood up, interested. Marina looked away from her shriveled body. "On," she scowled angrily. The little queen stood motionless, glaring at the old witch's naked body, and she finally morphed into a hag wearing a tattered dirty dress soiled with ground. Vritritra sat down in front of her.

"I have made allies with them. I will gain their trust and learn more."

"How possible?" She knew that the witch had been hunting for these colorful Mejuarian; nevertheless, the same powers that kept the Arvunglies out of the Mejuarian Kingdom too kept out Vritritra. "There might be a way you can enter their lands now."

"Say so?"

"Yes. The king and the rest of the villagers have left their kingdom. They live in the lands of the Dragonors now."

"The barriers might be down now," Zacharias added, which made the old witch's demeanor seem to brighten a bit. Of course, the thought of horror gave her pleasure; nothing else would, Marina knew this all too well.

"Imp queen and scamp, good job."

"Their lands will be vacant for some time, and they have no guards protecting it now." Vritraita grinned evilly at her. Terror in the witch's condemning grin made her want to back away. Marina remained still but looked away from the two crooked brown rotting teeth she showed.

"More?" the old witch whizzed giddily, staring at her, missing the doubt she held before for the queen.

To her relief, she realized the witch did not have the nest. She was sure if she had them, she would have mentioned that fact to her by now. Zacharias gazed over at her, and she understood his stare. There was no way she was going to mention the missing nests or their help with the dragon. Since she knew that the witch could read her thoughts, only idle ideas of clothing and food stuffed her mind. "Lady of Darkness, I came all the way myself to give you this news. I thought you would like it."

Her head bobbed up and down, "Do."

"I am glad this news makes you happy," she grinned. "You must come to my wedding!"

Chapter Fifteen

Blessing for the Lost

Hubert sat at the kitchen table, eating a burnt toast piece, and having his first coffee of the day. The coffee was strong and dark and tasted like it had been sitting all night and only warmed for his benefit. Tiny particles in the liquid floating in the coffee, the grounds filled his mouth, giving the morning drink a terrible taste. This was odd because, typically, Mrs. Cheasemina was careful to remove the grinds mingling with the coffee because of the old percolator's futile operations. Breakfast was terrible this morning as well. Runny eggs, and half-done bacon, was the morning start that the old woman delivered today.

Mrs. Cheasemina must have missed her happy bath last night; Hubert chuckled to himself, reminding himself of his son's comedic remarks since the old woman told them, "Bathing helped release negative energies." Hubert was alright with the release energies statement. Many people loved baths; however, she takes at least a forty-five-minute bath in cold water every night because the freezing temperatures washed away the filth of the world's diseases.

Mrs. Cheazemina was strange but was a good housekeeper, and most of all, he felt sorry for her, and Hubert hated the thought of firing her since her husband died right after she started working for him. The old lady almost begged him to keep her job once when he discussed the possibility of letting her go after his death. Ren did not know this and wanted her gone. Brooklyn did not mind either way, but some part of him could not let the old black lady go. In this sense, Hubert felt it was his responsibility to ensure she was taken care of because she was a widow, having no other family. Mrs. Cheazemina was like a grouchy mother-in-law you did not want around but felt accountable for her well-being.

For almost five minutes, Hubert pretended to read the paper while he listening to her blame Cecil for dying. Speaking two languages, alternating between broken English and some type of strange speech, Mrs. Cheazemina gripped in tears for being alone. Hubert was familiar with this behavior initially; when the old woman started her rant, he would listen to the foreign language, trying to determine what she was speaking. It was pure rubbish, and he actually believed she was not uttering an authentic dialect. Mrs. Cheazemina was very religious, so he even thought she might be speaking in spiritual tongues; nevertheless, he had never seen it done in such a way.

"Good Lord, Cecil," Mrs. Cheasemina cried out, startling Hubert, and the coffee spilled out upon the newspaper. It seemed as if she had forgotten that Hubert was in the room, and he did not want to interrupt the old woman from her rant. A moment later, she lazily padded over to him, her small feet dragging against the floor. Angrily, Mrs. Cheazemina refilled his cup with more grainy coffee.

"Mrs. Cheasemina, can you please make sure that the eggs are cooked hard for the children?" Hubert told himself he would not say anything, and he hoped this had not been a mistake. The eggs were just too much for him, he had to say something. Again, she began to rant, and this time he thought he heard his name.

"Them chillins is spoiled, Mr. Hoobert. Ren haz no responsibilities, and he won't even listen to you. I brought in the paper this mornin."

Hubert stirred the runny eggs with a piece of bacon and bit off a part of the meat.

"By the way, Mr. Hoobert, you shoulda not brought in those creatures. I feel demon evil." The old woman went on talking, and intent to let him know how serious she was. "Mr. Hoobert, I have been sent to take care of you and them chillins, and I feel there is bad things gonna come from them. The bible talks about evil."

Hubert could no longer hold on to his laughter; he burst out in loud chuckles. His grandfather an evangelist, and his father a reverend, created quite a fuss in the family when he chose to become a vet; he was quite versed in God and the bible. Having read through the bible his first time at age seven and many more times since then, he was quite informed enough to debate with the old woman. "There is nowhere in the bible where it says thou shall not bring pups into thou home." Laughter again escaped his lips.

"Mr. Hoobert, do not laugh. They's will be trouble," she said sadly, and he actually thought he saw sorrow when the old woman glared at him, not anger this time but with worry in her eyes and upon her face. "I know evil. Where's I comes from, evil was there. Now, yous home will be hunted by that evil." Mrs. Cheazemina's index finger on her right hand moved to her chest, and she crossed it from left to right, giving the sign of the cross.

How could she see so much evil in these two pups? The old woman was worse than Ren with the UFO fantasies. Mrs. Cheazemina was like most seniors, and Hubert was not going to change her mind. Sometimes beliefs were hard to break. Besides that, he did not know where she was from. "Where are you from that has all this evil, Mrs. Cheazemina?"

"That's no matter. Mr. Hoobert, listen to me."

"If you remember, I am a veterinarian, and I found nothing that concerns me. They are my children, and I will never give them anything to harm them."

"Mr. Hoobert, I had a dream. Something black and dark was coming to this house."

"I don't know what this evil is you are talking about, but one thing I know, Ren and Brooke seem truly happy again." Bickering from the old woman began to get on his nerves, and everything she said about Pinky and Bracket was wrong.

Brooklyn was his beloved; he and Irene adored her more than anything in the world, even more than Ren if he were honest. Not because she was a girl or pretty, but his angel was sickly. Hubert hoped his daughter would grow out of her epileptic seizures. Doctors told him not to expect her to heal, and it was possible she might suffer from SUDEP. Still, he was hopeful. Last night, he was not sure what happened, and if he had not seen it himself, Hubert would not have believed the actions of the little pup.

Last night when his little angel played with Teddy, she ran happily around the room, stopping to take a bit off a cherry on her travels. She had not overexerted herself in her joy; a symptom of her malady coming upon her, she fell and was lost to him for a couple of moments. While Hubert watched, dropping in the middle of her stride, she lay in the middle of the floor quivering, and his precious daughter foamed at her mouth. Seizures were expected in his little daughter. Hubert would never get used to them, though, and the rolling back of her eyes, so only their whites were showing, made his heart stop. Every incident, the doctor's words ringing out in his ears, he prayed for her to come back to him.

In his mind he remembered, before he could reach Brooklyn, the pink pup bounced off the couch; running up to his daughter, she lay her tiny body upon her trembling chest. Grasping her claws into her clothing to keep from tumbling off, the little pup held on while she jerked around. Quickly, Hubert reached his daughter, and like before, planning to grab her in his arms, he intended to hold her until she broke free of her brain's disorder. To Hubert's surprise, she sat back up, grinning at him; she had Pinky tightly clasped in her arms.

"I am alright, Daddy," she told him. Hubert grabbed her up anyway, and playful giggling came from her, as if nothing happened.

"Mrs. Cheazemina, enough of these superstitions. I don't want to hear you talk about this again. Not at all. I don't ever want to hear Brooklyn mention it." All he needed was for her to frighten his daughter with talk of dark spirits. "Please cook more eggs for the children."

Mrs. Cheazemina mumbled to herself for a moment, turned and said, "They says..."

"I do not care what they say, Mrs. Cheazemina. Those old wives' tales are just that, old tales of superstitious people. They are unsupported and serve only to scare the ignorant and uninformed." Hubert realized he just called her ignorant, but at this moment, he did not care. "I need a cup of coffee. Fresh with no grinds, now. Please."

Mrs. Cheasemina grunted and flipped the bacon over as it fried in the pan.

Ren came into the room, with the little purple pup following behind him. Hubert quickly placed the newspaper in his lap so that Ren could not see it. "Ren, did you get the newspaper today?"

"I have not yet, Dad, I am running late for school, and I don't have time right now," he said, sitting down. Bracket jumped up into the chair next to him and then onto the table, waiting for breakfast, with a very precious grin on his face.

"Are you going to feed Bracket? He needs to eat, also, and you both agreed that you would take care of them." Ren grunted and walked to the refrigerator. "Another thing you promised, and you did not get up in time."

"Geeze, you got the newspaper already, I see it. Why are you asking me about it?"

"That is not the point."

Ren smirked, shook his head. "The paper is in the driveway, and since she has to come right past it, I don't see why she can't bring it in any way."

Mrs. Cheazemina grunted. Before the old lady could speak, Hubert stopped her saying, "It is your responsibility. Not Mrs. Cheazemina, and tomorrow I want it."

Ren filled Bracket's bowl with the freshly mixed fruit and sat back down. "She just needs to complain about something because she just does not like me. My friends are afraid to come to the house now because she is here."

"Ren, I hardly doubt that Mark or Franklin are afraid to come over here."

"They are, Dad, for real. Ask Mark, she threw the dustpan at us one day."

"That's causin the two of you locked me in the closet out there in the hallway, Mr. Hoobert. I knows how to get out, though."

"It was a mistake, Dad. We did not know she was in there. I closed it by mistake."

"Humph," Mrs. Cheazemina groaned.

"Ren. You are still grounded, and I don't want your friends here. You have Bracket now, enjoy. I want your chores done, no more excuses or you will be grounded until you graduate."

"Yeah, whatever."

"Ren, I want you to come to the clinic after work today and every day until I tell you to stop. I know where you will be then," Hubert forcefully told him, then grinned.

"Dad..."

"Subject closed."

Ren saw that he was serious this time, and Hubert could see by his expression he grasped that he was not winning this argument. "Ok, Dad, I will get my work done, and I am sorry, I did not mean to disrespect Mrs. Cheazemina or you. I will get the newspaper tomorrow. Dad, I promise."

"Whatever," Hubert shrugged, winking at him. "Just be at the clinic this evening." Hubert turned when Brooklyn came running through the kitchen door with Teddy dangling from the crook of her arm and Pinky resting against her shoulder like a baby. Both she and Pinky wore pink today, and having dressed herself, his daughter's shorts were on crooked and her white sandals on the wrong feet.

"Daddy, are you going to work," Brooklyn asked, grabbing the fruit mixture out of the refrigerator and stuffing Pinky's pink bowl. Brooklyn placed the bowl on the highchair, gently picking Pinky back up; putting her in the chair, she sat the pup next to Teddy.

"Yes, Brooke, I have to go to work today."

"It is okay, Daddy. Pinky, Teddy, and I are going to have a tea party today." Brooklyn ran over to the old woman and gave her a pink bow she was holding, "Will you put this in my hair, please, Mrs. Cheasemina?"

"Chile, look at you. Mr. Hoobert, I tried to get her dressed this morning. She told me she did not need my help."

"I don't, Daddy. Pinky will help me now."

Crooked shorts, shoes on the wrong feet, and her hair not combed but only a band placed around the nappy ponytail, for the second time this morning, Hubert wanted to laugh. "Maybe, sweetheart, you should let Mrs. Cheazemina help you from now on, Pinky too."

Brooklyn looked up sweetly at the old woman; her large brown eyes like that of an angel, she asked. "Mrs. Cheazemina, will you make Pinky and me matching dresses?"

Maybe the eyes of Brooklyn changed the old lady's opinion about the evil in the two pups; her eyes softened. "You go over there and eats yous breakfast. When I finish cleaning this house, we will go down to Rose's and get some pretty cloth."

"Yeah," Brooklyn screamed, darting to the table, she sat down.

"Mrs. Cheazemina, please leave the pup behind. I know Brooke will want to take her."

"I will, Mr. Hoobert. Chiles, when I finish this, we gonna go change your clothes. Uh, uh, uh," she grumbled.

"Ok," his daughter nicely answered.

Hubert reached over and pinched Brooklyn's cheek, gently watching a beautiful smile come across her face. Even though Ren did not bring in the newspaper this morning, he was noticed bliss in his son. Brooklyn appeared over the moon with joy. Hubert did not know if an average dog would have given him the same results since he genuinely believed these little creatures brought more to his family than any other pet might. Practices in the field changed every day; new species were being found. These two are baffling now. Tomorrow, however, the little pets might end up as the next posh pup; grinning happily, he left the table.

"I am off. Don't forget, Ren, clinic."

"Bye, Daddy." Brooklyn never watched him leave, never bothering to run and cling to him; this made Hubert very happy.

"Cya," Ren told him, and the little blue pup was grinning.

A New Friend

Brooklyn sat in her bedroom playing with Pinky while Mrs. Cheazemina cleaned the house and made her shopping list for this afternoon's trip downtown. Wide awake from her morning nap, her new friend waited for her, ready for pampering when she opened her eyes. Excitedly anticipating the shopping trip to go buy fabric so that she and the little pup could have matching dresses, she brushed her pet. Pinky's coat was beautiful, so soft, and grooming its silky strands was her favorite thing to do now, and Pinky loved it as well. Pinky bathed with her last night, but her daddy said she should not bath the little pup every night. Not giving her a bath every evening was alright because her little pup had a pretty smell without adding soap, just like bubble gum.

Brooklyn dressed Pinky in a rosy lacy dress, similar to the pup's own coloring that she took off one of her dolls. The garment fit Pinky perfectly and matched the pink ribbon that she tied about the little pup's long pink hair on the top of her head. The silky locks, bound between her ears, flowed down into her eyes like a rolling fountain in between her two small upright ears. Short bell sleeves, the pup sat on her behind while she dressed her like a prized doll.

Hubert told her that Pinky would get agitated if she always played with her all the time, and the little pup needed to sleep to help her grow. This was not the case though, in fact, her tiny pup thrived on the constant attention and wanted all that Brooklyn had to give her. Brooklyn had a lot to offer. Pinky was her new best friend. She did not need much rest, either, like her daddy said. In the night, Brooklyn awoke to find her perched under the nightlight; she stared down at the picture of a woman in a long yellow gown in one of her mother's fashion magazines. Her father did not have the heart to cancel the magazine, so she took them because the pictures were pretty.

Pinky watched everything, and even when Brooklyn began to nap this morning before the little girl nodded off, she saw her pet standing on the bed next to her. Pinky looked around the room, as if she tried to figure everything out. While she nodded off, Brooklyn thought she heard Bracket enter the room, and the two of them started talking.

Oh, the peace and joy that Brooklyn felt when she hugged the little pup. Although she was still very young, it did not matter. Even if Brooklyn were a teenager, the girl could not explain the comforting sensations that submerged her from the little pup. Only her mother provided harmony when she put her to sleep and a warm aroma of love when the two of them said her nightly prayers she missed for a long time. Last night she and Pinky said their prayers with Daddy, and the well-being of her mother wiped away her tears. Brooklyn did not want to cry anymore because her new friend told her she would take away her fears. In her innocence in accepting the unforeseen supernatural of the world, the little pup shared a vow to protect the little girl as her own.

Brooklyn had a secret, too, that only the two of them shared. No one would believe her if she told them, anyway. Yes, the mystery the two of them shared was that she could talk with Pinky. Of course, the little pup did not move her mouth or talk like we know speech to happen. A mind link between the two of them, she telepathically transmitted her thoughts to Brooklyn, and the little girl spoke aloud to her. The two of them chatted all into the night until she could no longer keep her eyes open.

Brooklyn gazed down at a pretty lady dressed in fancy clothing. "Pinky, do you like this one?" Her little pup looked at the print on the dress. "It has lots of flowers on it."

Yes. It is like you, pretty. Pinky looked up at Brooklyn, grinning her lovely pink lips turned upward, and an infusion of bubbly happiness came over her. Immersed in pleasure, she laughed jovially. *You like?*

"I like it so much," Brooklyn gleamed. "I will take the picture with me to Ms. Harpins at the fabric store."

I will be pretty, like Mommie.

"Mommy was a princess. You will be pretty, like Mommie. Just like a princess, right, Teddy?" Brooklyn picked up Teddy and gently took Pinky in her arms. For a moment, she danced around the room. "I want to dance on my toes like the pretty ladies."

I will dance too, Pinky told her joyfully. *I am now.*

"I want you to go, Pinky. You can see the pretty materials Mommie used to buy."

I want.

Brooklyn placed Pinky on the bed; running to her closet, she found her church purse her mother got her the last Easter they shared together.

Lined in frilly lace, on its basket shell, it matched her white dress and plastic shiny flat shoes she wore to church that Sunday.

The bag was perfect; a rigid shiny box bottom and its top drawstring bag portion made it perfect. It was just the size she might hide Pinky in, and she was sure the little pup would be obedient and be quiet. That way, her friend could sneak a peek at the beautiful cloth and the handsome ladies downtown and on the bus.

"I found this," she screamed happily, putting the pretty bag on the bed. Pinky crawled into the bag and peeked out of its open flap happily.

"Brooklyn," Mrs. Cheazemina yelled.

"I am coming."

"And leave that dog up there."

"I will," Brooklyn yelled back, running to the door. "Shhh," she told Pinky.

To Be Continued